REMNANTS FROM THE PAST

PATRICK PIERRE

Patrick Pierre

Always Remember That God Can Transform a Sinner's "LIFE."

Published by PPP.
(843) 307-0450

ISBN: 9798323397976

DEDICATION

The Union Baptist Church United Ministries, Society Hill, South Carolina, Church Family, I thank God for You.

IN MEMORY Of:

My Father Fernand Andre and My Beautiful Mother Ena Pierre,

Uncle Rodrigue Casimir,

Father Edner Day,

Patricia D Pierre,

Mother Grace Fergus,

Trustee Claude Fowler,

Deacon William Waiters,

Mother Inez Johnson,

Mother Marie Swiney,

Irma Jean Alstom,

&

Ruth Byrd.

ACKNOWLEDGMENT

To My Lovely Wife,

Dr. Joy Roberts Pierre

To
Pastor Faye Waiters, Dr. Rosa Fowler, Dr. Diann Brown, Dr.
Yvonne Graham, All My Children, Grandchildren, Siblings,
Nephews, Nieces, Relatives, & Friends.

THANK YOU!

SPECIAL THANKS

TO

Mother Georgia Henry,

Jerneil & Natacha Pierre Hunter.

Valada Rhonda Morris

Table Contents

All Biblical Quotations were taken from the NIV Bible.

INTRODUCTION

"Remnants from The Past" continues the story of "Tears of Deception" and "Soul Out with a Kiss." The Power of God is portrayed in all three novels, revealing His interactions with believers and non-believers. These writings showcase the strength of sin, confession, forgiveness, and love.

Remnants from The Past explains how God, the Architect of the universe, helps us overcome the burden of sin.

The sequel emphasizes the importance of not dismissing sinners based on their sins, as long as they're alive, there's potential for change. In "Remnants from The Past," the focus is on the doctrine of sin and how it creates a divide between sinners and God.

Wherever sin is present, it always leaves a lasting stain. Removing stubborn stains is no easy task without an effective stain remover. Certain residues can only be eradicated by the Blood of Jesus, not any other means. The remnants of a troubled past should be used as steppingstones to break free from its influence before it corrupts the mind, body, and soul. To conquer the lasting effects of the past, one must focus on personal growth through Christ and leave it in the past.

Those who genuinely seek forgiveness are known to be forgiven by God. His mercy prevails, even though sin leads to death, redemption is possible.

Who is Mother Faye Esther? She's a woman deeply devoted to God who receives messages from Him. Filled with wisdom, knowledge, and understanding, she is a prophetess. She holds the role of the Matriarch in her family, as well as in other groups. God responds when she prays. The journey of this relationship spans from Tears of Deception to Sold Out with a Kiss. The more she grows older, the more God bestows divine revelations upon her.

In her Wisdom book, Mother Faye Esther established a contrast between a negative and positive past. She explains "Both are capable of dominating someone's life. It is up to the persons involved and their connections to turn the situation in their favor. Reflecting on a positive past can motivate someone to excel in the present. A beautiful past can spark a dream that ultimately becomes reality.
Positive memories tend to fade faster than negative ones. The objective of the path is to lead to a hopeful future. The power of a traumatic past can make it difficult for someone to break free and move on. This is a taskmaster speaking in an imperative tone. This feeling has the power to grip a person's heart and mind forever, but It's not invincible."
"The victims' connections determine the outcome of the defeat. There is a possibility for the victims to have hope and move beyond their past. Having faith in God can help them escape the weight of a difficult history. If they don't know God, they should make themselves familiar with him. The inability to let go can turn the past into a heavy burden. It is possible for the victim to feel that forgiveness and repentance are unattainable for them. Just like a skilled hunter, the past will always chase the victims and catch up. A miserable life is sometimes the consequence of feeling remorseful about a dreadful history. The saying "You reap what you sow" perfectly captures the essence of the past. If every part of the plant is harmful, the

harvest will be nothing but evil. Over time, the remnants of a haunting past once again become whole. Always remember that confessing your mistakes and seeking God's forgiveness has the potential to transform situations. Thank God for that!

CHAPTER 1

CONCERNED

There was a time when Pastor Leslie spoke about her concern for Mother Faye Esther's welfare. Pastor Leslie is related to Mother Faye Esther as her daughter-in-law. She married Pachouco the baby boy who is a preacher and a famous Gospel singer. Their love story depicted in "Tears of Deception" was totally unique.

It was a mystery to Pastor Leslie how Mother Faye Esther, being her age, handled all the family problems, and sometimes at once. During their crisis, they all sought counseling from Mother Faye Esther.

"How do you manage? Aren't you fed up with the amount of trash we produce?" Pastor Leslie asked her Mother-in-law. She answered Pastor Leslie with an unforgettable smile, saying, "When you enjoy doing the task that God gives you, the word tiresome never comes to mind because His joy is your strength. Without God's divine permission or guidance, stopping will result in missing out on His blessings."

Pastor Leslie said, "More power to you, Mother!" Immediately she kissed her mother-in-law with a holy kiss, took her pocketbook. While walking towards the door Pastor Leslie uttered, "Mother, someday, I aspire to be like you. Had my niece Miriam still been alive, she would have surpassed me by now. I miss both her and Moses, but only the Lord knows how much." Angela and her two girls, Patrice and Patrica, caused a stir in the family by mistreating Moses and Miriam. Even in that situation, Mother Faye Esther's godly wisdom shone through. She emphasized to the family that in challenging times, those who have faith in God will receive abundant blessings.

Several years ago, Pachouco and Pastor Leslie went back to the Island of Haiti. At that location, they established one of Haiti's largest ministries ever. Society Hill, South Carolina has been their destination for the past three years, as summoned by God.

Upon arriving in Society Hill, South Carolina, Pastor Leslie met with Claude, the driver of Mother Faye Esther whom she considered as her own son. Pastor Leslie was eager to discuss the shameful disturbance that had affected the family for many years. She knew that only Claude could provide an explanation for what was happening. Pastor Leslie met with him privately, while everyone else believed she was still in Africa except for her husband.

Seeing Pastor Lesly at the restaurant in Cheraw made Claude incredibly happy. He shared everything from start to finish.

A tranquil day had suddenly arrived with lightning speed. Mother Faye Esther, a 90-year-old woman, woke up from a dream at three am one Saturday and hurried to her living room. She summoned her chauffeur, Claude. Claude and Tamara got married recently, but Tamara wasn't familiar with Mother Faye Esther's approaches. Tamara immediately recognized Mother Faye Esther as a wonderful boss for her husband. Mother Faye Esther was the person on the line when Tanara answered the phone. "How are you, Mother Faye Esther? Is everything alright?" Tamara glanced at the clock. "Tamara, my lovely daughter, if I feel any better, I might just scream. I know that my son Claude is currently resting. Please convey to him that Mother requires his presence. Early this morning, he has to play the missionary adventure for his Mother, and it has to do with Moses and Miriam."

Tamara repeated the names "Moses and Miriam" and agreed to go get Claude. Tamara expressed in her heart that the situation is becoming both intriguing and incredibly challenging for her.

Tamara shook Claude, letting him know that "Mother is on the phone." His response was, "What does she want?"

"Something about Moses and Miriam," replied Tamara.

"My God, my God," said Claude, "Mother is ready to claim her mansion in Glory. She's stuck in the past." He got up and answered the phone. "Good morning, Mother. What's the story with Moses and Miriam," he inquired.

Mother Faye Esther responded, "I want you to visit the computer store for an urgent task of creating a huge banner" that says, "WELCOME HOME MOSES AND MIRIAM, ENTER WITH FORGIVENESS IN YOUR HEARTS." "Mother, where are you going to hang this banner after all these years? Is it possible that Moses and Miriam will return from the dead?"

"You're right once more, Son. Please hurry and carry out my command. I need you to come to the house and pick up the measurements. Don't forget to mention at the store that I need it by noon. I will give the manager a call right now," she inserted.

"Are you serious, Mother Faye Esther?" Claude inquired.

"My dear Son, I'm completely serious, as a heart attack."

Claude's end of the phone became completely silent. He made an effort to find the bravery to tactfully discuss his thoughts on Mother Faye Esther, but the term senile kept coming to his mind. He had to reconsider before persuading her to visit a psychiatrist promptly to prevent the problem from getting worse. Mother Faye Esther has been deemed delusional by Claude in his recent thoughts. Based on what she said, he believed she was out of touch with reality. Mother Faye Esther's words carried great power, and her visions and prophecies swiftly came true, a fact Claude was fully aware of. Claude appeared to have shifted his belief to doubt. In his opinion, Mother Faye Esther's advanced age has caused her memory to work better for past events than present ones. Not long ago, Claude tried to prove to Mother Faye Esther how ridiculous it was for her to place a camera in just one room of her mansion, keeping its whereabouts known only to herself and the technician. Due to this move, Claude thought that Mother Faye Esther's mind was playing tricks on her. Her actions would make sense to him if there were hidden treasures in the room. In the afternoon, she imparted to Claude the lesson of never underestimating the power of a praying woman, especially one who is considered wise in the ways of the Lord.

"Son, are you still on the phone?" She asked.

"Yes, Mother, I'm here thinking about your well-being."

"Son, don't you waste your time like this. For your information, Mother is Super Fine. However, son, there is one thing wrong with me. I can hardly wait to see Moses and Miriam. They look just like Yves and Ester."

"My Lord!" cried Claude as he said, "Mother Faye Esther, it has been years since they died."

.

"Claude, my son, you are highly mistaken. Whenever I was around these children, you were always there with me."

"Who me?" replied Claude. "Mother Faye Esther, I'm becoming increasingly worried about you. I've never been in the presence of the dead after they were laid to rest. I couldn't handle it emotionally. Mother, I have something I'm about to do. You might disown me as your adopted son or even terminate my employment as your chauffeur after I complete it. I'll call your children to inform them about your behavior of anticipating visits from the Deceased. Mother Faye Esther, I understand your hands are full of your daughter Rose's situation. The next time I take her to see her psychiatrist, it would be helpful for you to see him as well."

"Claude, you think that I'm losing my mind. Anyway, don't be late picking up the measurement for the sign. I'm looking forward to seeing you when you arrive. Let me make it clear, Claude, that our conversation is ending for now. Claude, the revelation is true. I don't want you to sow

5

any more doubt into my heart. I expect an apology from you to God and me when it becomes reality."

"Okay, Mother Faye Esther, we will see. Tamara wishes to speak with you."
Tamara got back on the phone. She asked Mother Faye Esther if she could tag along with Claude to view the banner. Mother Faye Esther answered with joy, saying, "Positively!"

Tamara developed an interest in knowing more about Mother Faye Esther's family. Whenever an opportunity arose, she picked her husband's brainer to gather more information about Mother. Tamara's concern was not sudden but developed over time. On their first date, she talked more about Mother Faye Esther than about Claude and herself.

Tamara has no idea that her husband will join the rich and famous family when Mother Faye Esther dies. He is one of her beneficiaries. Tamara won't get to enjoy her husband's sudden wealth, because she can't control her flesh. She will betray him with a charming loser, so he's going to divorce her.

Tamara wanted to follow her husband because she desired to know about Moses and Miriam. Tamara's curiosity was further piqued by one more thing. Mother Faye Esther's daughter Rose. Claude was unaware that Tamara was using him to gain proximity to Mother Faye Esther's family. According to Mother Faye Esther's Wisdom book, "A spouse who marries for reasons other than LOVE is a deceiver. It's like sleeping with an enemy."

She accompanied Claude. The moment Tamara arrived at the house; she was shocked beyond belief. Mother Faye Esther's strength and energy for her age surprised her. Her assumption of Mother Faye Esther's age was incorrect, as she believed her to be seventy years old. "Claude, look up there," she shouted. "Where," replied Claude? "On the ladder," responded Tamara.

Tamara was about to do something unusual from her husband's perspective. From her pocketbook, she retrieved a small camera. She owned a camera that her husband had no idea about. On the ladder, she captured Mother Faye Esther's picture. Tamara's actions, that morning, caused Claude's heart to be disturbed. Mother Faye Esther had a strong dislike for having her photos taken without her knowledge, and he knew that. He recommended that she refrain from developing the film and requested that she hand it over to him to guarantee its destruction. It was clear to Tamara that the film had come to an end. He took the rewound roll of film without any trouble and placed it in the car's ashtray. Tamara questioned why Mother didn't let Oscar, her cute garcon, climb the ladder.

Who's cute, Oscar? "He's a drunk," Claude replied. You wish to see him tumble from the ladder. The life of that young man is being squandered.

"To the best of my knowledge, he's undeniably handsome," continued Tamara; he will win the hearts of many girls when he finds himself.

Claude explained that Mother felt sorry for Oscar and hired him as her butler. She has his unwavering loyalty.

When Claude stepped out of the car. Tamara grabbed the film from the ashtray before his left foot landed and hid it in her bra. She returned an old one to the ashtray. She did not do it because of the photographs, but since Mother Faye Esther's business photo documents were in the roller. Tamara couldn't risk upsetting Claude that morning. Without it, she wouldn't have knowledge of the stories of Rose, Moses, and Miriam. She clung to her husband like glue. Even Mother Faye Esther picked up on this and responded on Tamara's actions, stating:

"Claude, your wife is up to something. Don't forget to bring some cash. Something special is what she needs from you."

"Mother don't put women's secrets out like that," Tamara retorted.

She leaned over, nuzzled his bald head, and kissed him. Mother Faye Esther jokingly exclaimed, "Claude, she got you!" and all three of them burst into laughter.

Tamara asked Mother Faye Esther, was it okay to use her bathroom? In a sweet tone, she assured Tamara that she could move freely around the mansion if she remained a member of the family through marriage. "If you mess up your clothes, I won't help you clean up, so use the bathroom.' Laughter filled the room. In a giggling stage, Tamara replied, "Mother Faye Esther, you're hilarious. I'm going to use the one in your bedroom because you said that."

Tamara was not kidding about using Mother Faye Esther's personal bedroom. It's an opportunity for Tamara to see how her bedroom looked after a long night's rest. The few times she snuck in there it appeared as if a stager came daily to stage the bedroom. Noticing the bed was unmade, she took out her camera and snapped pictures of the room.

Tamara was an experienced photographer. She kept her profession a secret from her husband. Tamara didn't utilize the bathroom. She completed her mission and stepped outside to join them again. Tmara expressed gratitude for the hospitality in a polite way. Without warning, Mother Faye Esther said, "You're welcome, and guess what?" I find it humorous that you asked to use my bathroom this morning. In my dream last night, a young lady named Tamara, who looked like she might be around your age, was in my bedroom. I granted her request to use my bathroom after she asked. She entered the room and took pictures of my bedroom without permission, even though she didn't use anything. A funny dream, isn't it?"

Tamara's idea to use the bathroom was an alibi. After she heard Mother Faye Esther's dream, she lost control of her bowels and ran into the car. An accident happened to her.

Tamara Baby, are you okay? "We're departing," Claude confirmed.
Mother Faye Esther replied, "When women have to go, they need to go."

Claude got into the car and Tamara told him she had an emergency. She had to return to the house for a few minutes. Claude inquired regarding the emergency. "It's personal," she replied, but the smell gave her away and Claude knew what had happened. He drove his wife back to the house. Tamara was getting out, she asked her husband, "Do you think Mother Faye Esther is a witch?" "Leave this car with your foolish talk," Claude said.
Mother Faye Esther raised the curiosity of many when she wrote in her wisdom book: "Have you ever noticed that

those who are used powerfully by God are often accused of witchcraft by those who don't know God's power?"

"Make sure you take something for your stomach," Claude suggested. "My wife is absolutely gorgeous. She is incredibly beautiful," While thinking to himself.

Tamara returned to the car, gorgeous as always. Claude let her know what he's thinking earlier about her. She laughed and asked him, "Are you trying to tempt me? Somebody is yielding to temptation," replied Tamara. "I changed outfits because I want to feel sexy for you today, baby," she continued. She whispered to him, "Let's go inside for a few minutes, Claude baby," loud enough for him to hear. He was under the impression that the sexual embargo had been lifted. "My emotions are not a game," he said sternly. Three months have passed since our last intimate moment. Tamara interrupted him, stating that "I haven't seen the gold necklace that I wanted you to purchase for me. You know what won't be possible without the gold necklace. It is the magical key to unlock the shop."

It struck Tamara that she was on the verge of ruining the morning and compromising her investigation. "Don't worry, honey, I was just joking," she said to Claude in a hurry. "Get ready for what awaits you when we get back home. The world you inhabit will become mine. It might take some time, but I'll excel at it. As you pointed out, it has been quite some time. I am optimistic that you're prepared." Claude smiled and said, "Baby, my world is yours, so rock it however you want."

Claude retrieved the banner measurement from Mother Faye Esther. He and Tamara were headed to the computer store, although he was not willing. He directed his gaze towards her. A contented Tamara caught his gaze. "Why the morning happiness?" He asked.

"I'm feeling sexy and romantic," answered Tamara tenderly. With a wrinkled eye, she added, "Can you handle that when we get back home, Big Boy?"
"Can I?" replied Claude. I promise it will be as good as our first time."

Tamara had effectively placed Claude in the desired position, and she was conscious of her achievement. She wasted no time extracting from him the information she needed about Moses and Miriam. Despite everything, she kept toying with his emotions by touching him with her magical fingers. She ensured he maintained his focus on the road.

She boldly and suddenly inquired, "Who are Moses and Miriam that Mother Faye Esther is welcoming home?"

Claude responded, "It's a long and sad story that turned out to be a crazy one. Mother Faye Esther is completely out of it, and I've come to that realization after all these years. Her mental state is deteriorating every day. I am worried that she is losing her mind. Do you know what she did? She spent a lot of money to wire a single room in her house. In one room, there are cameras everywhere. That's crazy, don't you think?"
Tamara, as nervous as she could be, answered, "Claude Honey, not at all. She's entitled to place cameras in her bedroom. How do you think she would react if she caught someone sneaking and stealing from her bedroom?"

Claude glanced at her, saying, "I would hate to be in that person's shoes for three reasons. Mother Faye Esther, first and foremost, is an extraordinary woman of God who can sometimes see things before they happen. People don't understand her anointing. She is the target of some people's jealousy. She loves a God who is willing to lead her to the truth.

Secondly, she has a strong belief system. The person would be the subject of Mother's prayers. Ensure that justice is served by prosecuting the thief.

Third on the list, she possesses the financial means to accomplish it. That treatment would apply to everyone, even family members."

Tamara was disturbed by the news of Mother Faye Esther having cameras. For some reason, she insisted on knowing the exact room. The information she wanted could not be provided by Claude. He believed with absolute certainty that the cameras were not in her bedroom. He thought Mother Faye Esther's decision was crazy, silly, and a waste of money, and that's why he viewed it that way.

Claude didn't specify in which room those cameras were located. After some thought, Tamara determined it was in the bedroom. She called herself playing smart by shopping around. She had trespassed into Mother Faye Esther's bedroom three times, secretly taking pictures, and placing papers and jewels in her bra and pants. She brought back the jewels and important papers during her final visit to the room. Tamara had a knack for knowing exactly where Mother Faye Esther kept her crucial documents. Tamara's motives were a mystery, except for time. Tamara's action will surely come to light with time.

CHAPTER 2

WARNING

According to Mother Faye Esther's wisdom book, "The most dangerous enemy is the one with access to every room in your house."

Claude disagreed with Tamara, saying "You are wrong. One of the rooms is where she installed the surveillance camera. Mother's bedroom is not where it is, I'm certain. The camera was a secret between her, the cameraman, me, and now you."

Unaware, with this information, Claude lifted Tamara's burden off. Knowing that she had the freedom to complete the task she started in Mother Faye Esther's bedroom made her happy. Once again, she leaned over and kissed him on the ear, expressing gratitude for sharing the secret with her.

Tamara said, "Getting back to my question, who are Moses and Miriam?"

"I told you, Love of my life, that's a long story," responded Claude.
Tamara answered, "We have plenty of time, I'm listening."
Claude looked at her passionately and said, "You're spoiled? Do you know that?"

Tamara, an opportunist from her heart, answered, "Who spoiled me? You! Claude.

Like Mother Faye Esther said in her Wisdom book, "A good husband has no other choice but to spoil his wife. After all, she is one of his ribs. She will fall asleep in his arms each night and dream of happiness. Meeting her needs daily is all a wife ever wants from her husband."

Tamara persisted, "Tell me about them."

Claude laughed and interrupted Tamara, saying she was doing Mother Faye Esther's quote an injustice by ending it with a period."

How about the section that mentioned "A wife should ensure her husband's needs are fulfilled? You omitted that part, Tamara, darling."

Tamara answered negatively with her response. I deemed this portion unnecessary. It was just a tease. I did it intentionally to test if you would let me get away with it, but I got caught. Now, let's proceed with the rest of the story."

"Yves and Ester, who died in a car crash several decades ago, were Moses and Miriam's parents," Claude started to say.

"Let me tell you, Tamara, Yves, and Ester were the epitome of a happy couple. Many couples admired their pure love and modeled their own relationships after it. They achieved remarkable success in life. Yves and Ester fell in love during their high school years. The accident took the lives of Veronique and her son, Yves. Additionally, Ester, the daughter of Yvonne.

The act of Moses singing the "ABCs" caused Yvonne to lose her memory. Deafness was a condition he had had since birth. Moses was a child who could only be described as a miracle.

The doctor initially thought Ester was pregnant with a girl during her pregnancy with Moses and Miriam. The ultrasound had certain limitations that affected its effectiveness. Initially, the image depicted a girl, but when the moment arrived, she gave birth to a girl. Something intriguing happened in the delivery room. The doctor noticed something inside Ester. The surprise that was disclosed was the existence of another baby. A breech delivery took place. Moses encountered difficulties because of a birth defect and a speech impediment. The whole family learned sign language to communicate with Moses, but Miriam wanted to see Moses speak so they could sing the "ABCs" together. Miriam's overwhelming compassion for her twin brother during their childhood made her overprotective. Every day, she would lift Moses before the Lord. She possessed a slight knack for prophesying.

One day, Yves and his brother Derrick gave Veronique their mother, a surprise birthday party. Derrick, who resided out of town, was on the route to give his mother a surprise visit and meet Moses and Miriam for the very first time, with a special emphasis on Moses. He desired to lay his hands on him and prayed to God for Moses to speak. He preached the gospel with sincerity and had unshakeable faith.

"Tamara," Claude said, "You should buy a copy of SOLD OUT WITH A KISS whenever the opportunity arises." In the book, you will find out everything you need to know about this family. Read it.

In the living room, we waited for Derrick to arrive. Abruptly, Mother Faye Esther requested that everyone halt their conversations and commence praying. Miriam's father was the only one who could console her as she wept bitterly. Finally, Yves put her on his lap, saying, "Talk to Daddy." What's the matter with you?"

On the wall, there was a picture of Derrick wearing his preaching robe that Mother Faye Esther had hung up. Her uncle Derrick was someone Miriam never met. To everyone's surprise, she pointed at the photograph on the wall and exclaimed, "I saw a drunken man hit that man's car. The man with blood all over his body waved goodbye to me."

Out of nowhere, the phone started ringing and Mother Faye Esther told Yves to answer it. The person on the other end of the line was a police officer and a friend of the family. He passed on the message to Yves regarding an accident caused by a drunk driver. The drunk driver took the lives of both Derrick and his adopted child. The accident occurred just around the corner from the house. The drunk driver's identity would surprise you, Claude said."

"Who! who! Who was he, Claude?" asked Tamara.

Tamara remained anxious as she never received a response to her question and the complete story details. Claude had to stop the car because he became emotional. He attempted to finish recounting almost three decades of the story, but he was too overwhelmed. The stories from decades past were still vivid in his mind. Yves and Ester had a positive impact on him.

Claude shared a part of the story with Tamara, who was eager for him to continue. Tamara felt this opportunity might never come her way again. Additionally, she believed that every disgraceful aspect related to this family had been concealed. She continuously told her husband with insistence,

"Honey, let's park the car and finish the story, and take a deep breath."

Tamara didn't show any compassion to her husband. "Moses talked," Claude resumed his statement. "Using a fake will, Angela, Ester's younger sister, took Moses and Miriam from Mother Faye Esther and Yvonne. Angela resorted to using another fake Will to get hold of Derrick's assets. She was one of a kind. She made only one mistake-attempting to fool Mother Faye Esther, which proved to be the wrong decision. Angela assigned the responsibility of taking care of her twin girls, Patrica, and Patrice, to Moses and Miriam by turning them into maids. Angela received a sixty-five-year jail sentence for committing various crimes. She was responsible for the deaths of Moses and Miriam."

Tamara lost her temper, saying to Claude, "Let's forget about it. What you're telling me right now is confusing. The amount of information that's missing is excessive."

Claude echoed, "I told you if you want to know anything concerning Mother Faye Esther Esther's family stories," read "Tears Of Deception" and "Sold Out With A Kiss". Mother Faye Esther and her family are the subject of both novels. Mother Faye Esther sent me to get a welcome home sign for Moses and Miriam, but something seems off. The reason they died of starvation, Tamara, was because of Angela and her children." Tamara kissed her husband and said, "Let's pick up the banner."

They arrived at the store and the banner wasn't ready. The person in charge of making the posters was running behind schedule. Claude and Tamara passed the time by browsing the store. While Claude was browsing the video game accessories section, Tamara headed towards the books department. Tamara left the books department and called Claude on her telephone which she grabbed from her pocketbook. He answered the phone, She informed him that she would be in the lobby reading. "Don't throw away the newspaper after reading it," Claude told her. "Save it for me, okay baby?"

She ended the call and Claude returned to playing video games.

Claude and Tamara were both doing what they loved, so waiting didn't bother them. Nevertheless, Mother Faye Esther was not content. The delay had caused her to become impatient. She sensed that time was slipping away as Moses and Miriam's arrival was imminent.

Was Mother Faye Esther certain whether Moses and Miriam, who were presumed dead a long time ago, were still alive? If that was the case, how did she conclude they would visit Yvonne and her that day? Was Mother Faye Esther skilled in illusions? Claude thought that welcoming Moses and Miriam home was an insane idea. He thought Mother Faye Esther was delirious, because she prepared based on a vision she had that morning. She prepared a great family feast, claiming God instructed her to do so. She invited a few of her old friends to come and help welcome Moses and Miriam. They felt similarly to Claude that Mother Faye Esther was losing her sanity, so they didn't make plans to attend.

Her behavior concerned everyone, so they agreed to inform her children and get her psychiatric help before it was too late.

Mother Faye Esther's close bond with God led him to believe her words before her mind began to falter. Claude reminded Mother Faye Esther of the good old times she had with God. She wasted no time in informing Claude that God never stops being a parent, regardless of age. As one grows older, their conversations with God become more dependable and enjoyable if they belong to Him. Why is that? The lifestyle becomes more trustworthy with fewer distractions.?"

Claude's thoughts shifted to his wife. He left the video games to check on her in the lobby. Now Tamara was very tall. During high school, she was among the basketball stars. To locate her in a crowd, Claude frequently relied on her height. This technique failed to work that day. In the waiting room for customers, Claude searched for Tamara. She was nowhere to be found. He headed to the parking lot to see if she was in the car. The sound of someone crying was heard by him. The weeping noise guided him to the other side of the waiting room. His wife was on the floor reading "Sold Out with A Kiss" because "Tears of Deception" was unavailable at the bookstore.

Tears flowed from her eyes as she became emotional. Tamara, a quick reader, discovered her husband's vulnerability in sharing their family's story after reading over half the book.

Upon learning of Angela's actions, Tamara became angry. She had the urge to go to the prison and beat Angela up. Angela's combative nature makes it difficult for Tamara to accomplish something like that. Upon seeing her husband, she asked him why Angela was being so devilish towards her own family and friends. Moses and Miriam's life was ruined by my friend. She wasn't truthful with me.

"Wait a minute Tamara," answered Claude. "Why have you referred to Angela as a friend of yours? You mentioned that she deceived you."

Tamara responded to Claude, saying "I don't know what I'm talking about," adding that "The story had me so engaged I was talking without thinking. I'll close this book and won't read it again. I'm fed up with Angela's homicidal behavior, and I pray her twins don't have her greediness." Claude echoed, "Give me a break, one of them is identical to her. She's willing to do anything for just a few dollars. She aspired to become wealthy overnight."

"Are you talking about Patrice, the one who is a nurse," replied Tamara. According to her, Patricia would be in for a rude awakening if she thought she could stay in the house after Mother Faye Esther's death. She claimed the mansion would belong to her and her mother and concluded the conversation with the words "watch and you'll see."
"Who said that again," asked Claude?
"Patrice", answered Tamara.
"Patrica is a gem," Claude replied. "I should have realized it was Patrice." Concerning her sister, Patricia won't think

that way. The saying "like mother, like daughter" applies to Patrice and Angela, and Patricia reminds me of her classy aunt Ester. I have a good friendship with Angela. I have knowledge of how dangerous she could be. She's capable of being both sweet and manipulative.

"Who do you tell?" replied his wife. "Trust me, I know from firsthand experience. She found pleasure in blackmailing people."

Claude glanced at Tamara with a funny look on his face. Tamara responded promptly, "Don't forget, I just finished reading about her techniques."

Claude is pondering if Tamara and Angela are friends, given Tamara's frequent misspeaking about her. If it is true, what is his wife hiding? Angela promised to find him a wife when he was still a bachelor, and he remembered that. On that day, he inquired about how she planned to accomplish it while being behind bars. "Claude, what's my name? I'm still Angela Casimir," Angela clarified to him. "Being in jail makes me a greater threat to the outside world."

"Yves and Ester were the ideal couple. They were known and admired by many," continued Claude.

"I know," added Tamara, but they died so young. The novel claims that they invited death into their lives.

CHAPTER 3

SUSPICIOUS MATCHMAKER

"Claude, when did you last see Angela in prison?"
Tamara opened the door for Claude to express what he was wondering about   earlier.
"It was two or three months before we started dating. I enjoyed her that day. At first, she spoke briefly about herself. Angela was more concerned about me being celibate. To fill the emptiness in my heart, she vowed to find me a young and pretty wife. She was serious about it. I inquired about how she would execute this while imprisoned. She said, "Claude, my name is still Angela. My connections span both inside and outside of prison. Don't play hard to get when she calls."
I asked her, "There are no strings attached, right?"
Angela replied, "Claude, do you ever know I work for free? Dancing to my music requires payment from either you or her. I'm kidding."
"I have a different opinion; I know you're not."
A feeling of sadness came over Angela and she cried with remorse. She said. "I have serious problems Claude" and I couldn't hold back my tears because of her sincerity. Mistreating others appears to be the appropriate behavior for me. Claude, I have a habit of exploiting others for my own benefit. It seems like I'm bound by a contract with Satan to fulfill his malicious desires. I'm determined to break this covenant one way or another. Seeking prayers to terminate this malevolent contract with Satan. I don't

want you to come and see me anymore, Claude. If I ever need you, I'll reach out."

Tamara was glad her husband stopped talking about Angela's plan for his life. There were some questions she wanted to direct to him. "Tell me, Claude, did the girl call you like Angela had said, she inquired?"

Claude took a glance at Tamara and saw JEALOUSY in her eyes. According to Tamara, it took her husband too long to answer the question, so she asked it again. Then Claude answered, "No, the girl never called. Besides, I never believed she could arrange something like that incarcerated. I am glad it didn't take place. I would have missed the most beautiful wife in the world, Mrs. Tamara."

She looked at her husband and thought he was lying. Claude quickly defended himself, adding, "You were the only female who called me and no one else. Darling, I tell you the truth."

Claude received a loving gesture from Tamara as she kissed his right hand and said, "I love you."
"Lord, have mercy," "Claude, you know, Angela is better off in jail. She is in a place where she can't use her manipulative skills for her personal gain. Allow me to retract that statement. Her expertise in mischievousness slipped my mind."
Claude burst out laughing uncontrollably. He laughed at his wife's last statement, finding it pitiful and naïve. She wondered what was amusing about her comment. "My

love, let me tell you, wherever she's at, she's a nuisance," Claude said. I'd like to share with you what she did while serving time in a women's facility. She conceived and brought forth a baby. The baby is now between three to five years old.

Tamara's husband mentioned Angela's pregnancy while she drank water from a bottle. She choked for a minute or two as water spurted from her mouth. She couldn't wrap her head around what she heard. With anger in her voice, she told her husband to get out of the car. Joking is inappropriate right now. "I'm curious, Claude, are you serious? I assumed she was in a facility for females only, where this kind of dilemma would not arise due to the absence of males. The rules in those institutions are very stringent. No, something went wrong somewhere. It's a new information to me, she never mentioned it before."

Once again, Tamara made a crucial mistake, Claude heard it and said to her, "Angela mentioned what to you?"

Tamara corrected herself, clarifying that she meant no one else before. "I'm getting too engrossed in Angela's craziness."

With smiled Claude turned to his wife and remarked, "Angela is bad to the core."

According to Mother Faye Esther, "Some people make the choice to be a nuisance to society. Their actions suggest that they create for that purpose. Angela is one of them."

"Wow! Claude Honey," shouting Tamara with anger, "I hate to imagine the fear and the tension among the women in there, knowing there were a couple of men, rapists dwelling amongst them who were taking women by force."

Tamara, when Mother Faye Esther said that she was completely done with Angela. She never previously considered the notion of getting her out of jail. If she chooses, she possesses the skill to do it. That caused Angela's daughter Patrice to become a monster within the family. She created a monstrous being with the sole purpose of destroying her own kind, regardless of the cost. It's possible that she'll need to secure enough funds to hire top-tier lawyers who can convince the government to drop all charges against her mom. To Patrice, Mother Faye Esther's money seemed to have ignored her mother. Mother Faye Esther had faith that Angela's time behind bars would change her for the better. Mother Faye Esther had no idea about Angela's plan to outsmart the prison system until she discovered Angela's rape and pregnancy during her time behind bars. Mother Faye Esther's briefing caught her off guard. She found it unfathomable that rape or pregnancy could take place in a women's prison. According to Angela, she was reportedly raped by a couple of men in the middle of the night. The women's correctional facility was faced with a particularly tough accusation. The situation was sensitive and needed to be approached with caution.

"Wow! Claude Honey, shouting Tamara with anger. The fear and tension among those women must be unimaginable."

"Oh well, Tamara, I'm sure the fear and tension in the prison was frightening. Women, regardless of their status as inmates or workers, were all in jeopardy of harm, violation, and suspicion. They had illegal hand-made weapons under their pillows while sleeping. Angela gained some supporters as the atmosphere turned negative. Among them, there were thought to be a couple of men who dressed and acted like women. The prison's official staff quickly administered a lie detector test to Angela to discover the source of the scandalous story that had brought shame upon the prison community. The tension increased as inmates and others waited for the test results."

Angela's passing of the lie detector test became widely known very quickly. The rage was palpable, both internally and externally, largely due to the involvement of the two men. Fear became inevitable among those who viewed the lie detector test as an exact science, bringing the staff to their knees with the results.

The institution suggested that Angela take a pregnancy test six weeks after the results were made available. Her hunch was right; she was pregnant.

Angela enlisted the services of a criminal attorney from Society Hill, South Carolina to act as her representative in a lawsuit against the women's penitentiary. The lawyer's name was Junior Jeffery. His reputation was built on winning hard cases.

"You know," Claude said to Tamara, "I don't blame Angela for thinking about a lawsuit against the institution. Due to the complex case, I won't speak with anyone without my lawyer present."

"The prison atmosphere is getting confusing day by day," continued Claude. It sparked curiosity among everyone involved. The breaking news made all the inmates have a one-track mind. She had the sympathy of many of the female prisoners in the institution. Angela received a positive result on her pregnancy test. The unanimous test result convinced everyone in custody that Angela had been raped by two men who had posed as women. The announcement of Angela's pregnancy caused chaos among her followers. She held the position of their spiritual leader.

Since Angela's arrival at the jailhouse, she played it smart by joining the most powerful religious group in the prison. By doing this, she avoided being perceived as the spouse of a stronger woman in the realm of lesbianism. She quickly manipulated others with her beauty. If you're looking for a challenge, Angela is not to be trifled with. To initiate her, the toughest woman in jail groped Angela's private part. She failed hard on the ground at lightning speed. Angela whispered in her ear while on top of her, "If you do that again, I'll send you to hell." Angela is a black belt in judo and taekwondo.

Tamara my dear, that Angela is an incredibly beautiful woman. The more she ages, the more gorgeous she gets, and she's completely aware of it. Her intelligence is a gift, but it can also be a danger to herself.

Angela taught bible study and a year later she became a well-respected prophetess of God among the inmates.

The jailhouse had no hidden information. Angela's past as a high-class criminal was known by the inmates. They were cognizant of her past self. She claimed to be a thief to the core in her testimony. They knew she had been sentenced to sixty-five years but then had her sentence reduced to thirty-five years. Their belief in her stemmed from their faith that God could convert even the worst sinners into preachers.

Angela came up with an exceptional method of preaching God's teachings, which frequently brought tears to her eyes, and to those who share her beliefs. She vehemently spoke out against immoral sexual intercourse. Women avoided having sex with each other despite their cravings. Her convincing words led some of them to believe that their body was the temple of the living God. She frequently repeated one of Mother Faye Esther's motivational quotes to them: "A purposeful woman is one who possesses resistance, perseverance, determination, and dedication."

However, Angela opened the eyes of her congregants to the admissible fact of choosing masturbation over fornication. Because of her charismatic preaching, she had no difficulty convincing her parishioners. Angela's approach to conveying God's message often stirred up debates, with some agreeing and others not. Her embarrassing dilemma made those who knew her stance on premarital sex and living right for the Lord shed tears. Some believed she deserved what she got for all the pain she inflicted on people in and outside of prison before her transformation.

Angela didn't care. She realized that the official staff members in the institution were at her mercy, and that could help her get out of there. Quarrels among the staff led to the dismissal and resignation of the prison supervisor and ward chief.

Angela faced a multitude of charges. Her name was included on the list of the most dangerous criminals, despite never having committed murder. She got released from jail three times, but each time she stepped out, a new arrest warrant was waiting for her. The police had warrants for her arrest in multiple states. Angela's lawyer examined her cases. He said Angela might have to endure another 25 years before they can release her. Angela saw a lawsuit as her way to outsmart the system. In exchange for her freedom, she intends to drop charges against her rapists and the jailhouse. Any charges against her from the states, past or present, must be dropped. She requested something impossible, but it's not the first time impossible became possible.

CHAPTER 4

THE INTERVIEW

The interview with the inmates commences, but the detective team serving as interviewers fails to find any leads. There is no solid evidence to overturn the charges against Angela. On a daily basis, the matter became increasingly complicated. Listening to two inmates of the victims led the detectives to take a recess. Nicole and Eva, two charming women, testified under oath that they were raped by a couple of men on separate occasions in their cell at night. As a result, Nicole conceived. She shared her belief that the correctional officers at the prison knew who sexually assaulted her. She informed them that the staff at the institution lacked compassion when they discovered she was pregnant from one of her rapists. An investigator asked Nicole, "What led to your baby's fate?" and "How did your life turn into a living hell?" "Do you want to talk about it?"

Nicole nodded her head emotionally to confirm.

For the first time since her tragedy, she felt both compelled and free to discuss the situation. Unlike her previous experience, Nicole faced potential retaliation without fear this time. Nicole looked at them with teary eyes and expressed her concern about repeating the same mistake from six years ago. They sent me to a solitary confinement cell for four months. The detective, who appeared to have a crush on Nicole, asked what the mistake was. Nicole declared that she shared the truth with investigators who couldn't handle it. The detective, who was also attractive, gave Nicole a smile that she thought was the most beautiful a man had ever given her. Known for his charm in handling difficult cases that had the potential to be unsolved mysteries. He answered, "Not this time Nicole, you are in good hands."

Relief washed over Nicole and all her fears dissipated. She found safety in speaking truthfully, as she did with her friend Angela.

Nicole started her testimony by expressing gratitude to God for making this day possible. Meanwhile, the chief investigator attempted to comprehend why someone as beautiful as Nicole was in a maximum-security women's detention center. According to him, her beauty got the best of her, and she ended up with the wrong guys, resulting in a 45-year jail sentence from the judge.

"Mrs. Heavenly, the warden, called me six years ago to assist her in preparing the menu for her annual Christmas party," recounted Nicole.

Mrs. Heavenly said to me, "For the past four years, I have done a great job preparing for the party and this year she had a special surprise for me. I was going to respond to her comment, but she interrupted me."

"Nicole, I showed the picture you gave me to my brother-in-law, and he went crazy about you. He claimed he would do whatever it takes to hold you in his embrace. He declares that you are the most beautiful woman he has ever laid eyes on. Nicole, he's wealthy, good-looking, but drinks excessively and smokes strong cigars.

Likewise, she went through her wallet and presented me with his pictures. Isn't he so cute?" She said.

"I confirmed by saying yes, he is."

Nicole, said Mrs. Heavenly, he is a nut. He asked me for the impossibility."

"What is that, Mrs. Heavenly?"

"Something crazy, to have me fired and go to jail, Nicole. He offered me $10,000 to help him meet you, Nicole. He was as serious as a heart attack that could be fatal."

"Mrs. Heavenly," Nicole said, "let him know that if I could, I wouldn't, because I'm completely done with men."
"My beauty was used as collateral in dirty deals by a rich man who claimed to love me, leading to my imprisonment. Oh no, I'm better off in here with no man in my mind, and I'm not falling for a woman either."

Mrs. Heavenly told Nicole, "I understand you got a bad rap, and I don't blame you. Let's move on with the menu preparation."
"Can I take a rain check this time? Some of my fellow inmates already informed you about my decision not to get involved this year. Christmas doesn't seem appealing to me this year. Is it possible to find a replacement inmate for me? I did it for the past six years," said Nicole.

"Nicole, you can't do that, so find your mood where you left it. I won't choose anyone else. This conversation is over." Added Mrs. heavenly.

"Mrs. Heavenly, is against the law what you are trying to do to me." There's no compulsion for me to celebrate Christmas. My rightful place is in my cell, and I want to go there. The warden signaled for another guard to take me away from her sight after I said that. "Shut your mouth, Nicole," said the guard as he joined the conversation. "Show some respect when speaking to the Warden. Let's go."

Mrs. Heavenly added, "Put Nicole in solitary confinement until the day after Christmas for trying to ruin the plan and spoiling the party."

"They isolated me from others and confined me to a 5x7 cell alone. A cell I never knew existed in the prison. I spent almost all my day, 23 hours, in that place. For what, not wanting to be involved in anything related to the party. Honestly, I avoided getting involved due to numerous hurtful dramas. Some girls are raped annually. Even in your presence, they are still hesitant to talk about it. They are aware of the consequences that await them. During the party night, I was in my cell. I was awakened by a female correctional officer calling my name and asking if I was awake? I remembered answering her, what do you want from me in the middle of the night? I attempted to identify the unfamiliar voice I heard. The door of the cell swung open. They removed me from the cell and took me to the hallway. One of the correctional officers grabbed my hair and pulled me down, leaving me lying flat on my back. She repeatedly slapped my face and called me the most degrading name as referring to female dog. The other two officers participated in the abuse. Despite my screams for help and fighting, my strength was no match for them. To keep me quiet, they put a washcloth in my mouth. The guards held my hands and feet down on the ground and celebrated the moment with joy. Two men brutally raped me. I understand that you're currently skeptical about the involvement of any man in this situation. Indeed, there was! When they broke their code of silence, I was in a state between waking up and passing out. They disputed among themselves using their natural voices over the duration of time. They were reminded to stop talking by the female correctional officer who acted as the referee. The first man finished raping me and then helped the other man flip me over onto my stomach, resulting in the most painful and disagreeable rape experience. They pulled me back into the cell, and one of them accidentally dropped his cigars. I finally realized the reason behind their outrageous breath. The combination of natural bad breath and the odor of liquor and cigars was unbearable. When the second man got on my back, I passed out for good. My memory was last triggered by his statement, "Nicole, I've been waiting for that from you for two years, but your name never made it to the ballot. I paid $10,000, Nicole, for this moment with you."

"One of the guards tried to have her groove back with the first rapist, but she could not make his sun rise again. She pushed the first rapist away quickly after hearing the talkative nature of the second rapist. She got back into her pants and pulled the second rapist away from me to avoid him exposing the Institution's dark secret."

"I've repeatedly voiced my concerns about the prison's institution staff running a yearly prostitution ring, but no one seems to care enough to investigate."

'From her bra, Nicole extracted an item concealed in a napkin. She handed over the leftover cigar, saying, "This is the evidence, detective." One of the rapist's DNA is in it.

The other inmate let the investigator know two men also raped her on two consecutive nights. She knew without a doubt that they were human, not ghosts from a horror film. The interview concluded with both agreeing "I believe Angela" based on experience."
Both prisoners requested a lie detector test to authenticate their testimonies.

The fear of continuing with the interview of the inmates had placed the detectives in an uncomfortable position. Not knowing how to proceed, they were stuck with the information they received. The last two inmates testified with certainty, incriminating the facility severely.

While dealing with that situation, another one presented itself. Angela began to receive death threats through letters mailed to her from Haiti. Angela was given a clear explanation in the letters that she had twenty days to drop the charges and terminate the pregnancy. If she refused, she would wake up in hell. Angela distributed the letters to the inmates after making copies. Angela has gained more popularity among her peers, even those who were previously against her are now her fans. The inmates showed sympathy towards Angela. They formed a group to keep an eye on Angela around the clock. They vowed to carry out that task until the baby arrived. Sadly, the pledge did not get off the ground. Angela's allegation was initially doubted by two powerful leaders among the inmates, despite the evidence in the letters, but most of them still believed her. Bullying is what these two leaders seemed like at times, with their behavior and speech. They constructed nicely due to their daily enjoyment of weightlifting, and they opposed Angela's claim of pregnancy resulting from rape by one of the two male intruders. The leaders had no issue with the rape case and believed it happened without a doubt. Their tone sounded as if they possessed exclusive knowledge, surpassing even Anela awareness. The idea that Angela's rapist was a man rather than a resident hermaphrodite was disproved by them.

One of the two bullies named Amanda, developed an interest in researching secretly can hermaphrodite produce children? Amanda learned the answer to her question and convinced her followers to distance themselves from the other bully and her family. The liaison between them did dissolve. Amanda's group stood alongside Angela. Overnight, Amanda became excessively protective of Angela. She defended Angela's honor by fighting the other bully who called her a false pretender. From that day forward, the other leader stopped making inane comments about Angela behind her back. Amanda is now thoroughly convinced that Angela was impregnated by her rapist on the night of the assault. Amanda found herself becoming intrigued by Angela's baby yet again. Angela's worship service and bible study caught the attention of Amanda and her gang, who decided to join.

Angela had turned into a ball of fire for the Lord, an impressive speaker indeed. Others found her prophecies to be consistently accurate. Her interpretations of dreams for her fellow inmates usually left them impressed God worked through her. Should she ever be released from prison, it would be difficult for her to convince her family of her new life in Christ. "If Angela accepts Christ as her Lord and Savior, Mother Faye Esther believed she would lead many to Christ. It's too easy for her to manipulate others vainly and lead them to the devil."

She prayed for Angela to have a change of heart and come to the Lord's side before her incarceration.

Each passing day, Angela's panic and pressure over the institution grew stronger. Angela stood firm on her demand for complete freedom and no charges. Following the advice in the investigators' report, the institution was prepared to release Angela and dance to her tune. The institution concurred with the report, but their lawyer, upon careful review of the report, recommended they hand over the investigation to another group.

One morning, they brought another team of detectives to replace the first team for conflict of interest. They accused them of sympathizing with Angela's alleged rape allegation. Furthermore, one of them remembered that he went to school with her and once had feelings for her. Someone leaked the information.

The new team leader required a polygraph test from Angela. They picked up Angela early in the morning for the test, but she refused to go through it again, believing that they were trying to frame her. Don't forget, she survived the same test previously. The top investigator tried his hardest to persuade Angela to take the test. Bad luck struck him. Angela grounded and rooted on the negative "NO."

She found out that the polygraph tests do not have the ability to detect honesty. She wouldn't have opted for the first one if she had known earlier.

When the inmates realized how late it was and Angela was not back at the institution. They caused a riot, overturned tables, brandished weapons, and demanded to see Angela in 45 minutes. The temporary warden urgently contacted the police department and conveyed the seriousness of the matter. During that time, the prisoners created a melody that echoed, "We want to see Angela today before the sun goes down and we mean it."

They hurried up and brought Angela back to the prison that evening. Her mood was affected by a detective's persistent attempts to extract the truth through violent means. He suggested that she should see Dr. Lina. The institution's chief staffer will discuss how to proceed with the pregnancy for the benefit of all. Angela agreed to meet with Dr. Lina. Angela's doctor since her incarceration is none other than her.

Something important that was kept secret from the inmates and the hospital staff that Angela and Dr. Lina grew up together. They used to be close friends, but life's difficulties drove them apart over time. Angela's mischievousness led Dr. Lina to terminate their friendship. When Angela and Dr. Lina last saw each other, they were both seventeen. Dr. Lina fled from her father's house and Angela's pressure on the same day to avoid them forever. More than thirty years had gone by.

Angela fell sick while in jail three years ago. They admitted her to the hospital. Strangely, she identified Dr.

Lina by two rare birthmarks on her elbow and lower back. Without saying a word, Angela began her own personal investigation into Doctor Lina, doing what she did best. Angela's statement was accurate. She was, without a doubt, Angela's old friend. Angela approached her doctor and asked, "Doctor, do you remember me? The last time we met, we were teenagers, I remember. Your father and I were together at your house."

Doctor Lina replied, "You are highly mistaken. I lived in Irvington, New Jersey my entire life until I got this job. Unlike you, I'm not a South Carolina girl."
"Who said you were?" Angela replied? "Who inquired about your place of origin? Do I give off South Carolina vibes to you? I recall you vividly, Doctor Lina, but do you remember me?"

"Madame Angela Casimir, your mind is playing a trick on you. You are completely overwhelmed with stress. I will prescribe medicine to help clear your mind. You sound delusional," said Doctor Lina.
"If you don't know me, how do you know my maiden name? Angela questioned Dr. Lina? On my chart I have my former husband's last name. Explain to me from where you get Casimir. That's your wild guess."
Angela challenged Dr. Lina to show her lower back.
"What's for?" questioned Dr. Lina as she threatened to send Angela back to her recovery home with her guard."
Without delay, Angela entered the comment, cautioning Dr. Lina that "it would be your second big mistake. Doctor, there's some business left unfinished that we need to handle. If the birthmark on your elbow is not on your lower back, let me see your lower back. I'll apologize to

you on my knees if it's not. "Come on, girl, prove me wrong," Angela shouted at Dr. Lina.

Dr. Lina couldn't beat Angela's challenge and decided to come clean about her identity. The responsibility for deciding her fate lies with Angela. Relying on Angela for your fate is riskier than playing Russian roulette. Before disclosing her identity, Dr. Lina requested Angela to allow her to keep the past events between them confidential. The pain was too much for Dr. Lina to revive. Angela agreed to Doctor Lina's condition after entering a plea. She needed Dr. Lina's forgiveness for all the pain and turmoil she caused in her life. Angela's request was finally approved, fulfilling her long-held dream.

Tamara, when I first learned about the story, I could not digest the fact she denied knowing Angela. When Angela first lay down on the examination table, the doctor recognized her and remembered briefly considering murdering her out of vengeance, but ultimately chose not to due to her faith.

The confrontation happened two years before Angela's rape and pregnancy. Dr. Lina's birthmarks gave her away and Angela's beauty did the same because it's hard to forget someone as beautiful as her. For Angela's safety and hers, she requested that Angela keep their childhood upbringing a secret and pretend not to know each other. Doctor Lina documented every detail of her good and bad experiences in her diary. Recording all her secrets was the doctor's way of coping with being quite a character. She held the belief that her writing would one day lead her to solve a mystery, and she would become wealthy and famous. She believed she was among the most secretive individuals to have ever existed. While possessing a diary, how could that be? Sharing it with Angela resulted in laughter. Angela will hurt Dr. Lina again because Dr. Lina set herself up and hasn't learned anything about Angela. She had the same level of trust in Angela as she did in their childhood. During their private conversation, Angela begged for forgiveness and revealed to Dr. Lina that some desires never die until they're satisfied. Angela's plea made Dr. Lina laugh and reminded her of two things - the importance of keeping their friendship a secret and never underestimating the power of impossibility. Angela smiled and said, "Dr. In my opinion, the word "impossibility" doesn't exist in my book, but "possibility" is always an option, especially when it comes to unfinished business."

With laughter, Dr. Lina told Angela to go back to her cell with her crazy self.
In her heart, she found a room to forgive Angela. Her hate for Angela was so intense that she didn't think she could ever forgive her. She ensured that Angela didn't miss her monthly appointment at the office. Love's triumph over hate is a sight to behold.

The young investigator scheduled an appointment for Angela to see Dr. Lina after being granted the right of way that morning. Angela arrived early and informed Dr. Lina that abortion was not an option in her book. Dr. Lina informed her that she was pregnant, to which she replied, "Never mind, I was raped in my cell while in jail. I passed the polygraph and I'm keeping the baby despite not knowing the father. Inform them that this is my choice.

Angela discovered that Dr. Lina and her nurse Nica passed away while heading to lunch, three months later after Dr. Lina delivered her Will to her lawyer. The person driving the car that hit them was a young girl who said she was running away from home. The doctor and the nurse lost their lives instantly. Anyone who knew Dr. Lina and her nurse well was in a state of shock, including Angela. Angela knew how to feign sadness outwardly to gain sympathy from others, all the while celebrating her happiness internally. The reason for her happiness was not Dr. Lina's death, but the time they spent together to reconcile. Angela relished every second and minute of it, but she had to remain composed. The extent of their closeness over the past three months to everyone.

Angela led a class on the "Powerful Family's Unity," which was something she wished she had grasped in the last thirty years.

As Mother Faye Esther pointed out, no one is immune to the possibility of reforming their lives for the better. Nevertheless, he or she can be classified as a hero in his own right. The magnitude of this conversion deserves recognition and praise from eyewitnesses.

 The way she taught the class, if she meant every word she said, that girl could make her family proud of her conversion; and even "Bury the hatchet."

The death of Dr. Lina and her nurse Nica intensified the situation, even though Angela's prison record is intact.

The key player appointed to negotiate between Angela and the official staff was Dr. Lina. They chose her to bring up Angela's abortion for consideration. Dr. Lina was very smooth. She was a charmer. In a given situation, she had the skill to change the mind of a strong-minded patient. Dealing with Angela required caution because her actions were unpredictable. Angela had an advantage over her. Angela was aware of who Dr. Lina was and knew more than necessary about her. Dr. Lina's opposition to abortion prevented her from playing the mediator game. She was conservative, although she let her guard down a few times. Like anything else, an aggressive government may face pressure to hide their wrongdoing. The embarrassment of someone had the power to turn Dr. Lina, a diehard conservative, to liberal. The fundamental notion is to take a hit for the team's sake. All her attempts fail after speaking to Angela. Angela had no intention of terminating the pregnancy, mentally, physically, or spiritually.

Angela, overnight, transformed into a conservative who now despised abortion.
She advocated for women's rights and was pro-choice before being jailed. Angela believed that abortion went against God's principles for reform. Her right to keep the baby remains intact despite the circumstances of the pregnancy. Moreover, the pregnancy was her means to freedom. Angela desired only a plea bargain that would result in her immediate release. She did not demand any financial reparations from the institution.

CHAPTER 5

TURN OVER EVERY STONE

Understanding how the pregnancy happened was the priority for the new team. They began flipping over each stone, one by one. It appeared that the official staff didn't have enough time. Angela's death threat caused the institution to act by confiscating any letters meant for her. All those threatening letters Angela received were mailed from foreign countries, strange as it may sound. To ensure Angela's safety, an investigator proposed moving her to another female institution. To prevent tension among the inmates, the chief investigator dismissed the idea.

The situation took a turn for the worse. Prior to delivery, the staff read all the letters. The investigators attempted to match Angela's letter's handwriting with other received letters to determine if the sender had any links with other prisoners. As of now, there has been no tangible evidence found.

What's the reason for someone threatening her life if she invited the media world to it? It's an undeniable fact that the story would make headlines in every nation's newspaper. The violation of inmate protection highlighted the incompetence of the official staff. A women's facility that doesn't prevent a female inmate from being raped and impregnated is not worth having. An even better option is to make it unisex, and that was the general sentiment among the residents, sarcastically speaking.

The atmosphere within the jailhouse was terrible. Their limited freedom was taken away, specifically their right to free speech.

Angela used a note technique to communicate important matters due to suspicion of double agents among them. She asked everyone to promise to rip the note into small pieces, chew it, and flush it away. The system appeared to function well for a period. Angela secretly owned a working cell phone that none of the inmates were aware of. It's only usable by her when specific guards are on duty. Angela's fantastic manipulative skills are once again proving successful. The person responsible for the harassment letters and death threats against her was herself. I concur with Mother's opinion that Angela was born to subvert any giving system.

"Who are you telling? I know that sister mischievousness first-hand." Replied Tamara.

"Tamara Baby, I had my doubts about whether you were joking or not. You made it sound like there was something going on between you and Angela," Claude hinted.

"Big Boy, have you forgotten that I read "Tears Of Deception and Sold Out with a Kiss," she replied. "Her wickedness led to the death of Moses and Miriam."

"Oh I see," continued Claude. Angela's friends asked her a question to set her up on a bible study night: why are you declining to take another lie detector test?
"Why should I," answered Angela. "They wouldn't let me retake the test if I had failed it the first time. This is the principal of the whole matter."

45

Amanda joined the conversation, saying, "Taking the test again is a great idea. I think you will pass it again because you mentioned in our conversation a few seconds ago that truth is always remembered naturally."

"A game they want to play with my intelligence," Angela replied to Amanda's comment, "One important point they missed is that two can play by the same rules. They have the outcome of my pregnancy test. It's known that I am pregnant. What's the object of their search? If my sexual dilemma was consensual? Am I acquainted with the perpetrators? What more do they need to discover from me, sisters? Did I find it enjoyable? Please tell me. Meanwhile, they try to buy themselves time, hoping for my miscarriage. I'm determined not to be another Nicole. I won't allow them to cause me stress."

Amanda grinned widely and asked Angela "if she had enjoyed it in a serious tone?" "Enjoyed what," said Angela? "The rapist," Amanda replied with a good sense of humor. They all started laughing at Amanda's word choice. In laughing, Angela replied to Amanda's comment saying, "If I didn't know better, I would think you were the rapist and my baby daddy, Amanda."
Amanda added, "You never know, time will tell girl." She suggested thinking of it as an opportunity to pass the test and prove your point. Impart a lesson to them. "You can count on our complete support. We stand alongside you."

Amanda's words won the applause of the inmates and left Angela in a difficult position. She decided to demonstrate her teaching based on her belief. Angela had everyone's attention as they pondered what the deciding factor would be. Angela gazed upward to the sky, whispering a few words of prayer. After glaring at them for a bit, she looked skyward and mumbled something once more. Silence filled the room. Crying bitterly, Angela fell to her knees. Her tears contaminated the entire room. Tears welled up in everyone's eyes. They sympathized with Angela, who appeared to have a confession to make regarding her situation. She wept and apologized to God, asking for forgiveness for her sins. Worshiping God, Angela sparked contagious worship in others. They confessed their sins to God and reaffirmed their love for Him before leaving the room. They left without knowing what Angela had decided to do.

The detectives scheduled another interrogation with Angela the next day. During her prayer time, they sent the guard to pick her up. The guard interrupted her before she could say Amen. She hurriedly escorted Angela out of the cell and took her upstairs. Upon her arrival, the three detectives flirtatiously offered her a chair. Angela's plain beauty made it impossible for them to resist. They encountered an Angela in the room who declined to speak with them. She handed them a business card from Junior Jeffery, her new lawyer. "Yesterday, you annoyed me so much that I almost lost control," she said to them. "You guys would be delighted if I miscarried. I think that is the reason you pressure and abuse me the way you do. From now on, I'll only speak to you with my lawyer present."

Was Angela's spotting genuine? Surprisingly, she managed to grab their attention, particularly when she shed tears. Even though they tried to reason with her, Angela remained tight-lipped. She will agree to retake the lie detector test if they promise to release her safely if she passes again. Angela did not get a clear answer. In fact, her demand rushed the meeting to its adjournment. The situation was on the verge of getting worse before it exploded. The official staff had no intention of negotiating with Angela. Later that day, they met and scheduled a meeting for Angela to discuss the situation with a team of counselors in depth. It happened the very next day. Angela's counselors paid close attention while she vehemently rejected the notion of abortion due to her religious beliefs, and instead embraced the idea of having the baby no matter the cost.

They never explicitly asked Angela to terminate her pregnancy, but the message was conveyed indirectly through the favorable options presented to her. The counselors had a different opinion than Angela, but they warned her about the seriousness of having a baby with an unknown father and how the memory of the rape would stay with her forever. Following delivery, they made her aware that the baby would be put up for adoption. Angela stood up and said, "The devil is a liar." "I need to talk to my lawyer. I've spent so long in this institution that I almost forgot what a sexual relationship between a man and a woman is like. The thought of dreaming about having a baby would have seemed completely insane to me at my age. In your jail cell, I got rape and pregnant. I'm carrying a rapist's baby in your women's jail where men are not allowed. Since I arrived here, I haven't had a face-to-face conversation with any man except for you guys who have been mistreating me since my ordeal. All of them, the doctors, the nurses, the guards are women. How does one get pregnant? Can you explain it to me? Please enlighten me. I need to get in touch with my legal representative. I want you to understand that I'm not in this state miraculously, but because I got pregnant by a man. When will you discover his whereabouts? My crime is clearly solvable, yet you're doing everything you can to make it an unsolved mystery."

The counselors were perplexed about what to do with Angela besides sending her back to her cell. They signaled the guard who came to gently lead Angela by the arm. "Should I contact my lawyers, or will you set me free to reunite with my family?" Angela inquired while rising from her seat. "I will be three and a half months pregnant tomorrow, and it occurred at your facility for women. I'm expecting a positive response from you within 96 hours. Enjoy the rest of your day, Gentlemen."

The tension in the jail continues to rise as the two rapists who assaulted Angela and two other inmates still haunt the institution. Except for Amanda, all the women in the prison slept with their handmade weapons under their pillows, determined to catch the two male rapists. She rethought because she had a better understanding of the situation than Angela and the institution. They circulated malicious rumors about the rapists' identities. There were different theories about the identity of the malefactors. Some thought they were the ward's sons, others believed one of them was her husband. Angela had a hand in spreading these rumors, but Amanda strongly opposed them. She waited on Angela, taking care of her from head to toe, and made certain she didn't lift anything too heavy. Amanda was so invested that she even suggested a name for the baby. Angela jokingly suggested to Amanda that she could be the father of her baby due to her excellent care.

Amanda responded, "Who knows, only time can reveal the truth."

"Girl, you're crazy," Angela said to Amanda with a laugh.

The inmates and staff at the institution failed to recognize Angela's innate manipulative tendencies. Angela's stunning physique, combined with her brilliance in lecturing about the word of God and her strong conservatism, was what baffled them the most. Her pregnancy had nothing to do with those attributes. She was locked up in a women's prison for some years, and it's unclear how she became pregnant. She will give birth to the baby in another five months. Angela's behavior worsened as she declined to deliver her baby to prison.

"Who could blame her?" Tamara disrupted Claude with this question? She added, "The official staff at the jail seemed to have overlooked the fact that she was raped while in their custody. She ended up getting pregnant in her old age. I think Angela's friends, like me, believe she's paying for the hurt she's caused others, especially Moses and Miriam, even though they feel sorry for her."

Claude agreed, but some believed her past evil character made her the great preacher she is today. Angela has been causing pain to many people for decades, as Mother Faye Esther put it, "The word dirty was invented just to describe her granddaughter Angela, and no one else."

Claude continued that even with everything, her followers perceive her as a new being because of her connection with Christ. They refused to stay fixated on her past for this reason. They thought of Angela as an innocent dove and a truthful angel. There are those who have faith in her loyalty and are ready to sabotage the institution by strongly questioning Angela's honesty and denying her conversion into a truthful individual. They collaborated on a letter to the lead investigator, urging an investigation into some of the warden's sons, husband, and brothers. "If you do that, Mr. investigator dear," they wrote in the letter, "you will find both our rapists and Angela's baby father." The inmates are determined to sort this out, preferably before the baby is born.

Among the inmates, who instigated this belief? Who gave them the advice to write this letter that 75% of the inmates signed? Did Angela have knowledge of the letter and its accusations? Angela knew about the developments beforehand. The letter was crafted by Angela's mastermind. Her preaching and the power of the pulpit drove them to react this way. She already knew the outcome because she had done her homework. Some of the Wards' husbands and sons used to secretly visit the institution with the help of their wives, who would dress them in women's clothing to conceal their identities.

Upon receiving the letter, the investigator, who had the same suspicion as the inmates, immediately called a meeting. The protocol he had to follow was misleading him. He didn't know how to tackle it without causing any disagreement, which might have caused his removal from the case. Nevertheless, his detective intuition and expertise compelled him to begin where the prisoners indicated.

The letter granted him the chance to conduct a routine investigation, subject to the committee's consent. It was a fact that the board had rejected the same recommendation before, and he knew it. By eliminating some possibilities, he initiated a fresh investigation. The inmates were tested individually, and it was confirmed that none of them could have impregnated Angela. A ruling stirred up strong passion in Amanda's disagreement. After reviewing the files of everyone working there, he ruled out the hospital staff that inmates frequently visited for checkups and medical needs. They were all women.

The committee approved the investigation, and the lead agent and his team have received permission to question all institution employees once more. Tamara. For most of the workers, the interviews lasted three weeks. Four workers caught the attention of the investigations team as being valuable. The four females broke the institution's code of ethics by letting their male friends and family perform walkthroughs as birthday gifts. To successfully finish the tour, they need to dress up in the opposite gender's clothes by a professional cross dresser. This is to deceive the prisoners and safeguard their loved ones who arranged the dangerous trip.

However, the four officers insisted that their family had only visited once before Angela moved in. This being a one-time thing made it difficult for the detectives to believe. Although they held this belief, they viewed even one occurrence of this situation as too dangerous. One husband and one son spent a few days and nights among the inmates, leading them to believe it occurred more than once.

What led the prisoners to discover this secret visit? This information came from Angela. She knew it and she spread the rumor indirectly to her sister inmates through the process of gossiping. A few years ago, Angela investigated the code of ethics of a women's prison after hearing from two inmates who were raped by men in their cells. Angela, a new inmate at the Jail, became fearful and paranoid and started conducting her own secret investigation on the prison staff's family members. She became interested in learning about their husbands, sons, nephews, and so on. Little did she know that the information she collected would come in handy one day. She managed to solve the assault puzzle.

During a conversation with Heavenly, the chief warden, Angela stumbled upon a fantastic discovery. She shared with Angela about her family and how her two sons were crazy about beautiful women. "If they ever see you, Angela, they will fall for you."

Angela reminded the warden of her age in a hurry.

Heavenly responded to Angela by saying that her sons don't care about age since it's just a number to them.

Heavenly went inside her wallet and flashed their pictures at Angela.

"Very handsome men! Are they married?" asked Angela.

"No way" replied Heavenly. "My sons are players. They just love to play and nothing else. They cannot get caught," and she laughed.

Angela helped her laugh and said, "They haven't found the right women yet. Women who could hook them up like fish and those types of girls often use live bait." Both laughed again.

"Who that might be? I thought you said, you're too old, you're not a cougar, are you?" asked Heavenly."

"Please give me a break Heavenly, Hunter and Jacques are old enough to be my sons. That would be child abuse. On a serious note, have they ever visited this facility?"

Heavenly screamed! "Angela are you crazy? That would be a firing issue. This is against the law of the facility. Angela, do you have any children? Wait a minute before answering. Angela, how do you know the name of my boys?"

"A few minutes ago, you mentioned that Hunter and Jacques are your sons and players," Angela said. "Beautiful women usually recognize players. There are many who think my two girls are my twins."

Angela went back to her cell feeling extremely happy. The conversation between her and Heavenly gave her a clear starting point for her investigation. Angela required only the assistance of her daughter Patrice as an undercover agent.

The guards on duty that night were the right ones. Angela retrieved her phone from its secret spot and dialed her daughter Patrice. She urged her daughter to join the most powerful and popular social media site to become friends with both of Warden's sons, Jacques, and Hunter. She gave her daughter and best friend all the necessary details to carry out the task. Angela explained the purpose to Patrice, who became excited and ready to embark on the adventure. Angela instructed her to keep everything confidential from the entire family, particularly from Patrica, her twin sister. The task given to Patrice was to find the Warden's sons on social media and add them as friends. Knowing their love for beautiful women, Angela was confident that Patrice and Patrica would win them over. Angela hoped Patrica would join the mischievous deal to hook both brothers but knew her integrity wouldn't allow it. Angela expressed her concern to Patrice, who revealed her plan to deceive both brothers by also playing Patrica.

Patrice heeded her mother's advice and went through their pages. She noticed their handsomeness. A new page was made under Patrica's name and two friend requests were sent, one under her own name and the other under Patrica's. She planned to go out with both separately and talk to them. The brothers immediately responded to the friend's request because the twin girls were stunningly beautiful. Patrice, being as smart as she is, informed the brothers that she and Patrica are twins. She sent them pictures of themselves.

Patrice and they developed a great online friendship. Every day, they felt the desire to meet the girls face to face. Hunter, one of the brothers, believed he was in love with Patrice, which seemed madness. She gave him her number because he talked a lot and she saw that as an advantage for her job.
 Patrice scheduled a double date with Patrica, Hunter, and Jacques two months later. Two days before the date, she requested Hunter to come alone because Patricia would be on a business trip, and Jacques knew already. Hunter droves for four hours to make this happen while feeling anxious. His brother Jacques was highly disappointed.
Patrice was without a doubt Angela's daughter. She persuaded Patrica to go with her to meet Hunter and leave.

The reason for Patrica's presence was unclear to her, so she inquired about it. Patrice confided in Patrica her apprehension about going on a blind date with an unknown man, asking her to meet him and depart. Patrice begged Patrica to stay for less than five minutes, and she finally gave in. Perfect! Patrice shouted.

She engaged Patrica in her deceptive act. She coerced her to come along so that Hunter could meet her twin sister and she could still act out Jacques and Patrica.

The two girls wore white skinny jeans with a yellow blouse and yellow and white heels that evening. Those girls were a sight to behold, so beautiful. They arrived in separate sports cars and parked in the restaurant lot where Hunter was patiently waiting for Patrice. It came as a surprise for him to encounter Patrica. When they walked up to Hunter after getting out, he thought he was dreaming about angels. Hunter was in disbelief and thought to himself, "My brother should have been here to see this."

Patrice walked towards him and embraced him in the most provocative hug he had ever received. He was left speechless, and Patrice knew she had already won his heart. Her sister was introduced to Hunter, and they spoke for a few minutes. As she was leaving, Patrica kindly asked Hunter to say hello to Jacques, which made her sister Patrice's day.

Hunter and Patrice entered the restaurant and took seats beside each other. Patrice received compliments on her beauty and outfit from the server. After looking at Hunter, she said, "You both make a great pair. You're blessed, sir, take good care of her." Hunter said, "I'm in love with her, but only if she's willing."

.

Feeling too nervous, Hunter asked to be excused to go to the bathroom without saying anything else. Upon leaving, the server returned to ask Patrice how she had done? They were great pals.

While feeling sorry for Jacques in the bathroom, Hunter sent a selfie he took with Patrice and Patrica to his brother. Before ending the call, he said to Jacques, "I think I have found my wife. Can you believe it? I'm in love!? I can't distinguish between them as everything about them is identical."

Patrice didn't waste any time going after the information she wanted when he returned to the table, and he had no qualms about sharing his thoughts on the female prison. Before that, Hunter left the restroom and made his way to the table, smiling as he noticed Patrice gazing at him fondly. "What's with that expression on your face?" he questioned her? "You make me blush," she replied. "I love everything about you, particularly your shape. Many women would go to great lengths to have a figure like yours. If I dressed you as a woman and put you in a women-only place, you could blend in for a week or two without being caught."

"I know," replied Hunter. He laughed and said, "We did that before, and got away with it three years in a row."

With an angry tone, Patrice asked, "We, who are we?" Patrice's eyes gave Hunter the impression of jealousy. "My brother Jacques, my two uncles, and I," he quickly responded, afraid of ruining the evening.

Yeah right! Patrice, who was acting, said to Hunter, "I'm not naive, so tell me everything or let's just end things here."

Hunter once again disclosed his secret like a whistleblower and caused trouble for his mother, the female institution and everyone involved.

Patrice came across some caveats that might be useful for her mother's release. It's a well-known fact that rich men who cross dress visit the jail for a weekend getaway around Christmas. Posing as women, they secretly sleep in the female institution. Regardless of how crazy they wanted her to sound, Nicole   spoke the truth.

.Meanwhile, a detective tried to bother Angela by urging her to redo the lie detector test. She gave him a look as if she could see into his soul and declared: "I'm willing to negotiate with you and your detectives."

"Really?" he asked. "Yes, call your partners," Angela replied.

He called his four partners and let them know that Angela was ready to make a plea deal. Anxious, they flew into the room. Looking at everyone, she smiled and declared, "I know some of you can't look me in the eyes, but I have an idea. Let's have three of you take a lie detector test to prove that you weren't pretending to be women while sleeping in this facility. We are aware that some of you are members of this criminal ring. I'll retake my test if you pass yours. If you reject my proposal, call my lawyer to come and get me or else three of you will be labeled as corrupt cops. With every passing moment, the 96-hour countdown to my release gets shorter. May I return to my cell now? I'll keep this conversation between us for the time being," Angela promised.

CHAPTER 6

PLAYING WITH FIRE

"Hold on, Claude Honey," Tamara exclaimed, "this is an incredible story. Let me use the restroom quickly, and I'll be back in a flash.

She got out of the car, took a few steps towards the restroom before realizing she had left her purse. Swiftly, she turned, sprinted, and grasped it as if she was shielding it from her partner. Was Tamara concealing something from Claude because he was not the type of man who would invade her privacy covertly? Tamara was on the verge of urinating on herself when she went back for the pocketbook, but she overcame the feeling. Curiously, what did Tamara attempt to shield from Claude? From beginning to end, she recorded their conversation using a small tape recorder.

Tamara opened her pocketbook in the bathroom and said, "Voila." She took out her tape recorder and verified if it recorded their conversation as desired. She listened to the tape for a bit and felt satisfied. She recorded everything Claude said about Mother Faye Esther and her family. Tamara surprisingly ran out of tape. She thought she had another one, but it remained on her dresser. She missed a fantastic opportunity because her husband couldn't control what he said. He planned to tell her stories spanning over two decades in just one day. Upon returning to the car,

Tamara was solely relying on her memory since the information was coming too quickly for her to keep up. She devised a plan for her husband to drive back fifteen miles to where he picked up the banner, so that she could buy some recorded tapes. Knowing her plan, she still executed it without upsetting Claude. She made a call to a friend before leaving the bathroom and requested them to call back after 25 minutes to exchange a brief greeting. "Hello, how are you, Tamara? Hang the phone."
"It's a deal," said the friend without hesitation.

Tamara's excessive interest in the story of this family may suggest that she had an agenda, but she needed to be careful. According to Mother Faye Esther, "those who take pleasure in rummaging through other people's garbage will eventually come across something so putrid that it will be the end of them?"

Tamara's lack of understanding led her to play with fire. Mother Faye Esther likely had knowledge of her malicious intentions and gradually lured Tamara in like a caught fish. Tamara was out of her depth swimming as a small fish among sharks. Those who break Mother Faye Esther's trust may face her vindictiveness. For this reason, Claude had regaled Tamara with tales of this dangerous family, covering all aspects of their notoriety.
For now, there are still numerous unanswered questions about Tamara's behavior. Tamara's prospects are bleak, with the clear message of "TROUBLE AHEAD.". Her espionage activities could lead to her becoming a pitiful and miserable ex-wife, having lost the worst divorce scenario of her life. One lesson she would learn from this

awful ordeal right or wrong, "The poor cannot expect to win against money."

The revealed fact is that Tamara spied on the Casimir family. Was it for her benefit or someone else's? She had a history in journalism. Perhaps she aimed to revive it by uncovering secrets about the family. Time, the great storyteller, will eventually unveil her disastrous motive.

Tamara returned to the car with a sad expression that caught her husband's attention. He inquired, "Are you alright, honey?"

Tamara replied, "My love, why do you ask?"

Claude replied humorously, "Sweetheart what happened to your manners? Asking another question is not an answer, what's wrong with my lovely wife?"

Tenderly Tamara pulled him away from the wheel, kissed him passionately and whispered in his ear, "Claude, I love you. I'm the luckiest woman in the world.".

"My goddess," replied Claude, "I love you too. We should leave this parking lot before we get in trouble for indecent exposure."

Tamara giggled and said, "Big Boy, are you afraid? This heat is not leaving anytime soon, it's on pause for tonight. Prepare yourself Big Boy."

Claude responded, I'm prepared to Rock'n Roll with everything I have and this time, I won't fall asleep, so bring it on, Big Mama."

They both shared a laugh before resuming their journey to Mother Faye Esther's house with the banner. After 25 minutes, Tamara's phone started ringing. "Hello," she replied, "yes... Oh my... I can't believe I did that. I'm in trouble - my husband is going to be livid. I will be right over to pick it up."

Her friend was the one who made the promising phone call to her.

Paying close attention to her conversation, Claude asked, "What's going on?"

"Claude, my love, I'm sorry I left my credit card in the store. They want me to pick it up now, and tonight I'll show my gratitude for taking me back, I promise."

Claude sought assurance. "You promise?"

He made U-Turn and took her back to the store. Tamara often forgets that "To love is to trust." She adopted a "Quid pro quo" attitude, using intimacy as a crutch instead of a marital duty.

She and Claude got out of the car simultaneously when they arrived at the store. Tamara rushed towards the driver's seat and gave Claude a kiss on the lips. She jokingly said to him, "Don't you move, Big Daddy. Just wait for me here. I'll grab those cassette tapes and come out soon. I don't want to be cheated out of what I deserve tonight, so please don't use the usual excuse of being tired, my dear husband."

Claude laughed at the mockery she directed at him. He repeated himself, "Cassette tapes! I thought you came to pick up your credit card."

"Oh honey," his wife responded, "tonight's excitement has caused me to misspeak. I meant my credit card."

Claude laughed wholeheartedly, oblivious to the deception. Does marrying someone who is old enough to be your child come at a cost? Yes or no, Claude is paying for it as a balloon mortgage, regardless of the price.

Tamara is indeed a liar who lies unbearably to play with her husband's true feeling regarding her.

Tamara arrived back in the car, equipped with a tape recorder, ready to capture the rest of Angela's peculiar stories, which Claude was fully aware of.

She said to him, "I didn't mean to interrupt our conversation. You know I must use the restroom also."

"Where were we in the story? Do you remember?" Asking Claude in a frightening voice.

"Yes, I do," replied Tamara, "where we left off at, Patrice went out with Hunter, the Warden's son and teased him until he spilled his gust out, putting his mother's job in jeopardy. She may even face jail time.

Tamara said in her mind, for some reason Claude is acting nervous, I wonder did I get caught deceiving my husband?

As he waited for his wife, Claude spotted a man at the gas station pumping gas into a burgundy and silver hammer, bearing a striking resemblance to the late Yves Day. He became extremely frightened, questioning the reliability of his eyes and mind, as they had just discussed Yves Day's death decades ago. Claude believed he had convinced Yves to come back from the dead. Claude bowed down his head and prayed. The burgundy and silver hammer vanished completely when he opened his eyes and looked up. Claude, as pessimist as he could be, had become emotionally incontrollable. He believed he had an encounter with Yves' ghost.

Hearing her husband shriek, Tamara came running to the car. She did not know what to think. She inquired, "Why are you behaving like a wild man?" Claude kept his silence, dried the tears from his eyes and drove. Ignoring her and refusing to answer her question, Tamara's husband

caused her to become upset and develop a nasty attitude towards him. Tamara formulated her question in a different way. This time, he added, "You won't grasp."
"Give it a shot," she responded. "Never mind," he answered. Tamara thrived on the back-and-forth response. She asked Claude to drop her off by the side of the road. She could catch a taxi home from there. Her reactions and her demands reached the softest part of her husband's heart. He remarked, "Baby, you always escalate things to a point where they become completely illogical. I know the minute I tell you; you will indeed laugh at me. Tamara, you might even think that I'm insane."
"No, I won't" replied Tamara.
Unexpectedly, he said, "I just had an encounter with Yves' ghost. It was very scary. I saw him pumping gasoline in a burgundy and silver hammer. I bowed my head, closed my eyes, and said a brief prayer because I could not believe what I saw. By the time I opened my eyes and looked up, the hammer vanished away, and I busted unto tears."

Tamara glanced at her husband with pity and burst into laughter, jokingly saying, "Guess what, Claude? It might be best for you to consider finding a new job, as working with Mother Faye Esther is detrimental to your well-being. You both should consider seeing a psychiatrist since you're mutually harmful. I need to stay away from you guys. Mother Faye Esther is looking forward to the arrival of Moses and Miriam, despite their deaths years ago. You had just witnessed Yves, Moses and Miriam's father who also deceased, fueling his truck. So Yves and his children were superhuman, just like his father Edner Day. What are you getting at? Let me stop teasing you, Claude. Before I start getting paranoid and thinking I see Ester, his wife sitting on the front passenger side of the hammer. Please forgive me. I don't mean to laugh at you like this, but you and Mother are funny."

What did Patrice do with the information? Asked Tamara, who tried to pick up the story where she left it.

Claude informed her that Hunter's information caused all the commotions, resulting in his mother and her staffers losing their jobs and facing jail time as they plead guilty during the ongoing investigation.

Angela did an excellent job spreading the news, using it as an alibi to explain her pregnancy resulting from a rape in the female prison.

Junior Jeffery, Angela's lawyer refuted the idea of retaking the lie detector test because they had too much evidence of sex trafficking in the prison.

Angela shared the news with her congregants, who praised her lawyer's expertise in criminal affairs. Amanda believed Angela should have countered the lawyer's argument. Amanda became deeply invested in Angela's welfare, even going as far as divulging the identity of the baby's father to fellow inmates.

Angela, who is five months pregnant, is anxious about her case as she doesn't want to give birth in jail. Each day, sadness would pay her a visit, particularly when she was alone. Angela only found happiness when preaching or teaching the word of God. Angela had a strong passion for God's word.

She fooled around and genuinely embraced religion. Angela earned the nickname prophetess Casimir from her devoted parishioners. By appointment, she would interpret their dreams and visions on a weekly basis.

One day, Angela was deep in her emotions, rejecting food, drink, and abstaining from fasting. She was overwhelmed with remorse. Having a baby in prison in her old age was unimaginable for her. Two inmates visit Angela's cell to uplift her spirits, but her self-disappointment robs her of her smile and laughter. One of them challenged Angela, saying, "I bet I can make you smile. Watch! guess what Amanda told us in a kidding manner of how she knew who your baby's father is?"

Angela got nervous like her secret was about to be revealed and she answered with a frown, "who did she say."

"Are you ready for this, Angela?"

Angela hastily replied, "Yes.".

."Look into our eyes," they said, and Angela did.

"Amanda," they uttered.

Angela's laughter attracted other comrades who came running to see what was so funny.

"For some reason," the inmate continued, "Amanda truly believed she is your baby's daddy."

Angela couldn't stop herself from snickering as she exclaimed, "You guys are so crazy, you might make me have the baby early."

They answered, "Angela, you better nip it in the bud before is too late," Angela questioned "how she could have possibly impregnated me and with what? If I have the baby here, I'll ask Amanda to be the godmother. I think she deserves that. She supports me in everything and is overly protective of me. She wants me to take it easy for the baby's sake. I told her one day last week, "if she were a man, I would think she was the rapist who impregnated me."

They laughed at Angela's sense of humor and added, "Do you know Amanda is…"

Angela resumed the conversation before concluding and asked, "Guys, do you remember what I preached about last Sunday during the evening services? Let's avoid spreading malicious gossip within the family and remember that salvation is for everyone. Life isn't about the past, but about the present and future in Christ Jesus. Once upon a time, my thoughts turned dark as I considered myself to be Satan's mother. Now look at me, God breaks me, places me into a mold, and shapes me all over again. Look, let me twirl a bit here for you to see the brand new me. God, the Chief Scientist, performed my heart transplant surgery."

They started shouting and praising God. Angela's power in God can ignite worship and praise in any believer. Amanda came to Angela's cell at the time Angela was twirling. Amanda was clueless about what was happening. As Angela spun in circles, Amanda shouted a reminder to be cautious of the baby. Amanda got upset and returned to her cell because Angela and the others were too engrossed in the spiritual realm to listen.

Tamara, "I believe Angela takes seriously her salvation. Through her witnessing, she has most of the inmates to convert to Christianity. They changed religion from left to right."

"Claude honey, not quite. She has a long way to go unless there is an overnight miracle taking place, and I know what I'm talking about, trust me."

"Wait a minute, my beautiful Tamara, if I did not know any better, I would think you were Angela's friend. Are you?"

"Yeah, through you," continued Tamara, "we talk about her for a minute now. By listening to you, allow me to form my opinion of her character concerning salvation. I have knowledge of her dirty deeds now and then. She needs a lot of repentance to reach God, even as we speak now."

"Tamara, I think you are right, baby girl." Tamara queried, "This is a fascinating life story. Let us continue Claude. Big boy, you are a true storyteller."

Tamara never missed a beat in boosting her husband's ego to the tenth power.

Claude resumed from where he stopped and informed Tamara that the baby was expected in four months. Junior, Angela's lawyer, organized a meeting with the six attorneys representing the Woman Federal prison to discuss reducing Angela's sentences to seven years. Something Angela and her lawyer will disagree with them. He wanted Angela to be freed, and all charges dropped, allowing her to give birth in her preferred hospital. He visited Angela to talk about her future behind bars, but Angela had different plans in mind, including hiring Junior to help secure Nicole's release and testify against the warden and her staff. Angela was the one who provided Nicole and the rest of them with the information that her daughter Patrice received from Hunter through manipulation. Angela's case benefited from the same information. Angela's brilliance is a double-edged sword, endangering both society and her.

One Friday morning, Junior Jeffery shared the good news with Angela. The board has approved your freedom, but it will take five months for the release form to be signed and approved by you and the institution.
Junior Jeffery noticed Angela's lack of enthusiasm about the deal and asked her about her mood.

"No deal," she replied, "The baby will be born behind bars in five months." I can settle for three months, and I want them to release Nicole as well."

Junior Jeffery responded, "They won't agree to that, you're pushing the boundaries of luck. Nicole is your escape route, as far as she's concerned. We must sacrifice her for your release and classify her as delusional and crazy to avoid another lawsuit. Remember, your release is contingent upon maintaining perpetual silence until death. I need to thoroughly review all the paperwork to ensure their legitimacy. I will communicate that we want to settle in three months instead of five. We will get in touch soon. Take care of yourself, beautiful Lady, and make sure you stay beautiful."
Angela answered, "You too, my handsome baby daddy."

Tamara urgently stops her husband and exclaims, "Claude, Angela's baby's father is her lawyer. Unbelievable! How that happened?"
Claude started to laugh and say, "There is a price to pay when males or females flirt with Angela. She will make t". She will make them pay, one way or another."

Tamara responded, stating that I know exactly what you are talking about and confirming its truthfulness.

"Say what?" Uttered Claude. "How do you know, Tamara?"

"Claude, my love, I'm great at listening. The manner you share the story which makes me feel like I know Angela. But you did not answer. Is Junior Jeffery, the rapist?"

"Tamara, girl, you are missing a screw. "You are funny," added Claude.

"But Claude, that sister, is capable of doing anything."

"Yes, you better believe it, Tamara."

Angela sadly went back to her cell. The inmates were introduced to Angela they had no idea existed all these years. Her demeanor was unapproachable, which piqued everyone's curiosity.

They interrogated Angela out of concern, but all she said was "Not now please and goodnight. See you all, Sunday, and be on time."

Rumors circulated among them about what was wrong with Angela. Many concluded that they denied her claim, an idea which crushed in pieces Nicole's hope to see the sunlight again.

No one has ever counted Angela out. She always hides something under her sleeve.

The determination to free Nicole from jail occupied Angela's intellect greatly.

She used her skills to find out all she needed to know about Junior Jeffrey her lawyer from one of his colleagues whom she flirted with online nightly while behind bar.

Junior's friend on the other hand thought that Angela was a law professor in a French country.

He shared with Angela Junior's deepest struggle to adopt a child and he wanted one as yesterday. How did she meet this man?

On Junior's social media pages and she realized both were lawyers and they were good buddies. Angela befriended him just to spy on Junior Jeffery.

Angela saw pictures of Junior's wife on his page and automatically fell in love with her, because she reminded Angela of her oldest sister Ester and her husband who died at least two decades plus ago.

She called Junior on that Friday evening and requested an emergency meeting at nine in the morning.

He agreed to meet with her the next Monday because he and his wife had an appointment with Maeva, the founder of a successful adoption agency who matched them with a baby for adoption. Before he could give her this information she replied, "Monday is fine."

Out of nowhere, she cautioned Junior about the meeting regarding child adoption, advising him not to attend as the child could be problematic for the future parents.

If it's God plan, I'll see you on Monday. On this note, she hung up the phone and left Junior Jeffery puzzled.

He immediately called the jail and instructed the answering guard to pass on this message to Angela: "She's truly a prophetess of God Almighty, just like my wife."

Regardless how the prison staff felt about Angela's connection to God, she did make a believer out of Junior and his wife.

Tamara added, "Claude, check this out. Do you think Angela got the scoop from Junior's friend about his meeting with Maeva?"

Claude responded, "She's far from being a perfect woman. The transition from bad to good takes time, especially for the old Angela. Trust me, Tamara, at this point of the story the girl is a saint now compared to when I first met her. I viewed Angela as one who is wrestled daily with Good and Evil, and Evil refused to let her go without an unforgettable fight. I believe one day she will truly praise God from where He brought her on that day, she will be a carbon copy of her grandmother."

CHAPTER 7

REFLECTION/REPENTANCE

Angela stayed in her cell all day Saturday. No one saw her. She spent the time with God preparing a message entitled "DEAL BREAKER" subtitled, "CONFESSION IS GOOD FOR THE SOUL" for Sunday morning services. The Day of the Lord arrived, and she began her message like this "No confession, no forgiveness, where there is no forgiveness, there is no love because love longs for the truth.

Overnight, she became one of the most powerful preachers' believers of God had ever heard. She had a particular style when delivered God's word. Pastor Angela asked them a few questions that morning, and of them was, "Let me see the hands of you who truly believed that Jesus saved you?"

Instead of raising their hands, they all stood up, giving God the highest praise that the jail house ever experienced. "From what I see, we are all saved in here, Hallelujah," continued Pastor Angela.

Her observation set the church up for true worship. While they were worshipping God in the spirit, she said, "Can God trust our worse enemies into our hands to pray for our salvation?" She continued, "Who will pay" "An eye for an eye or a tooth for a tooth." In that scenario? Who among you believe that "Forgiveness is greater than vengeance.?" She anointed who desired to be anointed with oil, and

Pastor Angela announced a three-day revival. She received permission from the acting warden to do so. The theme for the revival was "Let's Bury the Hatchet and Come Clean to Your Fellowman and Forgive Their Sins."

After the revival, everyone felt compelled to apologize to one another and begged each other pardon for doing wrong maliciously. In their plea for a new beginning. Something miraculously happened for the first time in the world penitentiary across the board since its invention. The residents of this female's institution unanimously agreed to live from now on an assault and drama free lives base on sisterhood's spirits. The revival that Pastor Angela preached that week pricked their hearts and soul. It unrooted all mischievousness associated with hatred and crimes. It disarmed them of their homemade weapons, no more stabbing, cutting, fighting, stealing, and killing. On the last day of the revival, they surrendered to the interim warden all harmful fabricated weapons they had for their defenses. The items that they stole from each other were returned to the appropriate owners.

The interim warden, a veteran of thirty-six years in that aspect was in the state of shock when she saw the high sophistication of armaments crafted by these women. Many questions crossed her mind. She became speechless wondering if the inmates were planned for a bloody riot against the institution.

"Tamara Baby, she was right in her thinking, they were about to attack the prison's staff if they caused Angela to lose the baby or if they refused to set her free," informed Claude.

Angela tried to change their minds and she could not deviate from their plans. Angela was conscious of this plan of action, prayed day and night for God to redirect their anxious and dangerous attack on her behalf. The Lord heard Angela's cries and supplications. He delivered in a way which surprised the petitioner herself, the prison, and the outside world.

This revival proved that Angela was truly a changed woman. The old Angela would encourage the people to riot on her behalf.

Monday morning arrived, and Junior was at the prison waiting room bright early to meet with Angela, his client. The female guard went to get her while opening Angela's cell she asked her to be good today for Goodness' sake. Angela responded as always.

The guard while leading Angela to chat with Junior Jeffery, she said: "Angela, why are you so happy today?" Angela wasted no time and replied with "Why not, I'm going to have a conversation with a man, right. Any woman living here would be pleased to see a man, regardless of his appearance or weight. As long as he's a man, who cares? Any woman who doesn't understand is as confused as someone wearing mismatched shoes."

The female guard replied, "For your knowledge, I don't have a problem, and stop throwing shade, So Called Woman of God."

Angela answered, "Good, whose woman's woman are you, woman?"

The walk toward the waiting room seemed longer than usual because of the friction existing between all the inmates and the guards.

Angela met Junior Jeffery that day who was in a jovial mood. He hugged Angela for the first time as her lawyer.

He thanked her for allowing God to speak through her to warn him and his wife about the adoption. He looked at her and said, "I felt good about the decision. I know God has a baby for us it's long overdue. I bring you good news Angela. Are you ready to hear it, sit down. I don't want you to hurt yourself nor the baby leaping for joy."

Angela acted like she did not care one way or another about receiving good news. She was more concerned about her soul than her physical freedom. She was starving and thirsting for living right, and doing the right thing was the only thing that crunched this urge. Angela had learned on her way to the waiting room to do right is a choice as well as doing wrong. She learned again there will be a payday someday by God Himself. Does the crime pay for it regardless of the sanction, and the times associated with it before meeting the Maker face to face.

"In that case, Claude, she has a lot for which to repent, Lord knows, but why give Junior Jeffery a cold shoulder," added Tamara.

Claude replied, "The situation was getting the best out of her to the point of introducing her to intense stress, anxiety, and sadness. The only time she felt free as a bird was when preaching or teaching the word of God. Outside of that, she found herself between a rock and a hard place. Nightly, she had nightmares about all the people she used, abused, destroyed, and the list was as long as eternity."

Tamara answered, "Especially Moses and Miriam. It was ashamed the way Angela caused those two children death."

Claude responded, "Yeah, Moses and Miriam were on top of the list from the things that haunted her daily since she gave her life back to Jesus. When she was living in sins stuff like that never bothered her. Sin is known to make its doers or sinners feel good about their lifestyles. The word remorse never entered their vocabulary until they repented and received their salvation."

Junior Jeffery questioned Angela about her mood, because he was so used to a cheerful Angela who was always happy and comical even when her going was tough. He said to Angela, "Relax Girl, you are safe now from the detectives, the institution, and their lawyers. Who else try to push you off the cleft or rub you the wrong way this morning?"

Angela, after sitting down on the chair, exhaled deeply with a sorrowful frown on her face and said to Junior, "I got to do the right thing even though it will cost me. It will be what I truly deserved to have peace with my God. The funny thing about that Junior Jeffery, God forgave me already, but I must come clean with those who are still living that I have badly hurt. You see Junior Jeffery; I'm talking to you in confidentiality as my lawyer. My two girls and the rest of my family don't know anything about my life behind bars. My carrying a baby is unknown to them. They knew that I'm incarcerated but ignore where. I led them to believe that I was in an institution near one of the West Indies Country, while I'm forty-five minutes away from them. I planned it that way, because I did not want any family members visiting me here. But anyway, tell me the good news Junior Jeffery."

"Oh well," started Junior Jeffery, "The good news is, you will be out three months before the baby is born. We won the lawsuit in twenty-five days you will walk out of here and have your healthy baby in a hospital of your choice. She is ready to come out I see her kicking in your stomach. I was telling my wife whenever I came to see you the baby kicks so hard like to say "Good Morning or Good Afternoon to me. She loves me. My wife swears you're carrying a set of twins."

Angela burst out laughing and saying, "Whenever you talk about my baby you always use her. Do you know something that I don't know?"

"Yes, this is a girl," responded Junior Jeffery.

"Tell your wife, she better have a couple cribs ready then because both will be hers. I wish that I could meet Mrs. Jeffery. I'm not asking you to keep a secret from your wife. As we speak, I have an open vision. God came to your wife and ask her to adopt my children, She is going to ask you to bring her so both of you can talk to me. But I only carry a child, but God says children my other kids are adults. Please don't tell her, let her share it first. Junior Jeffery, you are a man of faith, but you cause that faith to be limited. Let her tell you first, and it will increase your faith in the works of God. Between you and I, it was my intention to give the baby up for adoption anyway to a young couple."

Tamara, Junior Jeffery was speechless before Angela because his wife certainly told him that the babies that the woman from the jail carried belonging to them. He shouted with a loud voice before Angela saying, "Lord, keep on increasing my faith."

Then Junior Jeffery asked Angela, "Let me try to get some understanding here. Are you for real putting your baby up for adoption? Remember Angela in twenty to twenty-five days you will be a free woman. At first, they were willing to reduce all your sentences to seven years in prison. I entered a motion for a complete release or no deal in exchange for keeping your mouth closed. This immunity is one of the best deals I have ever seen or heard in criminal and civil court. You have what you wanted."

Angela leaned back on the chair with her hands locked together rested on top of her head and sighed deeply. Junior quickly recognized her distressful move and posture and he said to Angela, "I'm a lawyer not a mind reader. Please tell me what's going on with you besides wanting to give the baby away to my wife and me."

"Oh well, you caught me, Junior Jeffery, but you don't have enough time today to listen to my grievances. I was a Bad Girl, my entire life until yesterday after I was through preaching God came among us. He pricked our hearts, led all of us to repentance. Junior Jeffery, I'm a change woman. I'm feeling brand new. I'm not the same pragmatic scam artist anymore. I'm changed man, I change for the good. I used to think that I was beyond repentance, beyond receiving forgiveness from God. I have hurt so many people in my lifetime even here. I have so much I want to share with you as my lawyer, so many secrets but this room might be bugged. Sir, I need to come clean and confess some things with you as my lawyer, confident, and priest."

Junior Jeffery pulled out his phone, called the office and asked his secretary to cancel all his appointments. Then he said, "I'm all yours and it is safe for you to speak freely in confidential with me, right here."

"First and foremost, we need to talk about adopting my baby. After praying, I got the green light from God. I'm prepared to initiate the process, once I meet your wife who is dead serious. Are there any hindrances for you to adopt my baby?"

Junior clarified that they had concerns, not issues, and added that he and his wife were qualified to handle it without professional help.
As a lawyer, he can take care of the adoption independently, that's what he meant. He asked Angela, "What type of adoption are you seeking for, closed or open?"
What's the distinction," Angela replied with a question.

Angela, With closed adoption, there is no involvement or contact in the child's life. If the new parents, and the real mother were acquainted, they might not want to meet again following the adoption. But studies have found that children adapt better in open adoptions. It enables them to comprehend their adoption story. Questions about their birth parents can also be asked by the children."

Breaking through the conversation, Angela wasted no time in stating her decision for closed adoption. "After the delivery, I won't require any further interaction with the baby, and I'll keep her biological mother a secret.

Moreover, I still have seven years remaining in this prison."

Junior Jeffery screamed, "You haven't heard a word I said. Seven years!"

'They were settled for seven years which was the remaining of your normal sentences in this State. Now in twenty-fives days you will be free from jail. The sound of freedom is amazing, Angela. Can you hear it?"

"Junior Jeffery, I heard every word you said earlier. For reasons related to my faith, I'll opt for the seven-year choice. Let's not worry about that for the time been because in twenty-five days, God might change my mind."

Junior Jeffery asked, "About what, the adoption?"

"Oh no, continued Angela, it's a done deal. I'm waiting to see your wife before starting the process. Earlier, I spoke about my release time. I have a lot to share about this unplanned and unwanted pregnancy once the judge releases me. One thing I know for sure without a shout of doubt. My baby will be in good hands with you and Mrs. Jeffery. Junior Jeffery, you are a good man, and you will be a great father. Your kindness in adopting her is appreciated. Thank you."

Junior Jeffery answered, saying, "We will enjoy her. An open adoption would likely be favored by my wife, given her personality."

"I'm a hard no," Angela asserted, making her opposition clear.

Junior Jeffery, while listening to Angela, realized she hadn't been truthful with him concerning her pregnancy story. His intention
was to dig for the truth, but he hated to make her upset. He decided to push his luck and said to Angela: "You are a healthy lady; I'm praying for the baby to take after you. We don't know about the father."

 Angela mistakenly answered, "Yes, he's healthy and strong."
Junior Jeffery was in a state of shock by her statement but kept his cool. "If I didn't know any better, I'd say you have an idea of who the father is, I am your lawyer. Do you know who he is?"
Angela replied, "Between you and me, I plead the fifth. Let's not deviate from our topic."

 "Sorry Angela, I don't blame you for answering me like this. You are tired of this question. I understand, Okay my dear I must go. My wife and I will see you in two days. Stayed blessed Girl."

Angela replied, "See you later, my baby Daddy. Then she said to Junior, "Let me use a piece of paper and a pen."
He gave them to her, and she wrote on the paper "Yes" and handed it to him. "What does that mean he inquired?" She added, "It's nothing but a relief and it's also good for the soul, yes."
Júnior Jeffery left pondering on this three-letter word riddle,
Junior Jeffery's mind was haunted by the word Yes written on a piece of paper. The urge to decipher Angela's

Remnants from The Past

true meaning kept him up at night. He missed out on the fact that his client had a reputation for playing mind games to control others. She had experience in that regard. Angela was actually worse a few days ago, but she improved after accepting Jesus her Lord. Junior employed a process of elimination. What was it? For example, "Was she making a pass at me?" How, he didn't realize she was a flirter from the heart. Junior Jeffery determined the Yes signified full consent to continue with the adoption. Unfortunately, he had a lot to discover about his client. He hoped that his future daughter would inherit Angela's healthy lifestyle. Junior Jeffery needed to pray that the baby girl would not turn out like her mother. Otherwise, "Brace yourself, trouble is on the way.

Tamara found Claude's last statement so funny, she proposed Angela's story should be made into a movie.

"Right, Angela's story could make a great television documentary," Claude suggested.

When her husband mentioned the documentary, Tanara behaved suspiciously and appeared guilty.

. In speaking of documentary and movie, "Did I tell you about Mother Faye Esther's recent dream?"
"What was it?" Tamarra asked curiously.?"
According to her, "She had a dream about a known person who kept invading her privacy at the mansion. She captured numerous photos with the purpose of selling them to a documentary producer. The person was linked to another individual who was in federal prison. The person taking pictures in her bedroom was caught by

83

Oscar the butler. He informed her after his relationship went south with the culprit. She brought charges against both."

Tamara requested her husband to stop at a gas station so she could use the restroom, and he complied. She quickly exited the car and ran towards the bathroom, hoping it was available. She accidentally left her phone in the car. This time she forgot to lock her phone. To protect her privacy, she installed an app on her phone that captured images of anyone who tried to unlock it without permission.

Tamara messed up twice on the trip. At least six times, her phone rang. Claude finally picked up the phone. Someone was breathing on the other end, but he couldn't hear anything else. Women's voices playing basketball or volleyball could be heard in the background. Despite his repeated greetings, the person he was addressing refused to respond. The number he saw was from a jailhouse that was at least forty-five minutes away from their home. The phone call made him remember Angela, who he thought was thousands of miles away. He pondered who his wife might know in the prison. When he first mentioned the number, she said it was the wrong number.

Upon getting back in the car, Tamara informed her husband that she was feeling uneasy and suspected that her nerves might be the cause of her stomach discomfort.

Claude asked her, "What are you nervous about?"

"Mother Faye Esther's dreams gave me the creeps," she replied.

Claude responded, "I used to worry when she had a dream because nine out of ten times, it would come true. Her visions no longer hold any credibility with me. Just observe her efforts to resurrect Moses and Miriam. Just a heads up, the woman from the female prison called again." Tamara answered, "That's Angela?" "Angela who, Casimir," responded Claude. Tamara laughed so hard and added, "Boy, I'm messing with you. Her story is fascinating, and Claude, you are an excellent storyteller. I find you so stimulating, I could listen to you endlessly."

She boosted her husband's ego, causing him to forget about finishing the phone conversation with his wife.

He continued to recount Angela's story and his wife asked him to go back again to the store. He was too sleepy this time to question her motive, so he drove back to the store. He dozed off in the parking lot while waiting for her. Dreaming about the authentic ending of Angela's life story. Claude was unaware of the last three chapters of Angela's story in jail, which he had dreamt of about. What was it?

CHAPTER 8

BREAKING NEWS

Angela didn't have lunch. Her conference with her lawyer left her feeling full and satisfied. Amanda was furious that Angela hadn't eaten all day. She watched over Angela like a babysitter who was watching over a troublesome child.

Amanda realized that Angela was alone in her cell, and she entered saying, "Where have you been? You haven't had any food today. Can you tell me what's going on? You vanished without anyone knowing where you went. Angela, remember you're carrying our baby."
"Our baby" replied Angela. "Tell me Amanda, do you believe for real my baby is yours?"
"For sure,' added Amanda.
"Amanda, I thought you were teasing, but you appeared convinced. You and I are both females. With what did you manage to get me pregnant? I never came across to you because I am not one of those who play games and my love for a man is true. How did you arrive at this conclusion on a serious note?"

"Pastor Angela, I ask for your forgiveness after confessing the sin I committed against you. Are you prepared to see past my flaws and forgive me wrongdoing with love? I was moved by your revival messages to apologize to everyone I affected with my wrong actions. Forgiveness is something I haven't had the chance to request from you."

The long-awaited moment has arrived. "Here I'm, Pastor Angela, on my knees asking you to consider mercy after exposing my sin against you. Before we proceed, would you mind" saying a prayer for me?"

Pastor Angela knelt and embraced Amanda. Before Pastor prayed, she started to hum into Amanda's ears the same song Amanda sung after she received Jesus at the revival. "You're My Strong Tower and Fortress" was the title of a song written by Angela's uncle Pachouco.

Tears streamed down Amanda's face as she cried bitterly. She struggled with dealing with old sins committed against God, fellow inmates, senior citizens, and others she victimized without mercy. In her moment of remorse, she had a few outbursts saying, "Lord, am I beyond repentance? Could you ever forgive me for everything I've done? I believe I'm a nuisance to society and it would be better without me."

Although Pastor Angela's heart was touched by those words, she recognized that Amanda was a novice, Christian. For the time being, her understanding of God was tearful prayer to God on behalf of Amanda and herself.

"Lord, here we are on our knees talking and listening to you." Pastor Angela on the other hand was well versed in the word of God, began her prayer in this manner:

"Hear us as we repent and supplicate. By accepting Jesus as our personal savior, our transgressions were blotted out and our spirits were renewed. According to your word, Lord, you did teach us about this bless assurance in 2nd Corinthians 5:17 for a time like this." "Therefore if any man be in Christ, he is a new creature: old things are passed away; behold, all things are become new." "Lord reassures Amanda, which included her, I, and everybody else. Because of your divine nature, Lord, our former sins won't restrict the potency of our prayers. Lord, grant Amanda the courage to reveal her confession without fear of retaliation from anyone, including me. God, thank you for Amanda's redemption. She is deeply committed to being your warrior. If you search her heart, you'll witness the outcome of her profound transformation. Thank you for bringing her into my life to fill the sisterhood void I was missing. Lord, make my heart ready to hear her awful confession about me, as she perceives it. Lord, I confess that I may have trespassed against her in the past. Father, please grant Amanda a forgiving heart to accept my sincere apology for the sin I committed against her. Bestow upon Amanda the bravery to speak with a fearless heart. My God, I have already forgiven her for whatever she has done to me, and I pray that she remains my sister forever. We thank you, God, for touching our hearts and granting us forgiveness through Jesus. Amen and Amen!" After carefully listening to her pastor's prayers, Amanda hugged Angela tightly and expressed her desire to have known how she felt about her. "What I did to you, I would not have done it. I'm banking on your forgiveness, without it, rejection would be the end of me."

"Amanda, my sister, I give you my word a thousand times. My ears are ready to hear your confession, and my heart is ready to offer forgiveness."

Amanda cleared her throat with a sigh. She began, "Pastor Angela, do you recall the birthday celebration we threw for Nancy, so called your twin, six months ago?"
"What about it?" inquired Pastor Angela when she was reminded.

"I heard from Nancy that you two are close, and I asked her to connect us. She told me you didn't believe in lesbianism. I continued to convey my emotions for you to her. She offered herself to me in your place. Even though I was drunk, I jokingly informed her that I would never sleep with her. Upon reflection, Pastor Angela, I wasn't joking when I said that, and I still mean it today."
"Nancy's response was a joke, saying that "I will eventually make love to her and to trust her on that."

Nancy suggested a "quit pro quo" "where I had to give her a birthday celebration. That day, I had to make it appear as though I was truly in love with her. I agreed to the plan because my desire to spend at least one night with you overpowered my rational thinking. Nancy wanted me to be intoxicated, because she claimed you like having sex with a drunk lover. Once again, Nancy was able to coax me." She made a promise to surreptitiously spike your drink with a sexual stimulant. Once again, the plan sounded great to me."
"Are you ok, Pastor Angela?"
"Oh yes," replied Angela, "Please continue, Amanda."

"The warden granted me permission to have Nancy's birthday party. Pastor Angela, when I gazed at you that evening, I couldn't help but think that you are one of the most gorgeous women God has ever made, Eve, being the only one who surpasses, you. As the evening arrived, everyone danced and sang, completely forgetting that we were in prison. I noticed Nancy dropped something into your cup, which you drank and then left. The rape was scheduled to happen at midnight, two hours after the lights were turned off, according to Nancy. Your cell would be left unlocked by the guards on duty. The plan was flawless. She advised me to remain silent and savor the moment."

"Silently, I entered the cell and played a recording that threatened to harm you if you made noise or resisted; however, it was only a ploy to obtain what I desired. I cherish the time when you cooperated as the best time of my life." While we were both enjoying the moment, I didn't connect with my own emotions as much as you did."

Pastor Angela was taken aback by Amanda's words and tried to end the conversation. Pastor Angela was not allowed to interrupt Amanda during her confession as she had promised not to. Amanda proceeded to provide more information about the rape. Pastor Angela was boiling with rage and longing to speak up.

"The following day," continued Amanda, "I overheard chatter about a rampant rapist in prison. Three additional girls were violated. I wasn't the one doing this, and you knew that. Two months later, I learned that you were pregnant. Pastor Angela, I imagine this may sound crazy, but I conclude I might be the father of your baby. There's something important about me that you should learn. I'm certain the baby is mine because I am a hermaphrodite. I'm sorry for causing you pain, Pastor. Please forgive me."

Pastor Angela's tearful eyes gaze towards heaven as she pleads for guidance in doing the right thing. "I'm confident that you heard her heart's desire before you and me, God." Pastor Angela prayed, "Is the truth always appreciated, even if it leads to undesirable results? Is the truth lethal in the present? I gained insight into my uncle

Pachouco after I read Tears of Deception. Please my God, do I need to let the true prevail? I need guidance on how to talk to my sister Amanda in a way that shows her love and helps her find for what she's looking."

Pastor Angela's prayers held Amanda's attention as she attempted to comprehend the request. Amanda's imagination started to deceive her like she often did to some of the inmates. She imagined her marrying Pastor Angela at the altar for the baby's benefit. The devil had set up his workstation in her mind. She forgot, is the Pastor attractive to men. In her life, Pastor Angela has never encountered an ugly man. If someone identifies as male, she will find herself attracted to him to confirm his cuteness.

Pastor Angela was grappling with one of the biggest dilemmas of her life. Her compassionate heart prevented her from indulging Amanda's fantasies. She insisted that Amanda was definitely a rapist and not a liar. She had a strong aversion to informing her that she was not the woman Amanda mercilessly ravished that night. However, this news could be a crushing blow to her mental and spiritual well-being.

A sudden realization dawned on Pastor Angela that she has a lot of explaining to give to others in the upcoming days. She often cites what she overheard from a movie star that: "Every sinner has a future, and every saint has a past."

Amanda waited with curiosity and enthusiasm for the pastor's feedback, not realizing there were lessons she needed to learn. There are consequences attached to God's mercies. Everyone must pay for what they do before God, it's a fact. Those who take pleasure in deceiving others will one day experience deceit. Those who anticipate forgiveness might struggle to forgive others. Those who deceive detest being deceived. In the upcoming days, Pastor Angela will teach about that subject based on her experience to fulfill God's request.

Pastor Angela waited for an answer from the Lord, as hurting Amanda's feelings was the least of her desires. Among the inmates, Amanda had the greatest physical strength. Most people were afraid of her, but there were few who cared for her. She held a position as one of the leaders in the gang. From the beginning, Pastor Angela instilled fear in all three leaders for a particular reason. They recalled the time when one of them attempted to slap Angela, and she found herself on the floor in no time. "I'll kill you next time," she warned as she lifted the leader from the ground. "Check my record if you're skeptical. Don't worry, I'm not interested in your position." Furthermore, pastor Angela is a tough contender.

Amanda sought forgiveness from her pastor for everything she had done to her. The pastor answered, "You did not sin against me. We never shared a bed together. I would track her down and make her pay for violating me if a woman were to rape me in my cell. Amanda, if you had pulled that on me, one of us wouldn't be here to talk about it. Hell would be the destination of one of us. I'm pretty sure it would be yours."

"Stop playing" said Amanda, "I'm not delusional, it was you, I sinned against."

"It could be a fallen angel," Pastor Angela suggested. "I'm serious, we never made love. You are aware of my feelings on this issue better than anyone else you know that. Your smile indicates that you doubt me."

"Correct," Amanda replied.

Pastor Angela briefly lost her temper became upset and revealed, "I didn't spend the night of the celebration in my cell."

Amanda said jokingly, "Whoever that somebody else is, the day I meet her, I want to make her my wife. Regardless of who that may be, I'm sure she'll be my soulmate."

The echo of another voice quakes the room, adding, "Yes, I'll love to be your wife. Our pastor Angela doesn't engage in such activities, it was me, you messed with."

Amanda and Pastor Angela are speechless. They thought it was a figment of their imagination. They were gazing at each other, but Amanda became angry on the spot. The voice persisted, stating that her love for Amanda was so intense that it caused her to behave irrationally. "I regret tricking you into engaging with me, just to please my curiosity. I stand by the fact that I was wrong. My friends saw how you humiliated me, Amanda. You made a declaration to both of us that you would never physically interact with someone like me. I advised you beforehand "never say never."

Nancy walked in and disclosed that she overheard the whole conversation. She apologized to her Pastor and expressed that "Curiosity can drive people to do unexpected things."

"You better be ready to face the consequences, Nancy," Amanda said."

"She's not going to," responded Pastor Angela.

Nancy, aware of Amanda's anger, fell on her knees and begged for mercy. Nancy accomplished her goal now worried about the consequences. Nancy would have been six feet under if Amanda's stare had the power to kill. Nancy trembled like leaves in the wind and confessed to Amanda that "I acted that way because I had a wild experience of untamed nature playing with my mind."
She asked Amanda, "What is it that makes it hard for you to understand my peculiarities?"

Pastor Angela was shocked because she never expected Nancy to have the audacity to do something of this magnitude. In her thoughts, she acknowledged Nancy's bravery in playing this game with Amanda. Pastor Angela smiled and shook her head when she realized that Nancy had borrowed some pages from old Angela's book. She saw Nancy as a reflection of herself before she was saved. The only difference, Angela would do the same exact thing to a man instead of a woman. She removed Nancy from her kneeling position. She requested that Nancy step outside for a moment to have and hold off on going back into the cell. Nancy paced outside while depending on Pastor Angela to soothe Amanda's anger towards her.

Pastor Angela attempted to hug Amanda, but she declined. "Understood." Pastor Angela repeated. Amanda's attitude didn't hinder her pastor from having a godly conversation with her. The pastor started recalling to Amanda the numerous women she had tricked in this location. Except for Nancy, she abused them shamefully and it was quite evident that she took her time doing so. Pastor Angela reminded Amanda once again of Amanda's belief that it was acceptable to drug the Pastor and rape her. Amanda's plan ended up backfiring on her. "Pastor Angela explained to Amanda why she should not abuse Nancy because she had love for Amanda in her heart. Nancy's over-the-top obsession with her is unreal."

Pastor Angela took her time reasoning with Amanda while reflecting on her own past devilish behavior towards the world. Amanda was extremely deceitful but compared to the old Angela; Amanda is a saint. Mother Faye Esther was the only one who believed in an eternal hope of redemption for Angela. At some point in the future, Amanda will find out, continued Claude. However, Pastor Angela vowed a vow to God that she won't revert to her former sinful lifestyle. Pastor Angela delivered a private sermon to Amanda regarding her unwillingness to forgive Nancy. She continued to remind Amanda of her heartless plan to violently take advantage of her. Still, she found room in her heart to forgive Amanda. Hence, she expected Amanda to reciprocate the favor for Nancy.

"Amanda and Pastor Angela reached an agreement to have Nancy return to the cell. Pastor Angela motioned for Nancy to approach. She cautiously approached the cell, fearing Amanda's reaction could be unpredictable. This behavior is not unfamiliar to her. Nancy relied on the pastor to protect her from Amanda's potential threat."

"Amanda kneeled and called on God, bitterly asking for forgiveness for her sins against Him, Nancy, Pastor Angela, her fellow inmates, and everyone she had hurt over the years."

Pastor Angela and Nancy approached Amanda and declared, "God forgives you, so have we." This moment of confession swiftly transitioned into a worship service. Behind those bars, many inmates were eavesdropping. All of them started to clap their hands upon hearing Amanda's confession and composed a new song, "We forgive you too, girl."

According to the women, the acting Warden was easy to get alone with. She treated the prisoners with utmost respect. Upon arriving at the scene, she saw everyone worshiping God. She refrained from ruining their worship and ended up joining them without understanding the reason behind their unorganized worship. Impromptu worship was proven possible by the warden.

As the hour was late, Pastor Angela embraced her fellow inmates to conclude the service. The Warden caught her off guard when she looked up. The Warden received an apology from her, who also took full responsibility for the action. The Warden inquired of the Pastor, "What's going on?" Amanda spoke before Pastor Angela could respond, stating "Warden, I have changed. I made a promise to God and my sisters that I won't cause any trouble for you again." "She is not the same as before," implied Pastor Angela. If Amanda is saved, the jail would become more peaceful because she was the disruptive and meddling one. Since then, there was no violence in that place and peace prevailed.

Amanda made three demands that shook the foundation of the prison, but two of them are unrealistic. With a smile that illuminated the hallway, she knelt and held Nancy's hands. She expressed that our love is mutual, intense, and passionate. Amanda had everyone in a state of anticipation, unsure of what she would do next. She caught their attention by creating suspense. It appears that Amanda has forgotten whether she was in jail. She shamelessly asked Nancy before everybody, "Will you marry me?"

Both the Warden and Pastor Angela were in a state of shock, as Nancy gave them a quick glance. They were taken aback by Amanda's actions Upon seeing Nancy's gaze, they diverted their attention to the ground. The crowd assumed command, created a new tune called "Nancy what will it be, Nancy?" She leaped into Amanda's embrace and said, "We should not consider marriage, which is primarily a religious institution, in this context. We both understand that marriage should only involve a man and a woman," according to God.

Amanda turned towards the Warden saying, "I was about to ask you, was it ok, please Madame warden, grant us this privilege? Come to think of it, Nancy is right. Isn't she?" The majority of the inmates agreed with Nancy, and some didn't. The ones who didn't agree with Nancy's belief tried to frame the Warden, and they inquired about her opinions on Amanda and Nancy's choice.

The Warden expressed that she doesn't approve of this lifestyle, but she respects "Your right to choose for yourselves. Though there may be consequences from Life, always follow your heart."

Nancy was familiar with Pastor Angela's views on same sex marriage due to worshiping with a different pastor but held her in the highest regard. Pastor Angela was questioned by one of the dissenters about "Whether she would have married them if Nancy had accepted. Knowing Amanda would consider it a great honor if you were the one to officiate the wedding."

The hallway was silent, which was unusual considering Pastor Angela's intense devotion to the rules. The inmates' silence suggested that it would take a miracle for Pastor Angela to say she would.
"Pastor Angela raised her gaze to the sky and implored for aid in her prayer. She expressed gratitude to God for affirming, through Amanda and Nancy, her course of action in the upcoming days for taking a stand for God ordinance. They fearlessly expressed their feelings, thanks to the boldness given to them by God. But please Lord, let everyone who hears her prayer have a mutual understanding that they are all sinners. Their opportunity to become saints in God's kingdom is due to their belief. Though imperfect, her righteousness is close enough. Their beliefs are unshakeable, and the same goes for her. Imbue them with comprehension to embrace my unbiased belief but fill them with your sacred scripture. As she concluded, she prayed to God for their merciful hearts to pardon her quickly. Her final utterance was Amen.
The inmates struggled to make sense of Pastor Angela's prayer conclusion."

"I would show my admiration to Amanda and Nancy by holding their shoulders. I would tell Amanda that I felt honored for thinking of me performing the wedding ceremonies. Despite this, I cannot participate because of her faith and beliefs."

Pastor Angela clarified that her refusal would not be due to her being homophobic since she is not. She communicated that no one in jail ever heard her say anything homophobic. According to her, most of them know her definition of marriage as between a man and a woman.

Despite Pastor Angela's love for Nancy and Amanda but stated her current opposition to same-sex marriages. The Pastor advised them not to leave her presence, suspecting that she would judge them. She would be unable to do so due to her imperfection, even if she desired it. Both heaven and hell exist, and it's a reminder. She believes that these beliefs will make her do the right thing in the upcoming days.

Amanda questioned what was going to happen in the next few days? Pastor Angela replied that time will reveal the outcome and advised praying fervently for her complete boldness in the meantime.

"Later in life, upon their release from prison, Amanda and Nancy chose to give up their lives through Christ Jesus. Amanda wedded her high school sweetheart, Pastor Serge, while Nancy married her lawyer, Rodrigue."

"Always remember that God can transform a sinner's life."

CHAPTER 9

MYSTERIOUS VISITATION

After pastor Angela had a few meetings with her adoption professional, who was hired by Junior Jeffery and his wife. The professional offered free counseling before, during, and after the adoption procedure. Junior and his wife wanted Pastor Angela to fully grasp the importance of what was at stake.

The exciting couple paid pastor Angela a visit for adoption discussions and paperwork signing. That morning, Mrs. Jeffery proudly wore her favorite color, red. As always, her dark skin, white teeth, and full head of hair beautifully complimented her red dress, shoes, and hat.

"Junior Jeffery looked at her and said, "Tell me honey, why are you more gorgeous each day than the day before?" With such a seductive way, she walked toward her partner and fell into his embrace, saying, "I know that I'm attractive."
He replied, "Yes, I am convinced of that, we do have a few minutes before us. Come burn me up with your hot self."
She answered, "tonight, make sure that you keep the fire department phone number near, because there will be an arson in our bedroom, and I will be the arsonist."

"Mrs. Jeffery can hardly wait to meet Pastor Angela. She told her husband that God desired her to adopt the children. However, she still maintained the right to perceive Pastor Angela as cruel, even without knowing her. Mrs. Jeffery claimed that her actions were more impactful than her words. Her husband promised that she would experience love at first sight upon meeting pastor Angela. Junior had nothing but good things to say about her to his wife. He presented pastor Angela to his wife as a truly reformed saint of God, but she seriously questioned it. Deep down, she recognized that she owed Pastor Angela an immeasurable debt of gratitude for the opportunity to be adoptive parents. Mrs. Jeffery, who could not bear children, believed that God had closed her womb for her to adopt the incarcerated woman's set of twins. She shared with her husband that God's purpose was far beyond her comprehension, and not knowing why this made her crazy. Upon hearing his wife's complaint, Junior Jeffery thought she was having second thoughts about the adoption. The gift of mind reading is possessed by Mrs. Jeffery, allowing her to understand her husband and others at times.

She said to him that she was not getting cold feet about the adoption. She knew the end result would be a surprising eye opener to many and everyone involved. "God did tell her that much," she said.

Junior Jeffery questioned his wife of her insinuation that Pastor Angela having twins, she replied "it's a known fact." She said that "if the outcome is different, you get to choose the baby's name. If they're twins, I'll decide on their names."

"It's settled," answered Junior Jeffery.

"To seal the bet, let's shake hands," his wife declared. His head shake conveyed the message, "You really believe in yourself, don't you, baby?"

With a happy laugh, Mrs. Jeffery corrected her husband, stating that she has faith in God rather than herself.

They reached the federal jail, and Mrs. Jeffery was unaware of its existence in this area. He parked the car, gracefully exited, and chivalrously opened the car door for his beautiful companion. He kissed her tenderly, whispered, and uttered, "Let's go do this in the name of the Lord of our God."

While walking towards the entrance, she unexpectedly started daydreaming about her traumatic experiences as a child. Her obvious discomfort reached her husband's attention. He misunderstood the overwhelming emotion that completely consumed his wife. He assumed she was hesitant to enter a place where violent offenders lived. She felt like she was about to confront the person who ruined their childhood and abandoned them to die. Her empty compassion seems to be a figment of her imagination. Her mind appeared determined to deceive her. At this moment, Pastor Angela's charm was expected to make Mrs. Jeffery laugh and bring happiness to her heart. Something that Junior Jeffery relied upon completely.

Junior Jeffery should have faith in his wife's strong bond with God. The Lord frequently spoke to her directly, just as He did with the prophets of old like Moses and others. In the future, Mrs. Jeffery will have a better grasp of her spiritual gifts. Eventually, she will come to realize that the gifts of God can be hereditary, from one generation to the next, because God's anointing is meant for His people, and it's a family matter that she hasn't grasped yet. If she ever took a good look at her brother's ministry and how God is using him, she would share this opinion. Mrs. Jeffery had multiple caveats that hindered her knowledge of her family history. Her parents and family members were completely forgotten by her. Within a few months of becoming an orphan, she managed to raise herself. The pleasant moments of her life were completely wiped out, and she was too young to retain them. She could remember all the abuse she faced, but not the names of her abusers and family members. She fought and succeeded in locating her brother, who became her only surviving family, so she thought. In spite of it all, she kept a picture that aided in her reunion with her brother.

The guards from the jail met them in the parking lot and took them to the checked-in station. Mrs. Jeffery was as nervous as a cat, especially when the steel gates kept closing behind them. They found themselves waiting in a visitor's room, anticipating Pastor Angela's arrival. In the room enclosed by transparent windows, they observed three inmates walking alongside three guards. She queried her husband, "Which one is Angela?" According to Junior Jeffery, "Pastor Angela is the one with a large belly, confidently strolling around as if she owned the place." Mrs. Jeffery expressed her awe at her beauty and sensed a previous encounter.

"It wasn't really an encounter, but you two had a striking resemblance. You and she could be related," her husband replied.

His wife exclaimed that if their babies resemble her, they will be stunning. I'm excited.

Pastor Angela walked into the room and said, "Lady Jeffery, I had no idea you were so stunning. I must say, I really admired your outfit. You look fabulous in red. It seems to be your favorite color as well."

"Yes, it is, Pastor."

Junior Jeffery's joke was about skipping small talk and getting right down to business due to their similarities.

Pastor Angela responded only after she hugged Mrs. Jeffery.

She held his wife in her arms and they both began to cry simultaneously.

Junior Jeffery was bewildered, unsure of what was happening as tears streamed down their faces. Pastor Angela felt the strong kicks of the infants and became convinced that she was indeed carrying twins, just like Mrs. Jeffery had said. The ladies felt those forceful strikes on both sides of their stomachs even Junior Jeffery saw it. They all leaped for joy to help the newborns celebrate their new parents.

Pastor Angela held both by their shoulder and stated, "God is pleased with my decision to give the babies to you guys, for some reason or another."

Mrs. Jeffery exclaimed that the babies kicking gently welcomed her into their lives, assuring Pastor Angela that they will be well cared for.

"Mr. and Mrs. Jeffery, "Pastor Angela inserted "Just to clarify, once I give birth, the infants will be all yours three days later. As my lawyer, I will only engage in strictly business-related discussions and have no desire to be involved with either you or them. Mrs. Jeffery, I hope your husband discusses my adoption request with you. I don't want you to think I have a cold-hearted and myopic perspective on motherhood."

"Pastor, rest assured that we understand your point of view, and all your requests have been duly recorded in the adoption document. We've already signed it, so please keep it and check for any necessary corrections," responded Mrs. Jeffery.

"No need," Angela replied. "I'm a fast reader and already on the last page. Moreover, I want to keep my personal affairs away from the inmates; they will never know who adopts my babies. Soon, I won't know who I am or remember being conceived."

She signed the document and handed it to Mrs. Jeffery instead of Junior.
Pastor Angela warmly embraced and congratulated them on their new role as adoptive parents.
Unexpectedly, she remarked to Mrs. Jeffery that they could pass as relatives. When Mrs. Jeffery inquired for a reason, Pastor Angela explained, "You bear a striking resemblance to my sister and brother-in-law who tragically died in a car accident. Their twin children eventually faced the same destiny years later. My twin girls also bear a resemblance to you."
Tearfully, she cried and tried to explain to the couple that she blamed herself for their tragic death. Junior Jeffery joined the conversation, eager to know why she took the blame for her sister's children's death.

Soon enough, she will inform her lawyer that he will discover a lot about her during her release hearing in front of the State Parole Board. Her lawyer found the conversation interesting, but his wife shifted the focus to her sole concern - the babies' father, a rapist. Addressing his wife's concern about the father's background, Pastor Angela requested a pencil and a small piece of paper from her Counsel. He gave them to her, and she asked if he could turn around to avoid reading what she wrote to his wife. She penned these words on the paper, "As a woman of God, I assure you that the babies will be safe, and their father is not a rapist in real life. Don't worry, your husband will tell you the truth when the time is right, and everything will be safe."

Angela discreetly consumed the note in front of Mrs. Jeffery after she finished reading it.

Mrs. Jeffery couldn't stop herself from laughing and jokingly exclaimed, "Aunt Angela, you're insane!"

"Aunt," Angela answered, and Mrs. Jeffery responded, "Yes, if I look like your sister, she must be my mother." They began laughing, and Junior, contagiously, started grinning without even knowing why.

The guard reminded him that Angela's time had expired, and they bid goodnight after five minutes.

Besides feeling happy and fortunate, Mrs. Jeffery left the jailhouse with an unexplainable emotion of becoming a mother and her husband a father to Angela's children. She revealed that part to her husband, but she couldn't articulate her discomfort unrelated to the children but specifically towards Angela.

Her husband grew worried about the statement and exclaimed, "You had me fooled with how much fun you two were having and how you teamed up against me. I thought you loved Pastor Angela." His wife stated that love is irrelevant for her in this matter. She continued to say, "God told me, "In my spiritual realm, I encountered Angela's evil side long ago, but now I embrace her good side. Prophetically speaking, the Lord's guiding hand is on this process, and we, along with others, will be shocked in this small world."

Junior Jeffery understood the reliability of his wife's revelations and decided not to pursue them. Since then, she has had an unsettled spirit trying to remember where she met Pastor Angela. Mrs. Jeffery had a hunch that she and Pastor Angela were somehow closely related. She showed her husband the sole black and white photo of her parents to compare Pastor Angela and her mother's resemblance. Junior Jeffery glanced at the worn photo and recognized a potential family member.

Mrs. Jeffery, whose angelic voice mesmerized, suddenly erupted with a song titled "I cannot stop Giving God the praise," penned by Pachouco. Junior Jeffery harmonizes with his wife using his deep bass voice. Worshiping God was a customary practice for both, so having church was nothing out of the ordinary whether in their car or elsewhere.

They finally made it home and Mrs. Jeffery immediately headed to their prayer room, inviting her husband to come along. They were both well acquainted with this routine, and her husband would often do the same when they needed to address a problem. Junior Jeffery's mind started to wander, considering issues that could impact their marriage.

After praying at their altar for about ten minutes, they twisted their bodies and sat facing each other on their prayer seats. Mrs. Jeffery questioned her husband about his readiness to discuss his relationship with Pastor Angela. She said, "Your face always brightens up when you talk about her, even though she's your client."

"Please tell me, Baby, where are you going with this? After all these years practicing law, this is the first time you've ever questioned my relationship with a client in my career," Junior Jeffery commented.

"Junior, Pastor Angela left me with the impression that you are aware of who fathered her babies. According to what she wrote on that piece of paper, the twins' father is not a rapist and is in perfect health. Following that, she commented that you would disclose his identity to me in the near future."

"Junior Jeffery revealed that Pastor Angela is quite funny but didn't say who she was referring. She may choose not to be released, despite our victory in the case. Nonetheless, her preference is to have the twins delivered at the hospital, and we'll collect them from there."

Mrs. Jeffery began laughing, and her husband asked curiously, "What's so funny, Baby Girl?" She laughed louder and warned, "Don't mess with me, Mr. Jeffery. I'll be your worst nightmare if Pastor Angela's twins are your biological children. She jokingly referred to you as her Baby Daddy, I overheard."

"I get it now, that's why you insisted on dragging me to the altar," Junior Jeffery remarked.

"Yes sir," Mrs. Jeffery concurred, "some things require us to seek divine judgment on our knees before the Man upstairs."

They chose to take advantage of the opportunity and nap together on the prayer mat to express their gratitude to the Lord for the new additions to the family. They finally rose from the floor and began preparing the nursery for their babies. The couple tightens their bond as they anticipate happiness filling the emptiness in their lives. Junior Jeffery's curiosity was getting out of control; he was desperate to find out how she would name the twins, knowing he had lost the bet. He mustered up his nerves and asked her, "How will we name them?" Without hesitation, she cleverly responded, "We'll name the first one secret and the second one Junior baby, mind your business."

"Girl, you're truly unique," her husband chimed in, "You won't let down a proud father in the name planning." Mrs. Jeffery let him know that the girl will bear her name and the boy will bear her brother's name and his. Upon hearing that, Junior Jeffery was filled with pure happiness. He invited his wife for a weekend escape to their mountain ranch to celebrate. Mrs. Jeffery clasped his hand and said, "Yes, let's go, we have four-hours' drive ahead of us." Junior Jeffery reminded his wife to pack their clothes before leaving, and she responded that she had already done it and they're in the car. Just make sure the fire department is informed and prepared; I'll deliver on my promise to set you on fire with my irresistible lovemaking. "I am eagerly anticipating it, Young Lady, and kissed her from the house to the car. In their overwhelmed state, they left the front door wide open all weekend, neglecting to close it. However, despite his excitement to be set on fire, Junior Jeffery was too exhausted to take any action. He granted his wife a raincheck and honored it the next day. Mrs. Jeffery delivered on her promise, no fire department necessary, but poor Junior Jeffery slept for two entire days. In his bed, he resembled someone in a coma on a hospital bed. Upon waking up, Junior Jeffery, was asked by his wife, "Are you prepared for the third round, Big Boy?" Like a person running for their life, Junior Jeffery fled from the bedroom. Mrs. Jeffery laughed so hard that tears streamed down her face.

With joy, they climbed into the car this time, with Mrs. Jeffery taking the wheel and Junior Jeffery looking forward to enjoying the journey home. Before shifting into drive, they took a few moments to worship God for a safe journey home. The couple believed that daily worship was crucial for any God-fearing family. As the car placidly left the driveway, Junior Jeffery started reminiscing about the Lord's goodness in their lives since meeting his wife during a praise service at his church. The first gospel song she sang in front of him at her brother's church stuck in his memory. Despite the presumption of her brother's death, she persisted in her search and eventually found him with grace and determination. The memory of the day he met Mrs. Jeffery and the first gospel song she dedicated to her brother stayed with him. How he begged her brother on his knees for her hand in holy matrimony. He daydreamed about the kind old lady who sponsored their wedding reception and gifted them $400,000 for their first home. Despite being married for twelve years; they still had no clue about the identity of the mystery donor. Mrs. Jeffery called her their guardian angel. The foreign bank provided the monetary gift, and, without exception, they were prohibited from disclosing the giver's identity. Junior Jeffery, as a lawyer, tried his best to employ all his legal expertise to discover the identity of the mystery donor but was unsuccessful in every attempt. He saw her face when she handed him the envelope herself and told him that day, one of his clients asked her to deliver this package to him. The second time he saw that face was during his wedding ceremony, as Mrs. Jeffery repeated her vows, and he noticed the old lady in the church as one of their guests. Following the ceremony, he sought her out only to find her gone. He started laughing by himself and Mrs. Jeffery asked why. He replied that he was thinking about their guardian angel; and his wife proposed that the angel in question might have a role in their new family adjustment. At this point, our life is just days away from being completed. Mrs. Jeffery expressed her reluctance to wait months, as it would appear too lengthy.

CHAPTER 10

TIME TO COME CLEAN

Pastor Angela organized a gathering with twenty or her followers to thoroughly deliberate her destiny behind the prison wall. Amanda, Nicole, and Nancy were among those present, as they were the ones she fully trusted as friends. Pastor Angela cautioned them about an imminent discussion of significant matters. Whenever they heard it, they knew it was classified information. Before diving into a more serious matter, she wanted to inform them that she was expecting twins, and she was unsure if they were of the same or opposite gender. They cheered at the news and inquired if she had considered their name yet. She declined to be involved in the process, so the new parents will have to handle it. The cheer transformed into sadness as they couldn't fathom her decision to put them up for adoption despite having family. Pastor Angela comprehended their silence and the expressions on certain faces. She pleaded, "Guys, please don't do that to me. Amanda, look at me and understand my concerns. I'm too old to raise two babies now. If I had the ability, I would do it, but I'm currently incarcerated. What would you like me to do? I'll be here in this institution for some time."

With tears streaming down her face, Nicole said to her, "I thought you'd be out in two months or less. You won't be here with us, but you can make a difference for the kids."

The majority agreed with Nicole's persuasive words and commended her remarks highly.

Pastor Angela responded, "Nicole, I understand your concern, but you're thinking, along with everyone else's, is incorrect. Without going into detail, a few of you will depart from here before I do. In time, I will reveal the covenant between God and me, which will spark controversy. To many of you, I may be seen as the worst and most foolish woman on earth, but God the Father will be proud of me, his daughter. Trust me, I didn't choose their adoptive parents, God did. Believe me, Amanda, the twins will have the best parents in the world. I don't feel like I'm handing my children over to strangers, but to family members. They want me to be a part of the twins' life. I considered their offer for an open adoption, but ultimately declined. The new mother resembles both me and my deceased sister. She reminds me of my sister in multiple ways; she and her husband are both God-fearing individuals."

Nancy listened attentively to Pastor Angela and couldn't stay silent any longer. She said, "You're the last person I expected to do something like that. Will we get a chance to see them before you give them away?"

Pastor Angela conveyed, "Unfortunately, the answer is no. Nevertheless, your genuine love and support for me and the wellbeing of my twins does not go unnoticed. It's a fact that the law won't allow me to raise children here. Let's be honest with ourselves and acknowledge that the decision is divinely orchestrated."

In an instant, Pastor Angela's being was consumed by a profound sense of remorse, evident to all her friends present. Overwhelmed with emotions, the Pastor's tears flowed while everyone's minds raced to grasp the situation. Some of them stood up to express their love, but in a pitiful voice she pleaded with everyone to stay seated as she walked across the floor. Yet, her mannerism clearly indicated deep shame. She started speaking to her fellow prisoners, stating, "They didn't even know half of the trouble I caused and how society saw me as their biggest enemy. Yes, I was, and quite a shame. I have a history of turning anything I touch into destruction, including my twin nephew Moses and niece Miriam. I completely shattered their lives until they passed away. I often wondered if I'm in this situation because I was responsible for their death, which could be why I'm now expecting twins. Back in the day, I was driven by greed and had no qualms about scamming people for financial gain. At Derrick's funeral, my brother-in-law and sister, Yves, and Ester Day, were accompanied by their twins Moses and Miriam, as well as Yves' mother, Veronique. Moses was unable to speak due to a speech impediment with which he was born. Our only option to communicate with him is to learn sign language. Miriam, his twin sister, never fully accepted his birth defect, convinced that one day they would sing the alphabet together. Tirelessly, she sang their A, B, C to him day and night, not through sign language. Don't forget, I used to date Derrick and I treated him poorly, even after he died. I tampered with his Will to create the illusion that I was the only one entitled to his riches. I must admit, I was dirty. While returning from the funeral, Miriam posed a question about what people would offer God to hear Moses speak. Yves, Ester, and Veronique answered, "They're willing to offer there to see it come true." That night, the unimaginable became real.

Miriam, the four-year-old, understood how terrifying this weather could be for her brother as the thunder rolled and lightning flashed. As she usually did, she started singing the alphabet to lull him to sleep. She had the mistaken notion that she was her twin brother's mother. While Yves was driving and assisting Miriam in singing to Moses, Ester and Veronica were napping until they heard a third voice harmonizing with them. God performed a miraculous restoration of Moses' voice. Moses delivered his greatest recital of a lifetime, filling the car with joy and happiness as Ester and Veronica woke up. Veronica immediately called her Mother Faye Esther and Ester's mother Yvonne. Yvonne, Moses' grandma, was left speechless by the show he put on for them, and she remains speechless even now. My Grandmother hung up the phone to take care of my shocked mother."

The inmates, who were attentively listening to Pastor Angela, erupted in shouts and praises to God for Moses' deliverance and his family's happiness. The realization struck them that Angela's tears were just the beginning, and this story continued. Pastor Angela struggled to finish her remorseful confession while they sat in suspense, awaiting the outcome. Pastor Angela continued, explaining that something unimaginable occurred while they were in the car. Yves Day's car was hit head-on by a drunk driver who ran a red light, resulting in multiple car flips and the tragic deaths of Yves and his mother. My sister passed away two hours later. Prior to her passing, she instructed Miriam to always look after her brother Moses. She then took out a photo of Moses from her purse and urged Miriam to never lose it. The unfortunate news is that Ester died, but Moses and Miriam managed to survive. This tragedy served as a reminder of how influential our words can be. The family began their grieving process three months after the tragedy occurred. Guess what I did, sisters? I unlawfully entered my sister's house, took their Will, falsified it, and added my name as the only beneficiary. According to the fake Will, Moses and Miriam must stay under my roof. The devil had me fooled, He outsmarted me big time by coaching me to go against one of the wisest women in the spiritual realms who happened to be my Grandmother Faye Esther. It's one of the causes behind why I'm stuck within these four walls, today. I visited my Grandma's house and used a forged power of attorney to remove Moses and Miriam from her care. I was doing all that just to get possession of Yves and Ester's mansion. I placed a sign indicating that the house is for sale by the owner. Without resistance, my grandmother acquiesced to my wishes, showing respect for my false intentions. I should have known that my days walking on the street as a free woman were numbered. After taking care of Moses and Miriam for a few weeks, I discovered that raising someone else's children, whether they're family or not, isn't my forte. I planned to hand them over to Grandma Mother Faye Esther for her to raise once I sold their chateau. The plan is for my twin girls and I to get away from this town, far away from the Casimir's and the Day family."

Sisters, "God has a problem with ugliness, and I'm not talking about physical appearance." A realtor reached out to me, questioning whether I would be willing to pay him an 8% commission for bringing a buyer. Unfortunately, my greed got the better of me and I agreed to a mere 2.5%, and he accepted. The mansion received an offer of $3.6 million from his buyer. In a heartbeat I accepted the offer. I listed my house for sale and immediately I got a cash offer I couldn't refuse, but it was contingent on me moving out in just five days. I managed to make it happen. I came across a rental house with three bedrooms on the other side of town, but it was too cramped. I had no other choice but to take it. My closing on the mansion was scheduled three weeks after closing on my own house. Getting rid of Moses and Miriam was something to which I was anticipating, but it depends on us closing on their parents' mansion. I was completely taken aback when I drove past my old house and saw it completely boarded up. I wondered why someone would invest in a place they didn't even want. I told myself that the timing of the sale was ideal since I really didn't want to move in with Grandma Mother Faye Esther because of foreclosure. Maybe she's already informed about my foreclosure. Sisters, I was shocked to discover that the mansion didn't belong to Yves and Ester during the title search. It belonged to my Grandma Mother Faye Esther. I received a certified letter from her, containing the message: "A deceptive person will eventually be deceived unexpectedly." "PS I was the one who purchased your house. This is intended for your two girls. Once they reach adulthood, they will become eligible to inherit it. I'm suing you for frauds and Grandma still loves you dearly." "Once I read the letter, girls, evil spirits entered my being. All aspects of my being are steadily transforming into evil. I attempted to run away from my grandma's fury. Leaving Moses and Miriam, who were 6 years old, behind, I took my two girls with me. Additionally, Moses had a difficult childhood due to health problems. I hope they will just disappear and be gone from our existence. Patrica, my daughter, unlocked her seat belt, opened the car door, and refused to budge until I agreed to go back home and get Moses and Miriam. I was looked at by the little girl who confidently stated, "Aunt Ester would never behave that way towards Patrice and me." Those words fueled my hatred for the devil that night but didn't push me far enough to completely abandon him. Miriam had Moses on her lap by the time we reached home. They both cried as Moses called out for his deceased parents, while Miriam sang him to sleep. Miriam waited until everyone was asleep that night, then escaped with her brother to the back of a pickup truck. Years later, they were believed to be deceased, as depicted in the novel "Sold Out With a Kiss."

Pastor Angela continued to talk to the sisters of the prison. "I feel remorse for not being held accountable for child abuse, and possibly even murder. I could have been healed from decades of daily nightmares, if I had been charged by now. Whenever I thought of my twin daughters, I couldn't help but think about the unfair treatment I had imposed on Moses and Miriam. For some reason, God denied me the ability to heal that specific pain. The pain I experienced every day was described as the typical agony of hell. I will forever carry the burden of causing the death of my nephew and niece while they were under my care. The children of a beloved sister who loved me without condition. Some of you may not comprehend, but I made those infants into slaves to cater to my two daughters in every way until their demise. Grace and mercy finally brought forgiveness into my life. God could have let my newborn twin be raised by someone as cruel and abusive as I was."

Despite leaving many unhappy followers, Pastor Angela effectively conveyed her point. None of the prisoners were able to provide a convincing argument to persuade the pastor to cancel the adoption and take care of her twins. Pastor Angela instructed the attendees to perform the secrecy oath sign, before discussing the adoption issue in more detail. What that means, at this specific moment, everyone in the group promised to keep the secret and demonstrated the potential consequence of sharing it by making a throat-slashing and heart crossing gesture. Pastor Angela and the rest avoided violating the oath, and aware of being the excruciating repercussions. A castaway existence awaited the guilty person, who would be beaten every night with fresh stitches. Thus, they held deep reverence for this pledge, sparing no one from its consequences when failing to maintain confidentiality regarding others' matters. The twenty-one individuals all agreed to enter the covenant that day as they all stayed in the room, with no one leaving to avoid the freewill pledge regarding this proceeding. Pastor Angela adjourned the meeting, invited the same group to meet with her lawyer Junior Jeffery and three members of the State Parole Board who were going to sign her release paper on Tuesday. She reached out to her lawyer to contest her testimony and agreed to withdraw the lawsuit against the institution. Her decision caught her lawyer off guard since it came just days before the final judgment. It was difficult for him to comprehend that she desired to release her case, in other words, relinquishing her right to sue. He tried to convince her by recalling his hard-fought victories in the federal civil rights lawsuits against the state officials. Throughout the facility, they violated federal constitutional or statutory rights. The officials violated a prisoner's basic right to be respected as individuals or valued as human beings. Many individuals in the same jail experienced various forms of abuse, including physical, sexual, verbal, and deliberate indifference or intentional disregard of medical harm to a prisoner such as Nicole. Junior Jeffery divulged to Pastor Angela where she had bestowed her blessings, she didn't allow herself to be frightened away like others. The staff attempted to pressure her into signing a waiver that would prevent her from suing them or the institution, but she was wise enough to decline. Despite everything that happened, she desired to grant them a victory despite their defeat in the fight and the war for wrongdoing. Junior Jeffery reminded her how she became the Moses of the jailhouse, leading the inmates to freedom against deliberate indifference. He emphasized the significance of attorney-client privilege and confidentiality between him and Pastor Angela. Let's cut to the chase and tell him how she came to this remarkable decision to stay in prison rather than have her freedom.

Pastor Angela looked briefly at Junior Jeffery, feeling ashamed to meet his gaze. Her head bowed down, arms folded, she lost control of her tears while looking at the floor. He recognized these gestures from his clients when they were about to confess or tell straight lies under oath. It was clear to Junior Jeffery that Pastor Angela was dead serious about meeting him to discuss the case. He trusted her tears were real, not a charade. Despite a thousand thoughts racing through her mind, she struggled to begin her plea and confession openly to her lawyer. She finally began by expressing her gratitude to Junior Jeffery and requested him to pass it on to his wife for adopting her twins. She requested that he promise her that her new confession wouldn't impact his excitement and willingness to adopt the children. He assured her, speaking on behalf of his wife as well, that nothing can prevent the adoption as it is ordained by God. Three months ago, the Lord approved that for reasons beyond their control. Angela agreed with Junior Jeffery that everyone would understand the reason, except her, as stated in the agreement. Pastor Angela clarified that once she gives them the babies, she won't be found anywhere, and he won't see her again. The lawyer's prophetic response was, "Never say never," pastor. He succeeded in getting her to laugh a bit.

She instantly became serious, letting him know that the following conversation would be based on attorney-client confidentiality.

Pastor Angela started her confession by expressing gratitude to God for saving her. He was the only one who could have saved and prevented her from looking up in hell. "I was born into a noble family, but I've brought shame upon them. My family has considered me their worst nightmare for as long as I can remember." Junior Jeffery, she explained, "When I was young, I caused harm to many people, particularly wealthy men who were captivated by my looks. During that period, I was unaware that the wickedness of one's youth could pursue and haunt them until it eventually caught up. Before dating Derrick, I dated a young man named Carlos. Carlos's faith forbade him from engaging in sexual activities before marriage. On the other hand, I portrayed myself as a virgin when I was sexually active. Whenever I was in his presence, I could sense his pure and sincere love for me. My parents adored him, as he resided with his affluent and morally questionable father, who happened to be a close family friend, particularly to my Dad. His father manipulated me into having sex with him rather than his son. In the meantime, Carlos's father persistently discouraged any sexual encounters before marriage. I confronted his Dad about his hypocrisy, and he admitted loving me too much to let Carlos sleep with me. As a teenage girl, I had faith in his father's love for me.

Carlos got a prestigious scholarship to study abroad, and I would visit him every year during school breaks. The night before his departure for school abroad, I visited his house to spend some quality time with him, but he went to the nearby store. His father touched me, and I mentioned the possibility of being pregnant due to my missed period last month. He proposed a plan for me to have a special goodbye moment with Carlos when he comes back. Carlos returned and his father went and talked to him alone. They left me in the living room for a long time. I began to question the situation when Carlos's father was aware that Carlos had intended to stay the night with his mother. Knowing that Carlos had to catch the last bus to Port-au-Prince, his father didn't urge him to depart promptly. He alerted his father to the possibility of missing his transportation, but his father granted him permission to use the car for a visit to his Mother. Prior to his trip, Carlos received an offer he couldn't refuse since he always wanted to drive his father's brand-new jaguar. Caught off guard by the offer, he believed his father's sincerity stemmed from his impending departure. He agreed and stayed for three hours before leaving for his mother's house. He finished his private conversation with Carlos in the bedroom, then he called me to join them."

"My son is leaving tomorrow," his father told me, "So you two should make the most of your time together."

"Unsure of what to believe, I looked at Carlos and could sense that something was amiss. I questioned Carlos about his bewildered look."

"My father attempted to be a cool dad since he knew I would be away for a while. He wants me to abandon his belief of no premarital sex for just one night with you. I told him that you are a virgin, just as I am," and he said, "Son so what, she won't mind, she expects it. My father's advice left me dumbfounded." His words were, "Sleeping with you is a significant gift from a son to a father, a welcome to manhood."

"Angela," Carlos said, "After talking to my father, a mere two seconds before you entered the room, I pictured how special it would be for us to lose our virginity to each other."

"Junior Jeffery," Angela said, "I felt ashamed of myself. I was kneeling between Carlos's legs, looking into his eyes, and saying I won't lose my virginity tonight. Knowing there is none to be lost, I still expressed to him once again my stance on premarital sex. At this point, I understood that his father had tried to manipulate Carlos into having a sexual relationship with me, hoping to shift the blame for my pregnancy onto Carlos." While touching Carlos tenderly, he whispered urgently in my ear, "Angela, let me be the one to make you lose your virginity. Please, make love to me."

"Emotionally, I answered, "Carlos, I wanted to, but I can't because your father tried to make you pay for his crime. Carlos, I've often wondered what it would be like if you were the first person I slept with."

Swiftly, he revealed to me that "Tonight is the night to banish my astonishment. Angela, you're seeing me naked for the first time while you're just wearing underwear. Angela, I want to feel the intense heat that your gorgeous body radiates."

"My desire to be completely naked like Eve in the garden with Adam was suppressed by getting my period. However, brace yourself Carlos for a night you'll never forget, something completely new, and remember your father is home."

Angela maintained her kneeling position between Carlos's legs, using her hands and mouth to guide him to an unexplored realm.
Carlos couldn't control his silence, and his father heard his joyful noise, as if he had reached the mountain top. His father's heart was perverted by a spirit of jealousy, convinced that Angela had slept with Carlos. If that sixteen-year-old girl was pregnant by him, he could claim the baby is his son Carlos'. Angela refrained from getting involved with Carlos despite her intense physical desire for him. She didn't want to be trapped in the dilemma of not knowing who the real father was between him and his father. Angela's parents despised statutory rape, whether it was consensual or not, and his father failed to grasp that. Angela's family, who hold conservative beliefs, are against abortion regardless of the reason. For this reason, he had to pray that Angela's pregnancy assumption was a sham. Carlos resented the fact that three hours went by in a flash, causing him to part ways with Angela, the best

thing that had ever occurred in his life. With tears in their eyes, they bid their last goodbyes, knowing they won't see each other for at least a year. Angela being an American citizen made Carlos doubt the existence of a particular time period, as it would have been simpler for her to visit him. Angela had made plans to surprise Carlos at the airport in the morning with additional goodbye kisses because she loved him much. Carlos took the key to the sports car and embraced his father, who whispered in his ear, "Son, I'm incredibly proud of you. Stay focused on your studies. Don't fret about Angela, my future daughter-in-law; she will be in capable hands." Carlos responded, "Dad, I can rely on you, I know she will be."

"Junior Jeffery," Angela said, "My embarrassing moment as a teenager had come. Carlos asked if I needed a ride to the house as he was leaving. Before I can answer," his father replied, "No Son, keep going it's getting late, because my daughter drove here."

"Carlos left and his father was curious about what happened between Carlos and me in the bedroom. I told him his mission failed; I couldn't fulfill his desire to sleep with his son because I might be pregnant with his child. It would be wrong to accuse Carlos of something he didn't do." He said, "I hope you aren't pregnant." "While I was heading home, he pleaded for me to stay, and his manipulative skills won, so I stayed. Then, he began exploiting my vulnerabilities and I succumbed. Meanwhile, Carlos droves for forty-five minutes towards his Mother, only to realize he forgot his passport and had to turn back to get it. The decision to return home remains the most heartbreaking one in our love story, and it still traumatizes me to this day. Upon entering the bedroom, Carlos discovered his sixteen-year-old girlfriend and his father engaged in lovemaking. He was in such shock that he lost movement in his legs and feet. We witnessed him kneeling, clutching a butcher knife, crying angrily. Carlos observed us, his head bowed in deep repulsion at our nudity. His father and I rushed towards him, but he ordered us to stay back, or he would take his own life before us, turning his death into a tribute for his father and me."

"He inquired about my actions that warranted such treatment and questioned my dishonesty about my virginity. Did the man I referred to as my dad take your virginity, and if so, how long ago? Angela, answer me truthfully if you know what the true meaning is."

"I grew a conscience and informed Carlos that his father was responsible for that action two years ago when I was fourteen." His father replied, "That little heifer is lying, Carlos."

He angrily exclaimed, "Dad, you're a criminal! Watch out, her father won't let you escape punishment. My hatred for you, man, is so intense that I will never communicate with you again."

"Angela, I curse the day we crossed paths, and you won't see me again. Angela, I once loved you deeply, but now it's surprisingly easy for me to hate you. You belong in the trash dumpster outside. You'll be the first and last woman to cause me pain; I'll stay celibate and a virgin from now on." Carlos tossed the car keys to the floor, and "Sarcastically paid me for the services I provided to him in the bedroom. He dropped five dollars and the knife on the floor and left. Once Carlos left, I took the knife from the floor and confronted his father, warning him to never lay a hand on me again. That night, I went home and recounted everything to my parents, I mean everything. The following day, my parents filed charges against his father, and he was convicted of statutory rape, molestation, and sextortion involving minors. To my surprise, many other fearful parents joined my parents in the lawsuits against him, on behalf of their abused teenage daughters. Seven years had passed since that day, and a rumor started circulating in our neighborhood that Carlos had tragically died in a helicopter crash. Through DNA testing, they confirmed it was Carlos. I couldn't stop crying when I heard the news, and one thing I always desired was to be intimate with him." Junior Jeffery is unsure how to interpret Angela's tragic love triangle story. He pondered the connection between this information and her refusal to sign the release form. The board unanimously decided that she fairly and squarely won the case. He patiently listened to Angela, even though her decision to confess and stay in jail was unheard of in his legal profession. Although he didn't know any of her acquaintances, he was aware that Angela could afford housing. Her behavior didn't stem from her not having anyone or anywhere to go. Junior Jeffery attributed her decision to God, as she had become a God-fearing woman.

Angela became overly emotional and lost her train of thought. Finally, she continued the confession where she left off, giving Junior Jeffery the shock of his career and a lifetime.

Looking at Junior Jeffery, she suddenly asked him, "Have you had the pleasure of meeting Dr. Lina?"

Junior Jeffery said, "Yes, she died in a car crash not too long ago; she was a friend of the family. I spoke to Dr. Lina about your case when you first got in touch with me. Angela, she advised me to handle your case. I miss her, and she had no living family on earth, as she knew they all died. Her estates were confiscated by the government as escheat. Believe you me, the day she died, she was on her lunch break. On her way back to work from my office, she left me with the information I needed to do her will and she died right around the corner. My wife and I still are not over her death. I've kept her document sealed in the envelope, too afraid to open it as it won't make a difference." Angela replied, "If I were you, I would open just to be nosy, and you never know."

After contemplating for a moment, Junior Jeffery confided in Angela, "My wife and I are still mourning her loss. Her deep voice that we found incredibly sexy was often the subject of our jokes."

Pastor Angela's sadness vanished when she heard Junior Jeffery's last statement, replaced by a big laugh that left him wondering what was so funny. He questioned this behavior, and she told him, "You really don't know Dr. Lina." He held back his disagreement and allowed her the opportunity to complete her confession. She cast a pitiful glance at him, her face creased with a frown as tears streamed down her cheeks. With a deep breath, she addressed him as "Sir" for the very first time. This address even caught his attention. "Confession is good for the soul," Pastor Angela said, "Referring to individuals like me who have a checkered past. I'm tired of outsmarting the system, now God wants me to be honest with you and everyone else."

I fabricated a rape incident in jail to advocate for women who were violated by intruders.

Junior Jeffery surprisingly yelled, "Are you fabricating that, pastor, to stay here? Don't tease me, just tell me who you are playing." "Unfortunately, I'm not Junior Jeffery, even though I wish I were. I remember mentioning before that I knew the identity of my baby's father and he was not a rapist, as I was using blackmail to engage in sexual activities with him."

Junior Jeffery was shocked and asked her how she managed to get pregnant in this female prison.

Pastor Angela responded that it was at a hospital for female inmates. The same hospital where Dr. Lina worked.

"That's impossible," exclaimed her lawyer, the hospital is too strict for such a thing, and how did this man have so much freedom to get you pregnant?

Pastor Angela replied, "Your observation seemed right, yet wrong at the same time."

"Pastor, cut me some slack. The story doesn't make sense, and the parole board won't believe it. When it comes to male visitors, this hospital has the highest level of security in the country. Pastor Angela, I hope you have a clear understanding of your decisions. Can you provide information on the twin father's whereabouts and residence?"

"He died," she responded with an attitude.

Her lawyer is a lawyer from the heart, he intervened like his badgering her on a witness stand saying, "Yeah right!"

Pastor Angela repeated, "Yeah right, believe whatever you want. By you Adopting the twins, this will bring joy to their father's soul. He was a friend of yours. Pastor Angela, you understand that I would always have your best interests at heart. Should I suggest that you see a psychiatrist?

"I'm not crazy, my head is firmly on my shoulder," said Pastor Angela. "Junior, are you ready to discover who is responsible for my pregnancy? Promise me you won't have a heart attack when you find out."

"Having seen it all, I am now free from shock at my age. Pastor Angela, try me and to see, I'm ready for the information. Who is the father of your baby?" Junior Jeffery asked. The pastor's face turned serious as she told Junior Jeffery, "Dr. Lina is the father." The lawyer discovered that the world and its people are full of unexpected surprises, and no one is immune to shock. He dropped onto his seat, uttering, "Pastor, what in the world are you talking about? She is a woman like you. As I suspected, you are completely crazy."

Pastor Angela's serious demeanor caused him to become concerned. At this point in the conversation, he knew she was telling the truth, but he was extremely confused. From a scientific perspective, he attempted to understand the possibility of a woman impregnating another. Only in a dream from a deep sleep can such a thing be possible.

"Was Dr. Lina a hermaphrodite? Please answer this question." He continued.

"No, sir, she was completely a man. I'm the only woman he slept with for the first time at his age; I took his virginity before getting pregnant," replied Pastor Angela. Dr. Lina was Carlos, my childhood boyfriend. He was the one who caught me in bed with his father. From that day on, he struggled to deal with the deceit until he decided to change his identity after the death of his mother, and his father who died in jail. Carlos lived a very longtime pretending to be a woman until his death. He was good at it.

Junior Jeffery couldn't believe how Dr. Lina managed to escape scrutiny all those years, from college to her time working as the attending physician at the hospital for female convicts. He agreed that she did an excellent job covering her gender. Junior Jeffery understood why Dr. Lina refused to have a love affair with his lawyer friend, who was deeply infatuated with her. He smiled and shook his head, reminiscing about the double dates he had with his wife, his lawyer friend, and Dr. Lina. Their efforts to match those two together resulted in wasted energy. Junior Jeffery was unsure of how to break the news to Mrs. Jeffery and his best friend. He was under the impression that he saw them kiss passionately once. "Please, someone tell me, I didn't witness that," he said out loud. He looked at Pastor Angela and asked if she was confident that they would discover Dr. Lina's true gender if her body was exhumed. She replied, "Yes, all day!" and if they do a DNA test on the twin that you carry, they'll see he's, their father. "Yes, and I would like for you to shoot for that in due time." He mentioned to Pastor Angela that the possibility of exhuming her body might arise if she presented the story to the parole board for the sake of truth. Confidently, she agreed that it was the right thing to do, and regardless, it wouldn't affect the adoption since Dr. Lina had no living relatives. Junior Jeffery is struggling to understand that she deceived everyone, including himself, except Angela, and he made his feelings clear to Pastor Angela. She informed him that Dr. Lina had also deceived her for a couple of years until she observed a distinctive birthmark on Dr. Lina's wrist that resembled the one Carlos had. The birthmark was incredibly unique, shaped like a flying dove, and he had an identical one on his back too. When Pastor Angela first saw Dr. Lina at the hospital, the doctor displayed nothing but hatred towards her. However, Angela felt love from within her heart. She was surprised by her unexpected sentimental feelings, as she did not believe in lesbianism. Angela was puzzled by her sexual attraction to a woman because she resembled Carlos. The lingering effects of the past haunted her thoughts and emotions as she continuously reminisced about how Carlos' father and she treated him. Seeing Dr. Lina's wrist, the way she played with her nose, and her look, which resembled Carlos' last look that night, made her believe that the doctor was Carlos who had altered his identity. During one of Pastor Angela's fake sickness appointments, she confronted Dr. Lina. She dared the doctor to show her back to confirm if the birthmark on her wrist was also on her back. If Dr Lina didn't comply with Pastor Angela, she would expose her accusation publicly. Alternatively, if Dr Lina agreed, their secret would be kept forever. Dr. Lina opposed Pastor Angela's request and threatened her with a civil lawsuit for defamation of character. Pastor Angela advised Dr Lina to seek out competent lawyers as she planned to make the information public. She informed Dr. Lina that there were unresolved issues between them. They will see each other in court at the lawsuit hearing. Before Angela called her guard, Dr. Lina asked for a minute to confess to her high school sweetheart. The blame for the gender identity change was placed on Pastor Angela and her father by Dr. Lina, who questioned the unresolved issues, implied by the Pastor. Dr. Lina accused Pastor Angela of attempting to destroy her career, just as she had done to her life. Dr. Lina, in a fit of anger, exclaimed, "Yes, I'm Carlos, the one whose life you and my father shattered. I find myself despising you increasingly every time we cross paths. Angela Casimir, tell me what you desire from me?"

"Forgiveness," she replied, For causing harm through deceit." Carlos agreed to disregard her childish fault and promptly forgave her. Pastor Angela urgently told Carlos that he needed to make love to her that day as proof of her forgiveness. The unresolved issues she was referring to, were this idea. Despite agreeing to be Carlos, Dr. Lina was unwilling to comply with Angela's request because he was a virgin. He contemplated becoming a priest or a eunuch due to the trauma of that night. Angela used her knowledge of his weakness to easily overpower him, assuring him it would only happen once. Burying the hatchet that day was a risky decision that also put an end to their wondering and curiosity about how things would feel. Dr. Lina's revival of something previously considered dead, her manhood, placed her career, along with everything else, in jeopardy due to false pretenses. Prior to her death, she made another attempt with Angela, which led to Angela getting pregnant. Angela's twins father went by the name Dr. Lina but was also known as Carlos to Angela. It was Angela who was the rapist and blackmailer, not the doctor.

Angela became the Pastor of her flock and received her calling after navigating the challenges of pregnancy. As a result, her newfound faith prevented her from participating in the charade of pretending to be raped in her cell and she rejected the idea of manipulating the system. In accordance with God's mercy, she must admit her crimes and be honest with herself and God. She made the decision to be honest with the parole board and all those affected by her falsehoods. Junior Jeffery was stunned by the presence and behavior of Pastor Angela and the inmates she invited to her hearing with her lawyer before the board. He's excited to share the meeting outcome with his wife, which involved twenty-one inmates, including Pastor Angela. He admired their unwavering faith in God and was amazed by the pastor's courageous confession and her readiness to accept the consequences for her actions in prison. Dr Lina's body was exhumed by the state, and it turned out to be Carlos. The embarrassing state of the poor vetting procedure of both institutions forced this revelation to be swept under the rug. Consequently, both the female hospital and the female prison now have new management. Pastor Angela and her guests were granted immunity in return for their silence and had their sentences reduced by five years each. The judge gave her a seven-year sentence, the same number of years God revealed to her. Junior and Miriam Jeffery fulfilled their promise by adopting Angela's children. Angela stuck to her decision not to have an open adoption, even after her sentences ended. She stood by the decision to never cross path with the Jeffery's, and she was not interested in knowing their names. The Jeffery's did respect her wishes. Based on the DNA, the twins' father was Carlos, and Angela couldn't have chosen better parents than Junior and Miriam, who believed they were raising close family members. The twins were different genders; she named the boy Moses Junior after her brother and husband, and the girl Miriam Angela Jeffery. The inmates spent a day with the twins, and Angela left the decision to the Jeffery's. The inmates' dream was made true and strangely enough, the twins looked like Esther, Angela's sister. It was the last day Pastor Angela would see the twins, unless the good Lord changes things seven years from now or longer.

Pastor Angela, in a display of her seriousness, prematurely agrees and signs a no-contact order between the children and the Jefferys, beginning after her seven-year sentence. This restraining order could be considered a lifetime record in the judiciary system.

CHAPTER 11

CONFRONTATION

Tamara chuckled when she returned to the car and heard her husband snoring loudly. She shook him, and instantly he was wide awake. On their journey back to Mother Faye Esther, Claude coincidentally noticed the burgundy and silver hammer parked on the side of the road. Nevertheless, the man whom Claude mistook for a ghost; this time tried to wave him over. Pressing the accelerator to the floor was not a problem for Claude. In an attempt to flee from Yves' ghost, Claude ended up being pulled over by a highway patrol officer who turned on his blue light and issued him a speeding ticket. Before the officer left the scene, he told Claude to say hello to Mother Faye Esther and asked her to call because she needed to know how careless Claude was. Tamara questioned Claude's motives for speeding, and he replied, "I saw the ghost again this time he tried to flag me down." Tamara laughed until she infuriated Claude. His lips were sealed as a silent spirit took over, causing him to not utter another word to his wife until he got to Mother Faye Esther's house. Once they arrived in the driveway, they pretended nothing had occurred to avoid attending yet another Mother Faye

Esther counseling class. Her frequent statement was that "If a couple had a private disagreement, it should stay private even in the presence of others, to prevent confusion and malicious gossip." Upon meeting in the driveway, Mother Faye Esther inquired if Claude had acted like a good old boy that day. Instead of answering the question, Tamara responded with a smile. Mother Faye Esther answered her own question, stating that Claude was being bad. She had a vision where she saw him getting a speeding ticket for driving 100 mph in a 45-mph zone because he was afraid of a ghost who turned out to be Moses. Tamara was amazed by the ghost part and believed that Mother Faye Esther might be a psychic and a witch hiding behind Christianity.

Mother Faye Esther's comments went unchallenged before she turned to Claude and urged him to hang the banner. He responded, "You've already indicated where you wanted it to be." Mother Faye Esther praised the computer shop for doing a wonderful job. Claude responded, "Unfortunately, the people you are welcoming will never show up in this lifetime, Mother."

"Why is that?" Tamara inquired.

Claude remarked that "Moses and Miriam are no longer alive, decades ago."

"Tamara my daughter, you see my son Claude hasn't learned anything today. God's teachings are futile as his negativity obstructs his intellect, leading him to reject anything positive. Anyway, the sign looks good up there, doesn't it Tamara?"

"Yes Mother, it does."

Mother Faye Esther apologized to Claude and Tamara for leaving them alone with the banner, because she had to get dressed before her great grandchildren arrived. The couple didn't mind, even though they each had their own agenda. Claude aimed to convince Mother Faye Esther that she was hallucinating Moses and Miriam's death. In contrast, Tamara suddenly became extremely interested in Moses rather than Miriam. She acted like someone who got paid to study Moses' life. Claude's wife secretly disagreed with him, as she wished she could have met them. She concealed that feeling from her husband for some unknown reason. Claude hung the banner. Tamara took her cell phone out of her purse and snapped some photos of the banner, pretending they were for Mother Faye Esther. Meanwhile, she sent those pictures to someone else. Who could potentially receive this? Only time will reveal the answer. Mother Faye Esther frequently stated that time had a habit of divulging secrets when least anticipated. While heading towards the door to enter the house, a burgundy and silver hammer appeared out of nowhere. It was the truck he saw. When Claude turned around, he ran into the house and locked the door behind him. He deserted his wife outside, alone with the so-called ghost he was escaping from. The hammer frightened

Claude. In his hiding place, he prayed to God, begging for forgiveness for his feelings towards Mother Faye Esther and her intuition. Claude should have known better than to disregard Mother Faye Esther's words, but wisdom had finally found him. Tamara spun around and headed towards the hammer to talk to the driver who was already out of the truck. He greeted her saying "Hello my sister," and asked. "If this Grandma Mother Faye Esther's place."

Tamara quickly recognized that he was a man of God because the way he dressed and the manner he addressed her. She concluded that he was Moses, and one of the ladies was Miriam, due to their identical appearances. Tamara was quite unique, she pretended to be familiar with them and their parents, but she only relied on what others had told her about them. She answered, "You must be Moses the cute son of Yves and Ester?"

Moses was taken aback by that statement and immediately assumed Tamara was one of his cousins because they had a large family, despite his decision to be an outcast. He inquired, "How do you know who we are?"

"Say what," Tamara exclaimed, "You guys resemble Yves and Aunt Ester so much! We thought you two had passed away long ago since we haven't heard from you in decades. Allow me to capture a few photos of you and the family."

She took their pictures, and she asked them to follow her into the house.

She didn't give them a chance to ask her any question concerning the well-being of any of their relatives.

Moses and Miriam were not too cheerful to know about Tamara, because they were on a Special Mission. They came to visit Mother Faye Esther and Yvonne, their great grandparents. Moses and Miriam both were already afraid of the visit because they did not know what to expect. They had no remembrance of their great grandmothers at all.

The square footage of the mansion definitely impressed all of them. They drove past it four times that day, refusing to stop, because they didn't believe their Grandparents could afford such an expensive house. Moses spotted Claude in the yard and saw the red limousine with which he had fallen in love. He tried to flag him down to get the make and model, but Claude was not having that, Moses was wondering why the driver of the limousine drove like a mad man. Moses spotted him once more at the mansion, and once again he behaved oddly. Miriam repeatedly claimed that the house she saw in her dream was the same. Moses and Junior Jeffery ridiculed her a total of four times. Moses stereotyped their Great Grandparents. Both Moses and Miriam thought their Grandparents might be dead or one maybe still living. These thoughts were racing their faculties at the same time. However, everyone kept their thoughts to themselves. Every single one of them was anxious to get to the mansion for this great family reunion between the three or four of them in case one died.

Moses and Miriam felt fear in their hearts as they walked towards the back doors. The uncertain suspense of not knowing what to expect inside the house was toying with their minds. They had a fear of receiving news about the death of any one of them. Miriam suddenly looked up, saw the banner, and began crying bitterly while leaning over her brother's shoulder. Moses, Rose Marie, and her husband were all surprised by her unexpected reaction. They wasted no time in interrogating the reason behind the tears. Miriam directed her index finger towards the banner. Everyone glanced up to read the sign and Miriam's contagious tears engulfed everyone except her ten-year-old twins. Miriam's husband expressed shock upon reading the banner, exclaiming, "Oh my God, someone knew we were coming!" Miriam is grateful to God for those who willingly follow her in this blind adventure ordered by God.

The front door was locked, Tamara led them through the side door instead of the back. With singing on their lips, they entered the house. Tamara left the scene to go find her husband. While she was on her way, she sent a text breaking the news about Moses, Miriam, and their family visit, along with attached pictures as proof.

Tamara became so afraid of Mother Faye Esther now, but not enough to shy her away from her unthinkable and mischievous adventure. Tamara attributed the revelation of Moses and Miriam's arrival to witchcraft, rather than giving credit to God. In her mind, Mother Faye Esther was a root worker who received her divination from a medium. "Throughout history, believers who witnessed God's signs and wonders were often accused of witchcraft by jealous individuals." That was a quote from Mother Faye Esther.

In the mansion, they discovered Yvonne, who had lost her memory thirty-two years ago. Moses and Miriam began singing their A B C's, and as Moses hummed the song, he requested Miriam to pray for Yvonne. As soon as Miriam finished her prayer with an Amen, Yvonne's memory instantly returned and she told Moses, "Stop humming the song. Can you sing it for me? Your last performance was so amazing that it made me fall asleep. You and Miriam would have made Yves and Ester enormously proud and may their souls rest in perfect peace." The room was filled with happiness that day. They sang their A B C's and some amazing gospel songs written by their uncle Pachouco, who is married to Pastor Leslie. During a few instances, Miriam paused in the middle of a song to inquire about her great Grandmother Faye Esther. Nevertheless, her thoughts got derailed twice due to her grandma Yvonne's distractions. The exact same thing happened to Moses. Yvonne gave off the impression that she was concealing something from them. They were too caught up in their happiness to be aware of their surroundings. Miriam suddenly felt very uneasy in her spirit. She was overcome with emotion and haunted by the pain of her past. She began reflecting on Moses' teenage years and her own. However, she did not remember her Aunt Angela, and Patrice, and Patrica, Angela's children. She developed a strong hatred towards them that day because of the way they treated Moses and her. At this juncture, Miriam required someone to confide in about this unsettling sensation. The only person on her mind was her grandma Mother Faye Esther, whom she hadn't met. Miriam interrupted the song to ask about Grandma Mother Faye Esther's whereabouts. She desperately needed to speak with her.

Yvonne's silence for decades made it unbelievable when she finally spoke that day. Moses quickly grasped that something was not right. Miriam was determined to get a response from Yvonne, who ignored her. Miriam asked her grandmother, "Grandma Yvonne, please tell us the truth. Is Grandma Mother Faye Esther dead and buried?"

Yvonne began the day with enjoyment, but it has now transformed into hatred. This is the day I dreaded, and it seems I have no option but to confront it. I don't want to lose you and Moses again. She wanted them to make a promise to her. "No matter what, nothing can keep them away from this house, after all it belongs to all of us." Yvonne reference mainly revolved around their cousin Patrice, who had a nasty attitude. They exerted themselves to make sense of Yvonne's speech. Ultimately, they

concluded that Mother Faye Esther had tragically passed
away, possibly quite recently given Yvonne's tears. Moses
regretted how his foolishness had caused him to be
separated from a loving family. Miriam's presumption led
to her being inconsolable over Mother Faye Esther's
death. The joyful singing turned into chaos in an instant.
Junior and Rose Marie sought to provide solace for
Yvonne and Miriam. Yvonne kept them in the dark about
whether her mother had passed away or not, but she was
evasive. The excitement overwhelmed Moses and Miriam,
causing them to ignore their surroundings. Hanging above
the entrance they came in through, a sign proclaimed,
"WELCOME HOME MOSES AND MIRIAM, AND
THEIR FAMILY, ENTER WITH FORGIVENESS IN
THEIR HEARTS!" The words sounded just like Mother
Faye Esther because she frequently said, "A person who
can't forgive will live in misery." Nevertheless, why did
Yvonne behave in this manner? Miriam was eager to
uncover the truth at all costs. She persistently nagged her
grandma. Yvonne finally revealed, "Mother is in the room
handling a dire family crisis involving your aunt Rose
Casimir." All the information she shared with me is now
in my memory. Yvonne ended by saying, "She knew you
guys would be here today, and that's why Mother planned
a reunion between you two and..." "Lord has mercy."
Moses and Miriam asked, "Who are we having a reunion
with?" Moses and Miriam were confused, thinking
Yvonne was in a separate world by herself. Then she
advised them to read the welcoming sign at the entrance.

Moses deceived Miriam by falsely claiming he had a spy tracking Yvonne and Mother Faye Esther. The last time Moses knowingly encountered Mother Faye Esther, was at Irma's house, his parents' best friends who raised him. It was a wild guess for him to know who Yvonne was. Moses will soon learn another saying from Mother Faye Esther: "A deceiver will eventually be deceived by another deceiver or deceivers as life continues. Moreover, it's crucial to never forget that every person has the potential to deceive someone else."

Upstairs, Mother Faye Esther was on her knees, expressing gratitude to God for safely bringing Moses, Miriam, and their family back home. The singing and prayers triggered Yvonne's memories to come flooding back. Everything went according to her plan through God's revelation, except for one thing. Mother Faye Esther anticipated Yvonne's memory returning, but not on that particular day. Mother Faye Esther knocked on all four bedrooms doors down from hers saying happily, "Come down you guys, Yvonne's memory is back. Come down immediately, God has once again defeated the devil." The four individuals who lived upstairs quickly descended and found themselves in front of a house teeming with guests. Yet, their attention was primarily on Yvonne. One of Pastor Moses' loyal members was among the four people that came down, leaving him shocked and confused. Seeing she had a twin sister surprised him as well. Three sets of twins occupied the living room. Pastor Moses had a deep affection for that member. On a Sunday morning, she arrived with tearful eyes, pleading for his forgiveness. Moses at that time was a mega preacher who took things for granted. He never inquired about what she had done to earn his forgiveness. Regardless, he was left speechless, fixated on the upstairs, waiting for Mother Faye Esther's appearance. This member was known by Junior Jeffery, Miriam, and especially Rose Marie, Moses' wife. Why? People spread a harmful rumor about Pastor Moses having an affair with her at the church. Rose Marie, Moses' wife, did not trust Patrica around her husband. Due to their striking resemblance, Rose Marie found it difficult to grasp their connection. The room was filled with confusion. Pastor Moses inexplicably became highly nervous. As he was on the verge of saying a word, his grandma Yvonne shut him down. Who were the four individuals that joined them downstairs? One of them was Mother Faye Esther, who looked younger than she really was. Her daughters appeared significantly older than she. Her oldest daughter Rose, who is conservative by nature, recently had a mental breakdown following a devastating family crisis. All she did after the turbulent storms of deceitful love was cry. In her next counseling class, "Family does matter," Mother Faye Esther might use Rose's story as an example to prevent an indistinguishable situation from happening to another family member.

Pastor Moses and Miriam's ability to identify Mother Faye Esther might be affected by Rose's appearance.

They requested Yvonne to sing her favorite song, and she fulfilled their wish. They approved of her sharp memory, sealing the fact.

Mother Faye Esther walked with determination, acknowledging each person by name - Rose Marie, Moses' wife and their daughter Antionette, Junior Jeffery, Miriam's husband and their twins Moses Junior, Miriam Ester, and sweet baby Evonne, their third child. Mother

Faye Esther named all of them without Moses and Miriam introducing each one. All of them were astonished. Fear overwhelmed Moses and Miriam. They were consumed by curiosity and eager to uncover how she knew everyone and her identity. Mother Faye Esther introduced Patrica and Patrice, her Granddaughters who are the twin daughters of their Aunt Angela, Claude as her adoptive Son, her chauffeur and his wife Tamara, and Oscar her servant to everybody. They live here with us except Claude and Tamara. If any of them would like, they can stay here too, since there are still rooms available. Through it all, she still did not introduce herself.

The reason for Yvonne's evasiveness became apparent as she danced around the question. Miriam has asked for Mother Faye Esther multiple times. Conversely, Yvonne continued to steer the conversation in different directions. Yvonne's Mother, Faye Esther made sure to keep her informed about the family matters, including the feud between Patrica, Patrice, Miriam, and Moses, despite her memory loss. Mother Faye Esther held onto the belief that one day Yvonne would regain her memory. When her memory started failing, she talked to Yvonne every day for that reason.

This is Rose, my oldest daughter, continued Mother Faye Esther. She is in desperate need of prayers. The Supreme Being alone has the power to free her from her situation. Oh, and by the way, if we have the time, I'll tell you about Rose's interesting past. For now, forgive her actions and interpret them as a sign of affection. She is mentally unstable. Confronted with a family issue full of disgrace, she felt helpless and didn't know how to manage it. Subsequently, her sanity slipped away. Recently, she emerged from a psychiatric coma.

Mother Faye Esther's words fell on deaf ears as Miriam remained oblivious. Shock had overtaken her. The perplexing gaps in her childhood have been instantly located and are about to be pieced together. Standing in the same family room as the people who robbed her and Moses of their childhood, she could hardly believe it. Everything started to rebirth in Miriam's mind, she could hear the sound of Patrica and Patrice kicks on their heads. Miriam thought she had forgiven them, but her memory of their identity revealed otherwise. Another quote from Mother Faye Esther came to mind, "Forgiveness is a divine act. The victim may find it simple to forgive an offender who is not in their presence. It might just be empty words, or in other words, a blatant falsehood. It's possible that this forgiveness is not sincere. There are instances when the victim believes they have forgiven the offender, only to realize otherwise when they meet again. It dawns on the victim that they were still distant in forgiving the offender. For the offender to truly be forgiven by the victim, a face-to-face interaction is crucial for sharing the full story."

Instantly, Patrica's childhood memories came flashing before her as if it was yesterday. Now she did not have to wonder if Pastor Moses, Miriam, and her children were her first and second cousins. Whenever she was near to them, she always felt a strong family vibe but preferred to keep her silence, because Pastor Moses could be arrogant. What threw Patrica off, Pastor Unique Preacher often referred to his mother's name as Irma while he and Miriam reminded her of her Aunt Ester whom she still mourned.

Patrica ran, fell at Miriam's feet on her knees asking Miriam to forgive her for her childhood and painful behavior towards them. She said to Miriam, "I did not realize how cruel I was to you and my Pastor until the next morning. When we woke up that day and you two had gone. I saw stains of blood all over the floor, I felt so terrible. Please, would you two forgive me? I sinned greatly against you guys. I lived with this anguish for an exceedingly long time. I knew a day would come when we would meet face to face because we are family, and my prayer was for this future moment is for my apology to be accepted, sorry yes, I am. Until today and I don't care who knows it, I still blame my mother Angela for her disgraceful behavior towards you and the whole family at large. She destroyed our family bond to satisfy her own greed, and for this reason I have nothing to do with her. As far as I am concerned, she deserved to be rotten in Jail for all the grief she caused this family." For some reason, Moses and Miriam did not remember Angela at all.

Patrice inserted herself into the conversation with her twin sister, responding with anger and challenging her to cease talking about their mother in that way, revealing that their mother would soon be free. She entered prison wealthy and will exit wealthy.

Everyone ignored Patrica, but Mother Faye Esther gracefully knelt beside her, saying, "Look into my eyes, Patrica. Without realizing it, you are currently walking in Angela's old shoes. Your anger has caused you to sink to her former level. You are on the verge of betraying all my contributions to this family, especially for those of us who strive to do what is morally correct. I always pray for this family to grasp the true essence of forgiveness and practice it without being naïve. If it weren't for forgiveness, our existence would not be possible, Patrica. A heart that doesn't forgive nurtures vengeance, waiting for the perfect chance to strike. The act of forgiveness draws you closer to God, but seeking vengeance can lead you down a path to hell. Just so you know, your mother has completely embraced Jesus, the Son of God. Reject her previous behavior, adopt, and adhere to her new beliefs and ways. Needless for you, Patrica to ask Miriam to forgive you if you felt that way about your mother."

Patrica replied, "Lord, I thank you for my Grandmother for giving her so much wisdom to open our eyes. It's only now, as a believer, that I see how selfish I've been. I've completely misconstrued the real essence of forgiveness. I seek forgiveness from the Lord for the way I felt about my mother. Lord, please reignite my love for her and bless her in prison, as you know I have fallen out of love with her, amen.

Miriam knelt before her for compassion's sake, said to Patrica "I saw you in church one time, that day the spirit told me we were   blood related, but I was so happy finding my brother to act on the intuition. I forgave you and now I am certain of it since I am with you."

Moses, in a state of confusion, pondered why Patrica never disclosed her identity as his cousin. She made one attempt to talk about it, but his arrogance ruthlessly silenced her. "Due to his successful ministry and fame, everyone desired to be his relative, so he told her that day. His family consisted only of Irma, his mother, Rose Marie, his wife, and Miriam, his sister, and he didn't feel the need to add anyone else to the list. He concluded the conversation with the words "Good try, young lady."

At that time, he wasn't a saved preacher but rather an entertainer leading a mega church destined for hell.

Patrica approached him and apologized for not disclosing her identity despite his behavior. "But why?" Moses asked. Patrica received swift support from Miriam. "Moses, she would have faced the same or worse treatment as me, considering your past animosity towards the family. It's not a viable option for Patrica. Moses, you were excessively self-absorbed, even for your own liking." "Furthermore," responded Patrica, "I had no idea we were first cousins when I joined the church.

According to a malicious rumor, I believed that both Miriam and you had passed away.

When I moved in with Grandma Faye, she disclosed to me that you guys were safe and sound, and that God had a plan for you to come back home in due time.

Laughter filled the room, except for Patrice who remained as angry as a rattlesnake. She was aware that Mother Faye Esther was on the verge of handing Moses and Miriam a million-dollar insurance policy. The policy could only be claimed after reaching the age of twenty-five or older. Consequently, Patrice's hatred for Moses and Miriam intensified. She was truly the old Angela's daughter. They were two of a kind. The sole distinction was that Angela got saved. Thank God for salvation.

Moses responded bitterly, accusing Patrica of deceiving him and asking for Grandma Mother Faye Esther's whereabouts to chat with her before going home.

Rose Marie, Moses' spouse, interjected and advised, "Sweetheart, don't bring back the person you once were from the past." This behavior is the reason you were kept in the dark about so many things. Patrica would not receive forgiveness if she told you, so I don't blame her. He approached Patrica, embraced her briefly, and said, "Your pastor cares for you."

CHAPTER 12

TRUE REVELATION

In a sudden realization, Pastor Moses remembered seeing Mother Faye Esther multiple times in his church. "You contributed $250,000 towards our buses. I hardly ever get the opportunity to talk to you in person. You consistently departed prior to the conclusion of the service, and no one in the church was familiar with your presence. For this reason, we named you "The Angel Sent From Above."
Rose Marie recalled, "Oh, I remember now. You were the person who told me, at a worship service, that I would conceive tonight. I tried to let you know that I have been diagnosed with infertility. You interrupted me" and asked, "If God ever mentioned that to me." "No," I answered. "you said okay, and as a result, tonight First Lady, you will become pregnant. You had already left when I went to grab a bulletin. Grandma Faye, I found out I was pregnant from that night."

Miriam replied, "Lord my God, I remember you now Grandmother. You were the one who assisted me when the deacons pulled me out of the sanctuary, falsely accusing me of disturbing the church service. Your words, spoken with tearful eyes to me, still resonate with me as if they were spoken yesterday." Grandma Faye, you said to me in my ears. 'The light of understanding will eventually illuminate your reason, leading to a much clearer perception. All of us must endure suffering at the hands of those we try to lead to salvation. Alone, you must take on

this battle as a command from heaven, passed down from me to you."
Like a smoke-born angel, you disappeared, and I was left in a trance. Grandma Mother Faye Esther, why did you choose not to make yourself known to me?

Mother Faye Esther stated, "The Almighty commanded me not to interfere, otherwise your brother wouldn't attain salvation. The struggles that Moses and you have provided me with insight into God's emotions as He watched His son suffer and die for the sins of an unworthy world. Moses and you can't even fathom the amount of tears I've shed over my children's separation, including my grandchildren. There were moments when I could relate to Job's biblical perspective in my own journey. I was unaware of Moses' whereabouts at the tome and thought you, Miriam, were deceased. Yvonne and I were praying one night after bible study when I had a vision from the Spirit of God. In the vision, I saw a church with no address. I cried Lord what does that mean? The Spirit replied, "Moses and Miriam are engaged in a brutal war that could shatter the heart of a caring Grandmother." I inquired about the directions to the church. He gazed at me with a gentle smile and uttered, "My dear daughter, I care for you too deeply to subject you to this." "Lord, I cried and asked you to test me, knowing I can handle it with you beside me." "Not this time was his answer, If you're genuinely interested in doing this, I'll make no time to evaluate your abilities. However, there's something that is not allowed. No matter how tempting the situation gets, you must not reveal yourself to them. You have the option to quit whenever you feel it's enough for your heart. You are prohibited from providing any financial aid to Miriam.

Moses is not going through financial hardship, but he is headed towards damnation. Miriam, his sister, is the sole person on earth who can guide him to recognize me as his Lord and Savior. Interfering will result in death for both you and Moses." He provided me with the church's address. He instructed me to go to mass there next Sunday, where I'll meet you and Moses. I went and what I saw was beyond belief. I thought I had witnessed your father's reincarnation when I saw Moses preaching the Gospel. I felt a great sense of pride for Moses. I told myself, "This Gospel preacher is incredible, one of the best I've ever heard, but he must find salvation."

"My joy swiftly turned to devastation when I saw you stumbling into the sanctuary, intoxicated. I cried countless tears that morning. I was able to identify you because you looked exactly like Yves and Ester. I couldn't bear it any longer, so I got up to exit and the Spirit compelled me to remain and observe the harshness of life and your brother's treatment towards you. I personally observed all the embarrassing experiences you went through in that church. I couldn't find my voice to speak. I reached a breaking point and begged God to spare me from witnessing your misery. Despite having ample funds, I was forbidden from lending a hand to you. Your dress style caused an instant pang in my heart. I received a clear message from the Spirit of God stating that Miriam needs to confront this battle by herself as it serves as preparation for a more significant calling. The confirmation revealed that God continues to speak directly to those who obey and follow Him. We all emerge as pure gold from the fire, giving glory to God."

Moses, filled with shame, knelt before his Grandmother, and begged for her forgiveness for his thoughtless actions. He told his Grandma, Satan had me restrained, blindfolded, and surrounded by sins in a pit. I allowed Satan to reconstruct my heart with hate especially hate for my family. The unfortunate aspect is that I grew up with a mother who feared God yet taught me the values of love and forgiveness. Mother Irma mentioned your graciousness and preciousness in God's view. The mighty signs and wonders He grants you to do in His name. Mother Irma frequently assured me that she wouldn't force me to meet my family. If I were in your shoes, Moses, I would go for it since you belong to a noble family with a renowned grandmother in God's domain. My severe animosity towards my sister Miriam eventually infected our entire family. I felt she had sold me out with a kiss. How much of an idiot I used to be. Grandma, I became arrogant after making a fortune and getting caught up in the power of money. Despite everything, God never abandoned me. In a twist of fate, he allowed the sister I detest to rescue me from my deathbed, and yet I repaid her with ingratitude by rejecting her love. Following Mother Irma's death, I experienced a profound sense of loneliness, believing that no one above cared for me. Oh my God, was I wrong? In the depths of the wilderness, there I had a sister named Miriam who loved me more than everything in the world. She endured abuse and mistreatment from a heartless society, including me, only to discover I was her twin brother.

One of Grandma Mother Faye Esther's sayings about loneliness, often mentioned by Mother Irma, was: "Loneliness can be a fictitious illness that pollutes the mind's proper thoughts. Those who feel lonely often have a network of people who adore them and are ready to shower them with love."

I remember the last time I saw you vividly as a child, it feels like it was yesterday. I sought refuge under my bed, assuming you came to take me out of my comfort zone. I believed you came to retrieve me and return me to Aunt Angela. Even in my youth, this scenery has never left my mind, and today, it holds no bitterness because love has prevailed.

 I couldn't comprehend why you sent us to Aunt Angela to suffer mercilessly. I can't forget the time when my aunt picked us up, it was painful. That day, I experienced a deep sense of helplessness and abandonment. Tears streamed down my face, much like a child on their first day of school. When I turned around to see if you were coming to our rescue, instead you gave me an unforgettable kiss. With tears in your eyes, you whisper, "Goodbye Moses, someday you'll comprehend the purpose behind it all." According to Miriam, on that day you looked at Aunt Angela and stated, "Being greedy is one of the characteristics of being heartless; it shows a lack of concern for moral values and family. Being greedy in matters of family leads to the destruction of peace, love, and happiness. Dearest, my worry is that you won't go unpunished for this, as it goes against God's will. To get away with this, is creating doubt in the true existence of God. Have a safe trip Angela and give Grandma a hug." I struggled to grasp your intention behind embracing and kissing Aunt Angela as she took us away from you. I relied completely on Miriam, who was determined to reunite us with you. I was filled with excitement, but what did she do? Abandoning me in an unfamiliar spot, she instructed me to remain in place. "I promise," Miriam said, "I won't be gone for long. Keep in mind that strangers are often unsafe, so refrain from moving with them. Let me give you a kiss as reassurance that I'll return shortly."

That day, it felt that I shed all my tears and there was no one to dry them for me. I was under the impression that my own sister had used a kiss to deceive me. Moses started to cry after recounting this part, he continued, Grandma, how is it possible that you attended my church multiple times, recognized me, and yet never revealed your presence to me?

"Moses' replied Mother Faye Esther, "Like I said earlier I was in a divine mission. You and Miriam being here is the result of the mission."

Junior Jeffery, Miriam's husband, stared at Mother Faye Esther in an unusual fashion like he was amazed at her wisdom. His behavior left everyone perplexed.

Moses realized how strange he was acting, and he said, "Junior what is the matter?

Miriam intervened, "But what, Honey spit it out."

Mother Faye Esther wasted no time saying to Junior Jeffery, "Yes my son that was me."

"I knew it, I knew it repeated Junior Jeffery."

A complete silence took hold of the room following Junior's statement. Junior held everyone's gaze as he kept the remaining part of the story to himself. Everyone, except for Junior and Mother Faye Esther, was on the edge of their seats. Miriam couldn't refrain from speaking any more. She questioned her husband about her Grandma's comment. He responded with just a giggle. Miriam looked at Mother Faye Esther for an explanation, and she responded, "Don't give me that look, Miriam."

"But Grandma," Miriam exclaimed, "You both have a history. Spare me the details, please!"

Junior Jeffery laughed and said it was already too late and there was no point in dwelling on what had already been done.

Miriam became agitated despite her disinterest in knowing where Faye, Esther, and Junior had met. She repeated, "I hope not, no I hope not." Miriam's response is due to a recurring dream about a family member marrying a relative in a strange manner. Mother Faye Esther's reputation for staying close to the family made her think that she and Junior were possibly related. Regardless, her husband and grandma chose to honor her request and shifted the conversation. Miriam started contemplating her investment in the marriage, their three children, Moses Junior, Miriam Ester, and Evonne who was not adopted. Everyone was having a great time together, as if there had never been any distance between them. Miriam, who had been the life of the family reunion, became the melancholiest person at the same event. Worried, she asked to be excused so she could talk privately with Mother Faye Esther. She explained to Mother Faye Esther the reason for her concern by recounting her dream and expressing her fear of discovering a potential familial connection with Junior. Mother Faye Esther grasped her shoulders and declared, "Granddaughter, I truly believe that you are destined to inherit my prophetic gift. Years ago, God revealed to me how He favored you." Miriam, continued Mother Faye Esther, "Your dream is real Baby Girl, God is surely dealing with you, Baby Girl."

Miriam misunderstood Mother Faye Esther's comments. With great sorrow, she cried out, "I don't want to hear it, it's not true! Grandma Mother Faye Esther, please clarify that Junior is my husband, not my brother, cousin, or uncle."

Thinking that Miriam was her daughter Kote, Rose, who has a condition, went over to hug, and console her. Mother Faye Esther clarified to Miriam, "I wasn't referring to you and Junior, baby."

"Junior Jeffery and I were talking about how I paid for your wedding reception and the dress you wore. I made it impossible for Junior to refuse, even though he had never met me before."

Mother Faye Esther received a kiss from Miriam after becoming excited and jumping. Excitedly, she recounted, "He told me Grandma, but he thought you disappeared like an angel after giving him the directions. How are you aware of all the details about our wedding plans? Every store I visited to purchase wedding items had already been paid for. I initially suspected Junior, Rose Marie, or Moses, but they denied it, causing me to have faith in the angelic nature of Junior and Rose Marie. Grandma, you really pulled a fast one on us, and I appreciate everything."

Mother Faye Esther replied to Miriam, "Complimenting her on the beautiful wedding and commending her for her perseverance in helping her brother." She answered, "Grandma, why did you choose to remain anonymous during the wedding?"

She said to Miriam, "I intended to, but the Spirit advised me against it, saying that Yvonne would never speak again. The Spirit assured me that in due time, both Moses and Miriam would come home to learn about their ancestry. As always, the Spirit was correct - both of you and your families are present today."

Miriam left the meeting and went to share the amazing discovery with the group. Meanwhile, Mother Faye Esther trailed Miriam and took advantage of the moment to give blessings to all her Great grandchildren. Mother Faye Esther dedicated a lot of time to blessing and cherishing Evonne, the newest addition to Junior Jeffery and Miriam's family. As Faye, Esther, and Yvonne praised God for Evonne, Miriam whispered in Junior's ear, "I knew there was something unique about our only child from my own womb. We are blessed with three wonderful children."

Mother Faye Esther approached the TV, took an envelope with a million-dollar insurance policy, and gave it to Moses and Miriam. "Your parents loved both of you with perfect love," she told them. Make sure the money is divided equally between both of you."

Moses and Miriam received congratulations from Yvonne and everyone else, except for Patrice. Consumed by jealousy, she hastily ran upstairs. She seemed too overwhelmed to remain in their presence. She refused to apologize like her sister did to Moses and Miriam, believing she would repeat her actions if given another opportunity.

At first, she shared the same belief as everyone else that they were dead. She remained envious of them, despite being aware of this fact. Patrice didn't develop that personality overnight; she always believed she and her mother Angela and sister Patrica were outcasts compared to Moses, Miriam, Yves, and Ester, their parents. Angela informed Patrice about this rubbish, claiming that Mother

Faye Esther showed favoritism towards Ester's kids. Additionally, Patrice discovered the million-dollar policy during her upbringing, but she considered it a lost treasure due to the belief that the beneficiaries, Moses, and Miriam, were deceased. She often referred to herself as studying methods to manipulate the policy through identity theft of Miriam.

Mother Faye Esther informed Patrice about their upcoming visit, but Patrice ignored her. She believed that her Grandma had a psychiatric issue for expecting Moses and Miriam to visit. So, when she caught sight of them in the living room, jealousy consumed her. Running upstairs was a deliberate setup by her. Patrice's thoughts turned to cruel schemes for extracting money from Pastor Moses. Patrice immediately turned to her sister's diary, hoping to discover evidence for blackmail against Pastor Moses, as she was aware of Patrica's secret affair with the wealthy pastor. Observing the events downstairs, Patrice concluded that Pastor Moses was involved romantically with Patrica prior to discovering they were cousins. Going beyond, she unlawfully accessed Patrica's suitcases in search of incriminating evidence to back up her blackmail. Patrice, like her mother Angela, refused to give up despite her lack of luck. Patrica's safe deposit box keys were stolen by her. She was convinced there was evidence up there that would validate her assertions. Furthermore, Patrice recalled a saying by Mother Faye Esther that declares, "In a perfect love affair, there are no secrets." Its defining trait is to openly make foolish mistakes until they are caught.

She was putting in a lot of effort to uncover scandalous information about Pastor Moses, something that would raise suspicions about his character. Frightening to the point where Pastor Moses obeys her requests. If concrete evidence supports this accusation of a pastor having a relationship with his first cousin, it could ruin his ministry. Patrice was certain Pastor Moses would not tolerate such a rumor spreading in his church and affecting his wife. "This rumor can leave a lasting impact on all three groups of people. Those who have faith in it, those who doubt it, and those who are impartial." According to Mother Faye Esther, "Those who believe in malicious gossip are also publicists. Those who possess these qualities are more perilous, structured, and influential than those who do not."

Patrice discovered confidential information about Pastor Moses and Patrica. Patrica explicitly stated that she knew without a doubt that Moses and Miriam were Uncle Yves and Aunt Ester's children. She used a staple to fasten their picture to the letter she wrote for herself. Patrica knew that her sister Patrice thought that I was in love with Pastor Unique Preacher (Moses), but my love for him was purely a natural and deep family bond. This is something that my sister Patrice will never experience because of her greediness and wickedness.

Upon reading the secretive letter, Patrice became upset and tore it in a fit of rage. One of Patrice's plans is teetering on the edge of failure. Running upstairs, closing her bedroom door, she exhibited premeditation. She anticipated that Pastor Moses, both her cousin and preacher, would display compassion by following her alone upstairs to provide comfort. Patrice wanted to keep him upstairs to make her sister jealous or possibly seduce him. She knew Patrica didn't trust her around any man that looked descent and appeared to have a lot of money. Patrice took great pleasure in flattering herself, confident that she could seduce any man, including her own cousin or a religious leader, solely based on her physical features. She possessed a figure that was visually appealing enough to catch the attention of any man with functioning eyes. However, beneath that appearance was a woman who lacked understanding of LOVE, unless it involved money. That was the way Patrica felt about Patrice. Don't forget, Patrica and Patrice were indistinguishable.

Everyone was engaging in fellowship together. Claude emerged from hiding, took Tamara by the shoulder, and led her into the living room. Mother Faye Esther introduced them, and Tamara stole the show by sharing how Claude believed Moses was the ghost of Yves. Laughter filled every corner of the house. Claude recounted his version of the story to them. Tears of joy filled the eyes of every adult in the room. In a similar vein, Claude publicly expressed regret to Mother Faye Esther for assuming she had early-stage dementia, while also extending a warm welcome to Moses and Miriam in the land of the living. "Mother, I promise to never doubt your prophecies again, if my name is Claude."

 Then Moses and Miriam's Families chose to spend their two-week vacation with their Grandmothers. The sight of their spouses reuniting with their family brought immense joy to Junior Jeffery and Rose Marie. Mother Faye Esther invited Tamara to stay as well. Without any hesitation, she responded positively. Tamara secretly recorded everything, like a documentarian writing a script.

Pastor Moses was struck by a sense of compassion for Patrice as the laughter came to a halt. He felt the need to beg Patrice to join in and become part of the family during their enjoyable time together. A feeling of incompleteness washed over him, caused by the absence of his cousin

Patrice's laughter. He wanted to know; does she smile sometime? Patrice suddenly appeared downstairs, looking more beautiful than ever in her short skirt and mini blouse. She had complete confidence in her attractiveness. Both Moses and Junior, Miriam's husband, exclaimed in their hearts, "Wow, she's pretty but evil!"

She went to the refrigerator, had a drink, and returned upstairs, seeming troubled by the world. She determined to bring the preacher into her nest by playing mind's games. Pastor Moses made multiple attempts to go upstairs and talk to Patrice, but he kept getting distracted by his Aunt Rose. Amid her mental deprivation, he fell in love with her. Through compassion, he developed a unique interest in her. He inquired with Mother Faye Esther about the story behind Rose's condition. However, that night, Rose became a peaceful angel sent by the Lord to protect Moses from an evildoer's anger. Mother Faye Esther frequently emphasized that "The love of money and conscience are at odds. People who are obsessed with money often lack conscience; they don't recognize the word."

However, Miriam thought it was a great idea because she wanted to know about all her people. Mother Faye Esther assured them she would do it before their departure, cautioning that Rose's situation is embarrassing. To emphasize the gravity of the situation, she informed them that the family had enough secrets to fill a 500 ft pit. When Tamara heard Mother Faye Esther's statement, she lost control of her curiosity and answered "Go ahead Mother, tell us the story we do have   time.

Miriam expressed her agreement with Tamara, stating, "She is right Grandma, we can spare some time to listen to those stories." Mother Faye Esther smiled charmingly, but only Patrica understood the hidden meaning as she had spent the most time with her Grandma. Patrica had the opportunity to share with them the triumphant entrance of words brimming with wisdom. Mother Faye Esther faced Miriam, gripping her shoulders, and warned, "Miriam, please never reveal our family's private matters in front of strangers or so-called friends. When you come from a famous family, some relatives may use those stories against you to hurt your feelings whenever they are upset with you. The people who could do that are typically spouses, friends, friends of friends, the media, and unfortunately, family members with low self-esteem who don't understand the meaning of family."

Mother Faye Esther, being part of a famous family means you're always just a moment away from being in the headlines, not necessarily for the good things you do, but for any scandalous mistake you make, whether intentional or not. Beware, when you achieve fame, there will be individuals eagerly awaiting your dramatic and humiliating downfall. Fame can impair the judgment of choosing true spouses and friends, but selecting enemies for them is always spot-on. Miriam, there are people who would use a tape recorder to capture your words about your family and others who might shamelessly photograph your belongings to exploit you. In that case, you turn them over to God." Mother Faye Esther looked at Tamara and asked, "Tamara, am I correct, my beloved daughter?" In a choked voice, Tamara responded, "Yes, Mother, you're right."

Mother Faye Esther released Miriam's shoulders and then took hold of both Moses and Miriam's hands. Junior Jeffery, Rose Marie, Patrica, and the children held hands together. A circle formed instantly, as though preparing to offer a prayer. Everyone else had the same thought.

She omitted Claude and Tamara, and said, "Junior my Grandson, Rose Marie my Granddaughter I love you two so much. I won't reveal the family story to you, even though you married my grandchildren. It's up to Moses and Miriam to share it with their families. Junior and Rose Marie, I would appreciate it if you would grant me one evening with Moses, Miriam, Patrica, Yvonne, and Patrice, if Patrice is interested.

Junior and Rose Marie agreed with Mother Faye Esther. They felt this knowledge would mean a lot to Moses, who planned to write a biography and Miriam who thought she could be Mother Faye Esther, the Mother of the family.

Rose Marie before the circle break off, she said, "Grandma Faye, Moses and I would like to talk to you privately." Moses was shocked by her demand and said, "What for?" Miriam did not allow Rose Marie to answer to her husband, she said, "You know exactly why Moses." He answered, "This is the problem you two are always teamed up against me" and he began to laugh. Then Mother Faye Esther asked Patrice who was in a world by herself figuring how to blackmail Moses over the insurance money to pass her the appointment book. Patrice did, she opened it and showed them where she had already scheduled for them a counseling session for Wednesday. They were so amazed to the point all they could do stare at each other speechless for a minute. Finally, Junior Jeffery started to praise God thanking God for placing him in the presence of this great and powerful woman of God. Moses in the other hand fell on his knees praising God for his grandma.

CHAPTER 13

WHEN IT RAINS IT POURS

Goodness, something out of the ordinary happened in the history of Claude working for Mother Faye Esther. This was the first time Mother Faye Esther ever excluded him from something like that concerning the family. He felt he had been pierced with a digger to his heart when Mother Faye Esther failed to require his presence for the session. Later that day she said to Claude, "You're still my son but right now you're in a tough situation. Soon and very soon, you'll understand why I excluded you earlier." The explanation she gave him was not a legitimate reason as he was concerned and said to her, "I'll be in the limousine if you need me." This move indicated that he was in his feeling. Mother knew then he was going into the back seat of the limo to cool off.

On the other hand, Tamara felt like a worthless spy snooping on Mother Faye Esther. Tamara became aware that either Mother Faye Esther or God had exposed her behavior. She desired to thoroughly cleanse her hands of the situation. She seemed determined to continue with whatever plans she had, regardless of the circumstances. Tamara would be willing to jeopardize her marriage and more if Mother Faye Esther knew about her conniving nature. Sitting around the table, she somewhat controlled the atmosphere. After Mother Faye Esther arrived, the few comments that hit their mark silenced Tamara and filled her mind with concern. After her cell phone continued to vibrate, she politely left the table. Patrica echoed, "It has to be an emergency or harassment because not calling is not in this person's DNA." Tamara responded, "It's a little of both, and I'll address it right away, lightning fast." Upon stepping outside, Patrica cried out, "Someone is in trouble." "You're right on the money, Patrica," she replied. In search of safety, Tamara headed towards the limousine and leaned on the door of the passenger backseat. She forgot completely "That the universe has ears, and eyes. It's possible that people are not actually alone, even when they think they are. People need to be extremely careful where they spill their gust and to cover their dirt." This was another saying of Mother Faye Esther from her wisdom book.

She started the conversation after the greeting using Mother Faye Esther's comments. Tamara provided an explanation that Mother Faye Esther found out about her surveillance of the family. Thus, her best option was to resign. The conversation didn't go well for her as her life was threatened by the person she called. If Mother Faye Esther wasn't in the dark, Tamara would be in trouble by now, according to the person she called. Tamara's situation worsened due to the life-threatening situation and the advice given. Alone in the land of uncertainty, she pondered her next move. The person she spoke to insisted on two additional document photos or else the deal would be cancelled. The statement sparked a verbal fight before abruptly ending the call. Tamara lost track of her location and let the heated argument consume her. She expressed concern to the man about the escalating risks, claiming that Mother Faye Esther is a hellish witch capable of reading minds.

The guy who spoke like a possessive lover asked her something about Angela that she didn't catch, and she responded, "What about who?"

"Your friend Angela," he responded.?

"Don't involve her, she already requested me to stop spying on Mother. I regret not following her advice; I allowed you to persuade me. After this, I won't see you anymore because I don't want you to cost me my marriage," responded Tamara.

"It's too late for that," answered the fellow.

"Yes, I texted her those pictures of Moses and Miriam, and their family." She gave them back and warned them that she would inform Grandma and Claude about my attempt to ruin her faith. She brought up the $5,000 she paid me to spy on her Grandmother and then handed me Claude as a husband, even though I didn't deserve him. She warned me about your sorry self. She said, "If I don't stop taking care of you, she will tell Claude."

Then Tamara's lover got angry and said, "Tell that fake prisoner so called pastor to go to hell and be one of the devil's concubines like she was before going to prison. She's missing out because the commentary on Mother Faye Esther and her family will make us incredibly rich. What's the plan for Oscar the garcon? What should we do with him? He caught you once."

Tamara replied, "If ever caught me again, I would sleep with him, accuse him of raping me, and make Mother Faye Esther fire him. Listen to me sex toy, once I photograph Rose's medical papers and document her stories from Claude, I'll pause until I get paid, and this time I'm not referring to your body, but money."

Because he knew Tamara's lacked firm conviction, her lover was fond of that idea. Tamara brought up the fact that he hadn't revealed to her the writer's down payment amount for the documents she gave him exclusively on this family.

He replied, "Baby!"

"No more babying me, our relationship is officially over. I won't let you use my husband's hard-earned money to dress yourself up. Claude, my husband, is a good man who doesn't deserve me betraying him with a scammer like you. I want out."

"No, you can't leave me," he replied.

Tamara confidently stated, "I can't do it, but watch my smoke."

He warned Tamara that if she did that, she would end up in divorce court for adultery. 'I plan to send your husband all the intimate photos and videos we've ever taken, even sharing them on social media."

Furiously Tamara responded with rage, "Are you blackmailing me now. Give it a shot, young boy, and you'll disappear without leaving a single trace. Just a reminder, I am the spouse of a very powerful man."

Peacefully, he informed Tamara that "The chateau was bustling with guests, all eager to make up for lost time and get to know one another. That was the ideal moment for you to take pictures of those documents. You can fulfill my request by being in the room at this moment. Do you have knowledge of your husband's whereabouts now?"

"No," answered Tamara.

Her lover warned, "If I don't hear from you by this time tomorrow, the first picture will go up on Claude's timeline."

"Joseph, why are you doing this to me," inquired Tamara?

"Because I love you, my spiritual wife," replied, Joseph.

Tamara said before ganging up, "I see what I can do."

While adjusting her clothes, she accidentally left her phone on the roof of the limousine.

Tamara's decision to put the phone on speaker and talk to Joseph, her lover, was a mistake. Everything was going smoothly until she mentioned his name. The voice reminded her husband of Joseph, but he couldn't be sure. However, he rejected the notion that it was Joseph because his wife would never stoop that low. Claude, feeling down, sits in the backseat of a limo to discover his wife's affair with Joseph, the yard caretaker and the town drunk. Sitting there and listening to this painful story was something

Claude despised. Throughout the conversation, he frequently wanted to grab the phone away from her. He remembered the significance of this day to Mother and didn't want to be the one to ruin it with a scandal. Emotionally speaking, Claude's legs wouldn't cooperate when he tried to leave the limousine. He discovered himself praying for a rebuking stroke. He appeared to be in deep shock as his limbs grew inactive. In a million years, he would never have thought that his wife would be cheating on him with Joseph. If this information leaks, it will greatly astonish many, particularly those who were familiar with Joseph. Those who doubt that "Love is blind like a bat" will be proven wrong by this news. Tamara's physical appearance was in disarray, leading her to give up a life of wealth and fame for a less desirable one.

Meanwhile, Claude required assistance exiting the vehicle, but Miriam's memory slowly returned, and she recalled Claude, the uncle who consistently brought her and Moses' candy. She asked her grandma, "Where is Claude?" She responded from the backseat of the limo. With her anointing oil in hand, Miriam stepped outside. Upon opening the door, she confronted Claude for not bringing any candy despite knowing that Moses and she were coming. His response was, "When I witnessed Mother's determination for your arrival, I went to the store and bought your candy, let me go get it."

"Sorry," said Miriam, "I need to pray for your legs first as God requested, Uncle Claude." She took Claude's hand five minutes later and said, "Let's go inside. Uncle, The Holy Spirit mentioned that you acted with integrity and honor while supporting your adoptive Mother, all in the name of love."

Claude shared with Miriam that he believed he was having a stroke. "Uncle, believe in God's goodness but brace yourself for the imminent worst. I see it, I can even touch it. Keep what happened in the limo a secret, don't tell anyone," uttered Miriam to Claude.

As Claude and Miriam walked toward the mansion to join the fun suddenly Tamara's phone started to vibrate on top of the limo. Claude answered the phone and before saying hello, the person on the other end of the line began to rebuke Tamara. "Don't say a word and listen to me good Tamara. The pictures you sent me are a complete deepfake of Moses and Miriam, who passed away years ago. You should quit smoking marijuana with Joseph. By the time I'm released from jail tomorrow, you must confess the complete truth about your disgraceful lifestyle to your husband. Allow him to determine if he can handle a tragedy like you. If you refuse, I'll be the one to inform him. I feel remorseful for deceiving Claude by matchmaking him with you to benefit myself. I specifically asked you to stop spying on the family two years ago, and you assured me that you would. Yet, you have now started listening to Joseph, of all people. Your busybody soul will find a warm welcome in hell after my Grandmother is done with you, girl."

Poor Claude was utterly bewildered, like the two left shoes. He internally concluded that the voice he heard was Angela's. He thought he was trapped in a trance during his sleepwalking and dreaming. Tamara wasted no time snapping him back to reality, especially after catching him on her phone. Suddenly, she went berserk, yanked the phone from his ear, and hung it up, mistaking the caller for Joseph. Regardless, she found herself in a difficult situation. Her move left Claude stunned and took Miriam by surprise as well. Tamara was aggressive and embarrassed her husband by asking, "Why were you answering my phone? From now on, we'll both refrain from answering each other's phone calls." Miriam was left questioning if Tamara's reaction was driven by jealousy because she was talking to Claude outside. Tamara gave the impression of knowing her thoughts and brought her peace. Tamara said to Miriam, "Can you tell your Uncle Claude to stay away from his wife's phone?" Miriam asked Uncle Claude not to pick up Aunt Tamara's phone and to give her a moment to chat with her. Claude entered the mansion, but Mother Faye Esther sensed that something had gone awry while he was outside.

Miriam made certain that Claude was entirely indoors and described to Tamara how her husband retrieved her phone from the top of the limousine. She informed Tamara that they noticed the phone because it rang and vibrated, and Claude answered it. From Claude's expression, it was clear that he despised answering the phone. Miriam advice Tamara to interrogate her husband regarding the caller and their conversation that sadly changed his countenance The sight of a tear rolling down his face revealed the immense pain caused by their hurtful words. Miriam, who appeared to be in the Spirit, warned Tamara about her marriage. Once the Good Lord reseals it, expecting things to change while forgiveness is still possible, it is up to Tamara to seek it from her husband. "In most situation forgiveness has an expiration date," according to Mother Faye Esther.

Miriam told Tamara to never forbid her husband from answering her phone, and vice versa. In such cases, when one of them hides something, it raises suspicions about their character. If a husband or wife can't communicate with friends while their partner is present, trust becomes an issue. She held Tamara by her shoulders and uttered, "Auntie Tamara go and do the right thing for the sake of your marriage." Tamara exclaimed, "Miriam, my Niece, where have you been 2 years ago? My life, my self-esteem would have been in a better place. Niece, I have a feeling that I got caught or will get caught." Miriam with tears in her eyes responded, "I think so too, because your greed is stronger than your will." According to Mother Faye Esther again, "When it comes to bad habit, one last time or one last drop is known to destroy many people's live." They hugged each other and Miriam whispered in Tamara's ears "Auntie, the ball is still in your corner go inside and come clean with your husband. Tell him everything, I mean everything Aunt Tamara." She responded, "I will and thank you, too."

Claude's expression turned extremely somber until it caught Mother's attention. He was bombarded with an overwhelming amount of harmful information that evening. Mother requested Pastor Moses to come to her. Upon his arrival, she communicated to him that his uncle Claude was in dire need of a counselor. He faced a man problem that demanded the help of a divine man, and this was just the beginning of his challenges. Pastor Moses stated that the Spirit of God made it known to him as soon as Claude came in. He inquired of his Grandma what she desired him to do.

She called Claude and gave him the key to her prayer room. Instructed to go to the only locked room with his nephew, she commanded Claude to tell him what had occurred outside. Although shocked, Claude realized that Mother was determined. "Nephew, let's go," Claude said to him, expressing gratitude. The day you chose to come couldn't have been better. Pastor Moses confessed to Claude that he and his sister had been warned by the Spirit of the Lord that they had a mission to fulfill upon reaching their destination, expressing his urgent need.

Claude speculated in his mind that the room housing the camera is likely the prayer room, but its validity will only be known in due time. After opening the door, they proceeded to go in. They were astonished by the prayer room's beauty and spiritual theme. Both Claude and Pastor Moses displayed awe as if they had witnessed the ninth wonder of the world. They both attested to feeling God and His Heavenly Host in the room. Moses knelt and prayed to God, requesting three times the amount of faith his Grandma had. They performed a church ceremony before their session, during which Claude declared his acceptance of Jesus as his Lord and Savior. He got baptized in the chateau's pool the next day. From now on, Moses' ministry will never be the same. They were both caught off guard by something unexpected in the prayer room. Mother Faye Esther's achievements were revealed, including her status as a Doctor of Divinity and an ordained preacher. Claude discovered something he never knew and realized he had been taking Mother for granted.

Tamara watched the situation closely, attempting to stay informed about everyone's whereabouts so she could meet Joseph's demands and protect her marriage and reputation. Miriam's counseling seemed to have no impact on her. In simpler terms, it was unsuccessful in a challenging environment. Tamara found everyone when they gathered in the fellowship hall of the chateau, enjoying each other's company to the fullest during this fun-filled family gathering day. To everyone's surprise, Patrice joined in the fun after finding out about Mirian's plan to distribute the insurance money among all the twins in the family. Fernand, Andre, Reverend Pachouco, Pastor Leslie's twins, who were on their way to Mother in their private airplane. They were with Barbara, Yves, Natasha, Yvon and Michelle, and their twins Nya, and Moriah were all traveling with them. They were eager to see and meet Moses and Miriam, who were believed to have died decades ago. Claude and Junior Jeffery will pick them up in the limousine as soon as their aircraft lands. Get ready for a "Tears of Deception and Sold Out with a Kiss," novels' reunion.

At last, Tamara knows the location of her husband Claude and Pastor Moses. She didn't account for Oscar the servant until she spotted him napping in the corner. She skillfully slipped away from the splendid family gathering and quietly made her way to Mother's room, where she stored Rose's medical documents. Finding the folders was easy for Tamara, so she began photographing them.

Mother herself instructed Oscar, who had a strong infatuation for Tamara, to keep a close watch on her. His blushing whenever she spoke to him made it clear to

Tamara that he had feelings for her. Whether sober or drunk, he couldn't bring himself to look her in the eyes, especially when he was serving dinner or drinks. She frequently found it amusing to flirt with him openly, as if it meant nothing.

Tamara might t soon find herself singing the old cliche song, "When it rains, it pours. The ground is about to give way beneath her. "When it comes to breaking the law fraudulently, One should never trust one last time. The final attempt frequently lands the pledger in prison," this is another saying of Mother Faye Esther. While taking those documents pictures hiding in a corner, here came Oscar asking her, "What in the world do you think you are doing, I'm going to call Mother?"

According to Mother Faye Esther's wisdom book again, "Those who don't control their desires also fail to uphold moral values." Tamara was fully aware and had been cautioned about never betraying Mother, as no earthly refuge could shield her from her wrath except for God. Half undressed, Tamara summoned Oscar and beckoned him, saying "Look, then come back here." All timid and scared, he turned around and made his way towards her, keeping his head down. Too afraid to glance at her topless body. Tamara knew she had him right where she wanted him. With a firm grip on his hands, she led them to her breasts, ensuring he felt comfortable every step of the way. She used various types of kisses to break the ice in a provocative manner. He assisted her in storing those folders and guided her into an infrequently used room. Tamara didn't plan to get involved this much, but she ended up caught in Oscar's web. Filled with remorse,

Oscar lifted his face up and urged Tamara to get dressed, assuring her of his silence regarding the pictures and files. Tamara urged him to persist and continue what he was doing to her. He said, "Are you sure, Mrs. Claude?" "I'm positive," she replied, "And please stop calling me Mrs. Claude." Without hesitation he carried on with what he was doing, instantly driving her crazy. Oscar and Tamara were swept up in the excitement as arid landscapes encountered abundant rainfall for the first time. They behaved as if they were in their own private hotel room, oblivious to the fact that "Privacy was a thing of the past," just as Mother Faye Esther had written. They completely lost track of their surroundings and the mansion's owner. Furthermore, the place was crowded with guests. Tamara, in particular, embraced the mindset of a dog in heat. Through mimicry, they will come to comprehend the steep price of a life lived in mediocrity and the treachery of unrestrained desires. "To rein in a chaotic and untamed flesh, self-control is the only solution," said Mother Faye Esther in her wisdom book. Tamara risked everything she had - her marriage, luxurious lifestyle, and more - for a mere 15 minutes of pleasure, knowing the consequences if she were caught. Once more, the state of the flesh is messy. Is it worth sacrificing everything for a sexual affair that cannot compensate for what was lost? No matter the circumstances, pleasure seekers should never allow pleasure to ruin and destroy their lives, not even once. Does it hold value in the long term? The heart is shielded from breaking by self-preservation.

After receiving permission from Claude, Pastor Moses asked Junior Jeffery, the chairman of his deacon board, to join the meeting. Meanwhile, Mother and Yvonne focused completely on their grandchildren/ Patrice, Patrica, Rose Marie, and Miriam were having a great time together. Miriam impulsively sought out her Great Grandmother and pleaded for a companion to accompany her on a tour of the chateau, which featured twelve bedrooms, twelve full baths, and garden tubs. She responded to Miriam saying, "Baby this is your home too, you don't need anyone to give you a tour. If you get lost, go ahead and yell so Oscar can come to find you. You're welcome to explore every room except the castle, which I refer to as my prayer room. The boys are currently having their men's meeting." Where is Tamara? she inquired.

Miriam suggested that Auntie might be outside, talking on the phone. With a humorous tone, Mother laughed and said, right?

The tour started for Miriam, and she was blown away by every room she entered. She used to think her, and her husband's homes were beautiful, but now they see they can't compete with this place. The room designs and stages were stunning. Getting close to what seemed to be a conference room. A rumbling noise caught her attention, accompanied by a female voice pleading, "Please, make it stop!" Miriam, who was a black belt in both judo and karate, opened the door and witnessed Oscar on top of Tamara. She believed that what she witnessed couldn't be mutual consent due to Tamara's standing in their community. Miriam immediately associated him with rape because of his identity. She lifted Oscar and forcefully threw him to the ground, then sat on his back with his arms restrained. "You're about to break my arms," he pleaded, "please let me explain."

181

Tamara shamelessly whispered loud enough for Miriam to hear, "He raped me without showing any mercy. Oscar, why did you do that to me? Claude and I never treated as a maid but a son."

Miriam, in a fit of anger, used her belt to tie Oscar up with a Girl scout knot. Before contacting the police, she insisted on calling Grandma Faye. She directed her gaze at Oscar and expressed her strong hatred towards rapists. She shared, "During my time of homelessness in search of my brother Moses, I experienced repeated sexual assaults, happening three to five times a day or night. Throughout everything, God ensured that I remained free from any sexually transmitted diseases (STDs). Now in broad daylight, you had the nerve to rape my Auntie who is Mr. Claude's wife" and Miriam punched him again.

Tamara's accusation left Oscar speechless and feeling betrayed. His intention was to defend himself in Miriam's presence, but his words appeared to abandon him. At one point, to respond to Tamara's inquiry about his motive for raping her. He answered right before Miriam, "I don't know." On his stomach, tears streaming down his face, he begged Mother Faye for forgiveness for going against her instructions. Mother was not there to hear it. Upon hearing that, Tamara broke down in uncontrollable tears. During Miriam confrontation with Oscar, Tamara managed to tear up her underwear, blouse, and bra to stage the scene of her rape story. One might wonder if she accused someone else in the same manner before, given how quickly she tore them. Oscar was left on the floor while Tamara, who had difficulty walking, was escorted to the bathroom by Miriam. She told Miriam not to share what happened to anyone to prevent a family commotion as it was too embarrassing. Furthermore, it is important to shield the children from witnessing such conflict. Miriam, could you lend me one of your tops so I can go home and handle the start of this terrible nightmare that will haunt me forever? "Miriam instructed her aunt to take a hot shower, after which they would discuss the cover-up." Miriam returned to Oscar's location and asked him directly if he raped Tamara. He apologized to Miriam, admitting that he did indeed do it. Instead of washing, Tamara hid behind the door and listened to Oscar agreeing to rape her before quietly returning to the shower. Miriam freed his hands, preparing to exit the room, and Oscar inquired about his future. As she turned around, she exclaimed, "Oscar, my son, we can't let this type of crime go unpunished or ignored. Those who attempted to assist the wrongdoer are also liable for the identical offense. Son, acknowledging the crime means accepting the prescribed legal punishments."

Miriam gave Tamara a new top, bras, and skirt. She tried on the clothes, and they fit perfectly, so she packed her old outfit to bring home. Miriam was asked by her how they planned to keep that secret between the three of them. Miriam informed Tamara that she had faced numerous challenges in life and had decided not to compromise her moral principles for anyone. She won't risk her new relationship with her husband, brother, and grandparents over something significant trivial. We should let Uncle Claude and Grandma Faye in on this. If not, I had no other choice but to inform them about what I witnessed. Maybe Grandma Faye might already know.

The fellows concluded their meeting. Moses suggested that Claude should speak with Tamara. Forgiveness should be given if she came with honesty. Notify her that he was in the limousine, overhearing her conversation with Joseph. Junior and Moses encountered Miriam and Tamara while exploring the premises after leaving the prayer room. They paused to talk and noticed that Tamara was extremely distressed. They extended their assistance to her. Claude stepped away to use the restroom and intended to join us again afterwards. He followed the same path as Junior and Moses after leaving the restroom. He observed Miriam's attempt to console Tamara. He wanted to know what the problem was. Miriam responded to Aunt Tamara, explaining that she would be downstairs, and advised Uncle to be considerate, as it was not an opportune time. Claude thanked his niece for the reminder.

Inside the bag, Tamara retrieved the outfit she had been wearing earlier, showed it to him, and implied that she had been raped a couple of hours ago. Claude replied, "By who, Joseph." Tamara asked, "What do you know about him." "While in the limousine, I overheard every single word of your conversation with Joseph. Was he the person who raped you?" She shook her head to say, "No." "But who," Claude asked. She responded, "Don't you go embarrass me in front all the guests" and she said, "Oscar, the maid."

Claude's anger reached an unprecedented level. He expressed to Tamara the importance of not hiding this from Mother Faye Esther. Claude asked Tamara why she did not scream for help. She claimed she tried her hardest to seek help, but he threatened to strangle me. According to her, she attempted to fight him, but he was too strong to overpower. Claude began crying, and Mother heard the sound, so she sent Oscar to bring Claude downstairs. Miriam reasoned with her Grandma why she should not send Oscar near Uncle Claude. She recounted to her grandma the events as she saw them unfold. Miriam notified her that Oscar confessed to committing rape against Tamara. Mother reiterated to Miriam Tamara's lack of trustworthiness. She described to Miriam the location and room where the incident occurred. She confides in Miriam about Tamara being a manipulator and exceeding all previous actions. With the rope of betrayal, she chose to hang herself. Even though it's the biggest and largest in the neighborhood, the chateau only has one camera in one room for a day like today. God revealed to me in the past that I should position a camera at the exact location it occurred today. She told Miriam to come with her to the upper floor. The sight of Mother prompted Tamara to perform. At first, she claimed that Oscar raped her using a foreign object as well. When rang the bell, Oscar came running with tears in his eyes. Upon passing Claude, he swiftly seized Oscar by the neck, vigorously shook him, and Mother intervened, insisting that Claude release him. Mother questioned Oscar if she hadn't instructed him to keep an eye on Tamara today due to suspicious behavior. "Yes, Mother, you did and I'm sorry." "Oscar, did I not warn you not to fall in Tamara' trap today?" "Indeed, Mother, you did." "Can you confirm if you raped Tamara in this room?" "Mother, I'm sorry. I did it nonstop for one hour."

Just as Claude was about to punch him, Mother intervened and reminded Claude about the guests in the mansion. She requested Claude's phone, phoned the police Chief, and asked him to dispatch a couple of police officers to the chateau. Mother asked Tamara what she wanted to alleviate her pain and suffering. Her response was at least $50,000 for medical care, given her limited ability to walk.

Claude became angry at his wife for asking Mother for such a large amount of money. Tamara quickly reminded him that he was not the one suffering now. Mother told Claude that it was fine and to grab the   check book from the dresser. Claude sensed that his wife and Oscar were facing some kind of trouble. Mother instructed Tamara to file a police report against Oscar after explaining the details of the rape. Mother filed a police report accusing Tamara and Joseph of fraud. She instructed the two officers to stand guard at the door and prevent anyone from entering or leaving the room. The plan was for the five of them to watch a movie, as she mentioned. She asked Claude and Miriam if they could watch the film. Both responses were affirmative. Tamara stated her lack of desire to see it, to which Mother replied that she and Oscar were left with no choice.

Astonishingly, a voice reverberated in the room, it's Tamara's, confessing, "I fabricated the rape accusation against Oscar. I was the one who seduced him and began everything. Mother, I urge you not to let Claude watch the video for my marriage's sake. Miriam, I'm sorry for leading you astray. Mother, I ask for your forgiveness for invading your privacy and disrespecting your house. Claude, please be compassionate and show me mercy. I've been unfaithful to you with Joseph and Oscar. Should you find it in your heart to forgive me, I will shower you with love and devotion. Claude, Darling, avoid watching the film. I made a promise to Angela to be the perfect wife for you, which is why we secretly got matched together. However, I was all that to you until Joseph raped me in our backyard. That moment marked the beginning of my sexual addiction. Oscar, you're so young that I shouldn't have been the one to take your virginity. It's not you who raped me, it's the other way around. Please Claude, see past my flaws, and refrain from divorcing me."

Mother Faye Esther replied to Tamara saying, "Since I know you this the first time, I ever felt the presence of sincerity from your heart to your lips. However, to go unpunished is a crime against integrity and principal. If you knew that, Joseph, after raping you, should have been in jail until now. Nowadays, no woman after being raped by a man should not hold her peace in any circumstance otherwise, her silence is also a crime against his future prey and society."

Mother pressed rewind on the camera and then proceeded to play the film. While watching the video, they discover that Tamara was the one who told Oscar to pretend he was raping her. She was dictating his next moves. With tears in her eyes, Miriam expressed regret to Oscar for not understanding the situation. Meanwhile, Claude remained oblivious to his wife's untamed nature. It was disappointing to witness this perplexing pornographic video. Claude asked Mother if he could use the tape as evidence of his divorce since he couldn't bear to live with this nightmare. She requested that Claude accompany her outside. The others were instructed to wait for them in the room. Claude received an apology from Mother because

Tamara, his wife, chose to go to prison along with Oscar and Joseph rather than going home with him. Claude, she, and Joseph teamed up with a publisher to gather family information for a documentary. You were also recorded by her many times. I listened as you told her about Moses and Miriam today and she played the tape for Claude. Looked at the pictures she took of them when they first arrived here this morning, and Mother Faye Esther showed them to him. Three hours ago, she entered my bedroom and took pictures of Rose's medical record, she exhibited them to him. Claude asked how you manage to gather all this evidence. Unbeknownst to them, they unknowingly sent back all the stolen information about the family because I'm the publisher they are dealing with. Tamara assisted in gathering documents that could potentially harm all of us. Tamara was working with Angela before Angela converted. Angela secretly taught Tamara how to marry you without revealing her connection to Angela. Claude answered, "We should do what we're supposed to, Mother, they crossed the line." Claude went back into the room and sent Miriam out to talk to her Grandma. In five minutes, she requested Miriam to take the kids to the kiddy park behind the chateau. Joseph was apprehended by the police chief earlier, who then contacted Mother. The two police officers asked Oscar and Tamara to meet them outside. They handcuffed them and nobody else from the chateau knew what had happened.

Later that night, once the children were asleep, Mother Faye Esther gathered all the guests for a meeting to explain what had occurred. She kept the rape part a secret to protect Claude and let him decide the fate of their marriage. She disclosed to them the secret collaboration with a publisher to spy on the family for personal gain, to make a documentary. Pastor Moses lifted his hand, and his Grandma recognized him. He inquired about the way she stumbled upon this treacherous betrayal. She offered her Great Grandson a benign smile and said, "With the aid of competent authority I was the publisher. The document that was stolen from my family has been returned to me until I catch the person responsible. When you guys got here, you took pictures, and they were sent to me as the publisher. Look at them including Claude's conversation on his way to the store. My pictures on the ladder taking measurement for your welcome home banner this morning, you see them. Once I received Rose's medical records right here, I was certain about the identity of the criminals, and they were apprehended. Now they are behind bars. I have news to share with Moses, Rose Marie, Junior, and Miriam, which Rose, Yvonne, Claude, Patrice, and Patrica are already aware of. My love for you is unconditional, but don't ever deceive me." Junior Jeffery implied, now I understand why Miriam is the way she is. Mother Faye Esther adjourned the meeting amidst laughter, and Claude extended an invitation to the fellows to reconvene in the prayer room and discuss his marital status. When it rains, it pours.

CHAPTER 14

UNFORGETABLE REUNION

Junior and Miriam's twins, Moses Junior and Miriam Ester, captivated Patrice, and Patrica inexplicably. They formed a special connection with these two children, which everyone could see. Perhaps it was because of their similarity in appearance. They could easily be mistaken for siblings rather than cousins through adoption. Patrice and Patrica loved Antoinette, Moses, and Rose Marie's daughter, as well as Evonne, Junior, and Miriam's third child, but they're particularly crazy about the twins. The twins were drawn to the separate images of the same person in Patrice and Patrica's rooms. Whether together or separately, Moses Junior and Miriam Ester would passionately kiss the image every time they entered the room. At times, they would gaze at the pictures until they seemed frozen in place. The twins' attraction to the photos was shared with Mother Faye Esther by Patrice and Patrica, who observed them occasionally worshipping the images. Patrice inquired her Grandma about her thoughts on whether the kids had been exposed to any cults that worshiped human pictures. Why would the twins love my mother's photo so much without knowing her? Oh well, that's their Aunt. Patrice, to her amazement, couldn't stop talking, giving Mother Faye Esther a chance to speak, but instead burst into laughter. The three granddaughters, Rose Marie, Patrica, and Miriam asked their Grandma why she was laughing. Patrice, my wonderful great granddaughter, is brightening up my day with our joyful companionship. Mother Faye Esther's demeanor instantly changed as she solemnly said to Patrice, "God is Good, don't you think? Life is like a big puzzle that none of us, even the best among us, ever fully finishes, as Mother said. Why is that? Heaven or hell is where the remaining pieces are located. The choice between heaven or hell to find the remaining pieces of the puzzle depends on how mankind collaborates on earth."

One day Patrice, soon and very soon Patrice will understand why children do the things they do. Moses junior and Miriam Ester feel a divine connection with Patrice's mother's pictures, but too young to understand the effect of a strong bloodline. If their parents witnessed their behavior of theirs, junior Jeffery and Miriam would be shocked or past out for sure. They might also stare at the pictures too. Through all this Mother Faye Esther was having the time of her life because she knew through divine revelation her family would be reunited again and buried all hatchets.

Pastor Moses, also known as Unique Preacher, delivered a powerful sermon before Claude's baptism ceremony. Consequently, the entire household and all the guests, including children, willingly embraced Jesus as their Lord and Savior.

Every single one of them wanted to baptize along with Claude.

Even Patrice, who openly admitted to scheming for the past two days to smear Moses and tarnish his reputation. Even after finding out about their death, she still revealed her intense hatred for Moses and Miriam. Now, they were the absolute best first cousins she had ever had. She concluded her revelation by requesting Pastor Unique Preacher to baptize her in the water, either in the Name of the Father, Son, and Holy Spirit, or in the Name of Jesus. In perfect harmony, everyone shouted Amen.

Patrice and Patrica were the first to enter the water, followed by Claude. Following that, Jeffery Junior, and his family, which includes Yvonne and Rose the daughter of Mother Faye Esther, recommitted themselves to God. Rose's sanity was returned to her when Pastor Unique Preacher submerged her in water and raised her up in the Name of Jesus. It was a day when God's presence was undeniable and awe-inspiring. However, the story wasn't over yet; Pastor Unique Preacher had a personal request for himself and his family. He asked Mother Faye Esther to baptize him and his household. Without assistance, she entered the water, submerged Moses, Rose Marie, Antoinette, and lifted them all individually. Everyone was astonished by the strength of Mother Faye Esther, who is ninety-five years old. Miriam, who had a longing to be immersed in the water again, had her wish fulfilled by her Grandma. She baptized Miriam again. The chateau's pool on that day reminded many of the pool Bethesda because o's cure. They departed from the pool, convinced that God sent angels to agitate the water for them. The joyful commotion filled the neighborhood as people gathered to witness Rose's amazing spectacle. Her doctor who lived a few blocks away from the mansion was vacationing at Carrefour, Port-au-Prince, Haiti. Upon hearing the news he called Rose to make sure his wife knew what she was talking about. The first time Rose spoke to him on the phone, he cried and expressed gratitude to God and The Chief Scientist Jesus. Rose's mental dilemma prevented the doctor from discovering her humorous side. Before hanging up, she scolded him for not being present to celebrate freedom from Satan's prison. God freed me from the cage and used it to imprison Satan, tossing the key away. Doctor, there's no need to worry about Lucifer causing trouble now. He laughed and hung the phone praising God.

Long-standing community members were invited by Mother Faye Esther to extend a warm welcome to Moses and Miriam. Several of them were familiar with the narrative of their demise. Upon receiving the invitation, they labeled Mother Faye Esther as delusional. Rose's water baptizing miracle left them excited while Moses and Miriam's presence shocked them. The miracle happened through Pastor Moses' hands, exacerbating the situation. Mother Faye Esther's friends, who arrived towards the end of nearly everything, requested her to extend the ceremony by three days. She introduced the idea to Pastor Unique Preacher, whom most people had heard of or followed online, but didn't realize he was the little boy they knew with a speech problem. Moses asked his grandma to find a huge tent capable of accommodating a thousand people, promising to hold a five-night revival to express gratitude to God for miracles, signs, and wonders. The tent could be set up on the field. The well-preserved land surrounding the chateau covered four acres. Moses couldn't bring himself to deny his grandma's request, so he set an impossible condition. Junior Jeffery and Rose Marie shook their heads praising Moses' cleverness. Miriam, familiar with their actions, thought to herself that they are unaware Grandma Faye will make it happen to prove a point. Mother Faye Esther told Pastor Unique Preacher, "Grandson, prepare your sermons for the upcoming revival."

Mother Faye Esther had a deep understanding of both the power of God and the power of money, without making comparisons. She exited the spiritual party, entered the chateau, and initiated her phone conversation. She started off the evening by obtaining permission from the city for the event. She contacted the police department to ask for security for a crowd of at least two thousand people due to her Grandson's popularity. The tent, which they believed to be impossible, was provided by God's blessings. They offered to deliver the tent and chairs for free, only asking her to cover the cost of installation and removal. Junior Jeffery and Rose Marie spoke with Moses to apologize to his Grandma for leading her on a fruitless search. Moses thought she couldn't arrange it at such short notice due to her lack of connections. He responded, expressing remorse for his actions towards her, and planned to apologize in the morning.

Miriam's husband addressed Miriam regarding Moses' deceitful actions. She responded, "My Brother doesn't fully understand the immense power of God in Grandma Faye's life." Her husband retorted "Baby, to think she could pull this off was absurd, no way she could." With a laugh, Miriam remarked, "In the fleeting time I've been here, I've discovered that you should never discount Grandma Faye. Moses and You are in the same boat. The two of you must realize the struggles involved in deceiving one of God's elects. It's impossible."

Claude even though he left this good old gospel singing to go to the airport to pick Mother's children and their siblings. Moses and Miriam had no idea that people had flown to see them. Moses, his gospel choir, and his congregants in the mega church all enjoyed singing his uncle's songs. Moses was unaware of their familial connection. He recognized Pachouco from a photo on his CD.

Claude successfully kept the situation between him and Tamara a secret. The people in the limousine were curious about Tamara's whereabouts since they were used to seeing her with her husband when he picked them up from the airport. Despite the pain and shame she inflicted on him, he treated her with the utmost respect as a husband should. According to a Haitian proverb, "A leaking roof can deceive the sun, but not the rain." Everyone thought Claude and his wife were fine, except Pastor Leslie who knew him well. Yvon and his wife Michelle saw a spiritual aura on his face and inquired about it. Claude said that today, we all got baptized in the chateau's pool by Pastor Unique Preacher and Mother Faye Esther. In complete synchrony, they all uttered the same words. "Oh no, we missed it." They apologized for their tardiness and expressed their desire to have been baptized by their Mother and Grandmother. Pachouco eagerly asked Claude "If he mentioned that Pastor Unique Preacher, the beloved mega preacher, was at my mother's house helping her baptize people. I wonder how Mother managed to do that; I wish I could meet him." Pachouco's sister Barbara inquired "If he was the one who requested him to perform a concert at his church and then declined." Pastor Leslie agreed, but Pachouco politely declined, saying, "I believe I will meet Pastor Unique Preacher someday, but God has advised me to wait and be patient."

It didn't take long for Claude to realize that most of the people who followed Pastor Unique Preacher were oblivious to his actual name, which happened to be Moses

Pierre Casimir Day. It wasn't revealed by him that Pastor Unique Preacher was Moses, one of the people they flew to see. Claude also kept hidden the miraculous events surrounding their sister Rose and the ongoing spiritual services. Claude made a quick stop at the store to grab some drinks for Mother. Pastor Leslie accompanied Claude and inquired if he recalled the tale of Pachouco and her redemption in Tears of Deception, where Pachouco, Yvon, and Michelle forgave her transgressions.

"Who can forget this great love story filled with compassion, forgiveness, and the power of true love," replied Claude. Pastor Leslie emphasized that God expected Claude to forgive Tamara, given his newfound salvation. As Mother Faye Esther puts it in her wisdom book, "Being saved by the Lord Jesus Christ often entails navigating various territories to enter heaven, and forgiving others is the most significant requirement."

Upon their arrival at the mansion, they heard singing from behind the door. Barbara told Claude and the others that if she didn't know any better, she would mistake it for her sister Rose singing. Claude kept his silence. Right before opening the door, a person inside started singing Pachouco's song called "Just a little." Pastor Leslie gestured for Claude to hold on as she and the others, including their children, were astonished by the person's singing voice, which sounded like Pachouco's. Pachouco told them outside watched this. When the singer paused to take a breath, he waited before continuing the next stanza. Pachouco then took over and sang, "Time with Jesus, that's all I need to get my life right on time." Everyone on the inside was unaware of what was happening except for Mother. Moses continued singing in his mind, believing he was accompanied by angelic beings. Pachouco and

Moses sounded adorable, when they reached the chorus all of them from the outside started to sing the chorus, "The more they talked, the more they lied, the more I bend my knees Though they talked about me, scandalized my name I love them anyway." The sight behind the door shocked them when Claude opened it. The fellowship room was filled with a mixture of emotions, leaving everyone paralyzed. The immediate family of Moses and Miriam made a sudden turnaround. Miriam inquired, "Are you the famous gospel singer, Pachouco? Our church family is absolutely smitten with you, particularly my brother Moses." Pachouco replied, "yes and you're Miriam, he turned around pointed and you are Moses."

While the world knew me as a gospel singer, Moses and you should know me as your favorite Uncle. Miriam asked Grandma Faye if she had any more tricks up her sleeve. Mother gestured towards the sky with her index finger and exclaimed, "God always surprises me. It's possible that he has even more surprises in store for all of us." In my book, I mention that "Life is filled with surprises, but it's what you do afterward that truly counts."
Pastor Leslie and their twins were introduced to them, as well as Aunt Barbara, Yvon, Michelle, and their twins. It's hard to believe, but there were five sets of twins under one roof together.
Moses began sobbing uncontrollably and requested everyone to take a seat. Every person sat obediently, without a single person standing up. He implored them to hold off on stopping him until he made peace with all those present. "By being here , I truly understood the meaning of the saying" "Blood is thicker than water."

"Against my desires, I am here to appease my savior, my angel who I once treated poorly. I let hate take precedence over recognizing her value in my life. On my deathbed, she appeared and saved my life by God's grace. While she adored me, I despised her. Although I recognized her as my sister, I nearly divorced my wife, Rose Marie, for secretly supporting, feeding, and clothing her. I had a strong aversion towards the family even though I had no personal experience with them." Moses crawled on his knees towards Miriam, begging her forgiveness for keeping her away from their own family. Crawling on his knees, he went up to each person in the room, asking for forgiveness. Pastor Leslie and Pachouco prayed for him lifted him from the floor. Miriam did something out of the ordinary by gathering all the twins to encircle her and Moses. After tightly hugging him, she looked into his face and solemnly declared in the presence of God and a circle of witnesses that they would never speak of this again. "Moses, we located our family just in time. Could you imagine one of our daughters grow up and end up dating or Marrying Aunt Barbara or Aunt Lesli's son. Family needs to know each other . It's a must to have yearly family reunions to prevent this madness." Mother Faye Esther swiftly interrupted and redirected the conversation to prevent Rose from hearing Miriam's logical reasoning. It was something like that which drove Rose to madness in the past.

Rose, a playful trickster deep down, took pleasure in deceiving her sister Barbara, who loved pampering her with meals whenever she came to visit. Rose sat on her chair, waiting, as soon as she saw her sister. Barbara embraced everyone with joy upon seeing Moses and

Miriam alive. She entered the kitchen and made food for Rose. She began the task of feeding Rose. People who were aware that Rose was healed were laughing hysterically. Everyone else appeared foolish and clueless. Barbara's focus was to provide sustenance for her sister, who was unable to care for herself. Barbara placed the food beside Rose to prepare her milkshake. Rose captured everyone's gaze and silently signaled them to remain quiet. She quickly finished the remaining food and left the plate empty. When Barbara returned, she saw the plate clean, she asked "What happened to your food, Rose?" It crossed Barbara's mind that one of the children had ingested it. I'll fetch you another plate. Rose, in response to Barbara, happily declared, "I'm cured, thank you!" and immediately broke into dance. The entire group that came with Claude started praising God anew. Barbara and Leslie both started engaging in spiritual expressions; Barbara prophesying and Leslie praising God in an unknown language. In perfect synchronization, Rose Marie and Rose began singing Zion songs.

Finally, things calmed down and Yvon and Michelle were curious about Aunt Rose's healing. Earlier during the baptism, Patrica informed them that Grandma Faye had brought her to be baptized. When Pastor Unique Preacher submerged her under the water, Rose emerged healed. Another praise service was born in response to that. This family had a deep devotion to acknowledging God completely. Pachouco and Pastor Leslie expressed regret to Moses and Patrice for not having the opportunity to meet Pastor Unique Preacher, who reminded them of Moses. Patrice requested silence from everyone and asked them to repeat their statements. They reiterated and Rose suggested that Pachouco and Pastor Leslie will eventually meet him. They started to laugh. According to Pastor Moses, "Uncle Pachouco was at fault, for Pastor Leslie not to meet him. Pastor Unique Preacher invited him to perform a concert for the assembly. He turned down the offer. He mentioned that God had revealed to him that it wasn't the right time." They exchanged strange looks because they knew he had told them the truth. Miriam stepped in, questioning how Moses found that out. asked him, Auntie. "Right, answer that," said Pastor Leslie. He replied to his Auntie, mentioning that they were good friends and he planned to invite him over. Pastor Leslie reached into her pocketbook and revealed the tickets they bought for Pastor Unique Preacher's two-week crusade in Port-au-Prince, Haiti. They were amazed by how God used him in a powerful way and loved it. My husband has consistently believed that he could relate to him. Moses grabbed the tickets Pastor Leslie gave him, moved away, tore them into pieces, and asked, who wants to go to the crusade? He commented that it sounded great when all of them raised their hands.

Pachouco and his wife were deeply angered by Moses, but they pretended that tearing up the tickets was okay, despite everyone else, including his mother, finding it funny. Moses informed his Uncle and Auntie that he had moved away due to fear of their violent reaction to his joking behavior. He claimed that all of them would join him on the crusade because he is Pastor Unique Preacher. Pachouco exclaimed with excitement, "Baby, I was correct, he is related to me."

Claude was continuously asked by Pastor Leslie and her children about his wife. Mother noticed the discomfort it caused him. Before speaking negatively about Tamara, Mother stated that it was time for everyone to go to bed in preparation for the long days ahead. She declared that every party, whether spiritual or not, inevitably comes to a close. Upon that remark, Pastor Moses bestowed an Amen upon his grandma, which Pastor Leslie seconded.

In the middle of the night, Mother Faye Esther grew restless and heard a voice warning that "Tamara should not be in a women's prison, or she would be damned forever. Only Pastor Unique Preacher has the power to remove the Jezebel spirit from her. Urge Claude to trust his instincts." The voice persisted speaking to her, recalling her prayer for her Grand and Great grandchildren to come together with love in their hearts. The celestial being has a surprise in store that will leave everyone in awe, from adults to children. Ensure that any assistance Pastor Unique Preacher requires is provided. Goodbye, woman of God, and never forget that God speaks directly to those who trust and obey Him unconditionally."

For years, Mother Faye Esther developed the habit of keeping a dream journal by her bedside to record her dreams and visions. She grabbed it and began writing about her recent encounter, but her excitement grew when thinking about the last surprise and who it could be. In the morning, she called the judge overseeing Tamara's case and requested Tamara's release on bail. The ninety-five years old drove to pick Tamara up, just as planned without Claude knowledge. She left Tamara at her house to freshen up and promised to send Claude to pick her up by noon. As she arrived in the yard, Junior Jeffery and Moses stood up in front of the driveway discussing their joy in reuniting with an unknown family. They couldn't contain their curiosity about the identity of the person driving the new two-seater sports car with tinted windows. Mother Faye Esther stepped out of the car, wearing sunglasses in her eyes. The fellows were left speechless, and Mother said, "I tricked you, thought I was a young chic. Make sure one of you to park the car before Mother wets herself, Moses, have you explored the tent in the field yet?" she inquired. While Miriam was exiting the house, Junior Jeffery jumped into the car and jokingly invited her to join him for a ride. Miriam joyfully hops into the car, assuming it's a cute one for a ride. She had never seen the sports car before because it was inside one of the garages. Miriam fastened her seatbelt and her husband drove into the driveway, laughing and suggesting the journey was done. Miriam responded that's all, and whose vehicle is it Patrice or Patrica? Upon hearing Miriam, Mother inquired, "Are you insinuating that I'm old? God and I were the owners of the car." "Is this really yours, Grandma Faye?" Patrice, who came over to speak with Moses, joined the conversation and commented that Grandma had tricked numerous young men. Upon seeing the car and noticing a woman driving a gorgeous two-seater, they eagerly awaited an opportunity to flirt. Who they saw, a ninety-five-year-old woman, who looked sixty-five, emerged from the car and still goes to the gym to work out. Currently, she appears younger than she did at the age of sixty-five. God continuously regenerated her inexplicably. "Girl, you divulged too much about my love affair." They laughed and proceeded to view the tent as she requested.

Due to the absence of any commotion in the yard, they were oblivious to the fact that the tent had been pitched overnight. The tent had a beautiful appearance, similar to that of a large arena. Moses was in a state of shock when he asked his Grandma, "Who are you other than being our Grandma?" "Grinning," she declared, "A true woman of God, making the impossible possible through Christ, much to the surprise of Junior Jeffery, Rose Marie, and yourself," for example, she pointed at the tent. Miriam, Patrice, and Rose Marie are celebrating their Grandma's generous blessings from God, all thanks to her prayers. Miriam gazed at her husband in a remarkable way. He realized he had to apologize to her for underestimating Grandma Faye. Giving her a quick glance, he confessed that he had lost the bet because Mother managed to find a tent that could seat a thousand people at the last minute. "No," Mother replied, "It's not a thousand, it's two thousand. Don't try to cheat, Grandson." They burst into laughter at Mother's sense of humor. Moses acknowledged his mistake in misjudging his Grandmother's ability and capability.

The chateau was now empty. Everyone presents in the tent found its elegance enjoyable. Rose and Barbara both thought the neighborhood lacked enough people for the tent. At the very least, their mother should have selected a tent that can accommodate one hundred people. Moses asked his Grandma if she was certain about doing the revival here while holding his phone. She showed a positive response. He clarified to Mother Faye Esther that he had a contractual obligation to inform his followers about his preaching engagements. Once he tweeted about the revival and revealed the location, he cautioned all of them that this place would be filled with followers. He had

Mother Faye Esther approach the Police Department to secure a couple of police cars for the tent. Yvone claimed that Moses didn't need all of that, and Rose and Barbara agreed with their sister. Mother Faye Esther told her daughters what Moses asked was a phone call away. The tweet went out less than two hours before Pachouco began guiding people on where to park their cars.

The family encountered a completely unfamiliar Moses. He gathered everyone for a meeting in the mansion. Upon arrival, Junior Jeffery initiated the reunion by offering a prayer. Afterwards, He expressed gratitude to God for the privilege of living in the home of a powerful woman of God, whom we referred to as Mother. We gathered here to request a favor from those who only knew Moses, not Pastor Unique Preacher. Please refrain from calling Pastor Unique Preacher Moses from this point forward until the services conclude. "If not, he will not respond to you."

Pastor Unique Preacher's real name remains unknown to most of his followers.

Out of nowhere, an unfamiliar old man joined Miriam and Antonette as they descended the stairs. The elderly man motioned for Junior Jeffery to cease talking. Curious, Rose questioned him about his identity. Pulling up a chair, the old man whispered in a barely audible voice, "Try not to laugh too loudly, because behind this disguise, I am Moses."

Junior Jeffery warned that without disguising himself, the crowd would invade the chateau and fill it with joyful chaos. No matter what happens, don't reveal that Pastor Unique Preacher and his family stayed here. "Wow," added Yvonne, "I'm amazed."

Junior Jeffery acknowledged that your Grandson possesses the power of God, resulting in miracles, signs, and wonders accompanying him everywhere.

Yvonne replied, "when Moses and Miriam were born, that was the prayer my mother prayed when my daughter Ester gave birth to them." From the bookshelf, she grabbed her journal and read the prayer spoken by her mother, Mother Faye Esther, for them: "Lord, fulfill the desires of my heart, I present Moses and Miriam to you. Trust them with the gift of Your miracles, signs, and wonders throughout their lives, as long as they remained devoted to You, in Jesus' Name, I pray, Amen."
"God unquestionably responded to Grandma Faye's prayers for Moses and Miriam, who used her singing to perform countless healings. The whole family, regardless of age, is somewhat spiritually gifted," concluded Junior Jeffery.

Mother Faye Esther stood up and glanced out her window, noticing how busy Pachouco was directing traffic. She sent Junior Jeffery to inform him about the conversation they had regarding Moses. In a hurry, Junior applauded the idea and rushed outside to tell Pachouco. In the meantime, as cars parked, people walked nearer to the house hoping to glimpse the preacher. To take Moses to Claude's home, Mother asked him to drive the truck. In your yard, there will be a white limousine and she the key on the kitchen table. Bring Moses back to the limo to ensure the crowd remains unaware of his whereabouts. Claude did not think of anything besides that as a reason. He knew Mother had a key to his five-bedroom house and occasionally she would come to relax there. Prior to Claude's departure from the mansion, Mother informed him that Miriam, Pastor Leslie, Antoinette, and Pachouco would accompany them. Claude expressed his gratitude for driving a religious delegation and believed blessings were on their way. Mother answered, "The blessing was at the house bright early this morning. Claude, avoid angering God." Everyone in his delegation knew what was happening, except Claude. Yvon replaced Junior Jeffery to direct the traffic, making one more person in the group. The cane that Pastor Unique Preacher used as part of his disguise as an elderly man was accidentally dropped. Around sixty people set up camp near the chateau, and one of them rushed towards Moses, bending down to pick up the cane. He asked, "Sir, is Pastor Unique Preacher inside that house?"

He is better not be in there but outside, replied, the Pastor. The man replied, "Sir, he is trustworthy and beloved by many."

"Thank you, but I didn't say, he is not, replied Pastor Unique Preacher.

Claude left the yard, amazed by the crowd and there no parking place six blocks down and the event was four hours away.

Rose Marie cautioned her spouse against dishonesty. "Darling, the man asked, was I inside the mansion? I replied, saying I shouldn't, but I was already in the car. Can you point out the lie." Observing Rose Marie in the review mirror, Claude implied, "Niece, he outsmarted you." In addition to preaching, he may possess the spirit of an exceptional lawyer. The spirit of his Uncle Rodrigue Casimir.

CHAPTER 15

FORGIVE AND FORGET

Claude ought to have had suspicions that something was amiss. Every person in the group identified as a Christian Counselor, except for one lawyer. They all despised divorce and held the belief that "God gives second chances, and even more." The Matriarch of the family had orchestrated this mission for them to undertake. The objective was to maintain Tamara's marital status.

No need to speculate about how any of them would act in Claude's situation. Before finding God, all of them journeyed along this route. They healed and transformed together, becoming a powerful vessel for the redeeming God. The assignment didn't randomly land on their laps. Except for Miriam, every woman in that truck understood the messiness of flesh. They anticipated teaching Tamara how to convert her weaknesses into strengths and helping Claude overcome his pain to live a happy life. Rather than subscribing to forgive and forget, they embraced forgive and remember. Don't forget about the place God brought you out of. He may have to send you back to retrieve those who were left behind and trapped by Satan.

There was a serious battle between Claude's intellect and emotions. Claude attempted to appear strong and even made jokes around others, but when he was alone, he was overcome with grief. Feeling betrayed and humiliated by his wife, Claude began his revengeful prayers by saying to God: "Why I had been subjected to such treatment. I pleaded with you God in my prayers, explaining that my love for Tamara was too deep to grant her forgiveness. These imprecatory prayers revealed my strong animosity towards Tamara. I longed for a distinctive rendezvous between her and death. She must attend this meeting and endure the pain of death, there is no escape. Let the door to damnation swing open wider than ever to welcome her corrupted spirit. I despised hating Tamara but found solace in my feelings. The queen known for cheating got herself cheated and ended up in despair on the room floor. Within that setting, she educated me on loathing her frivolous existence. She broke my heart into fragments, causing lovers worldwide to mock my pain. Death why has not yet claimed Tamara, who finds the brimstone fire's unique appeal irresistible. Don't hesitate, move fast, and pull Tamara with her long hair to the center of the earth before the supreme Being has a change of heart. Her existence caused extreme anguish in my soul to the tenth power. Her every breath was a constant annoyance to me. Her being alive on this planet was just a nuisance to me and the more she continued to exist, the more I loathed her passionately. Escort her to the abyss and rename her from Tamara to perdition. Tamara erased the word love from my vocabulary and replaced it with a stronger force - hatred. To request my forgiveness on behalf of Tamara is equivalent to requesting that I end my life and vanish without a proper burial. I witnessed her indulging in her own desires, with my own eyes. From that moment on, I loathed her nakedness, which was tainted by sexual wickedness. My eyes and nose were instantly assaulted by her dirtiness and odor. I stayed true to our pledge of "until death do us part." Even though Tamara is full of life, she is dead to me ever since I saw her entangled with that worthless Oscar on the floor. Did she lose control of her youthful desires or was she lacking in character from birth to become the most despicable woman on Earth? Why is someone as cunning as Tamara included in my greatest creation, which I call "Woman." Did her rib come from a dog since her mentality reflects it? Does death seem too severe for her wrongdoing? What about letting her rot in prison? While she's in there, let strong women treat her as she treated Oscar - with abuse and manipulation. May she experience suffering and perpetual poverty until her death, even in the afterlife. I won't rescue her from her new living situation; I have too much regard for my finances to squander them on a duplicate of Jezebel or Gomar, Hosea's wife."

Tamara crushed Claude's ego, leading him to taste the bitterness of vengeance in his delusional imprecatory prayers. He was on the verge of finishing his orisons, saying the word, Amen! A voice shattered the sky, proclaiming that "Tamara had completed her penance. She regretted all the sins she committed against you and others. She has shown such deep remorse that it has reached the heavens, and I have chosen to forgive her. From my perspective, the decision to forgive her or not is yours to make, and both options will have consequences for Claude."

The echoing voice draws closer to Claude, causing him to question the fairness of requesting forgiveness for Tamara, who tore his heart apart. The echoing voice replied, "You might have the ability if you had the desire, but I believe you have the ability if you follow your heart instead of man wisdom. No matter how capable he may be, a man will never possess the same level of compassion that I show towards him, towards another man. Satan trembles in my presence, aware that mankind can be even more wicked than . My anger will consume modern mankind for thinking that my compassion and patience are limitless. If man possessed My absolute power, the earth would already be desolated. The person who remained standing would turn against themselves and take their own life, showing the extent of unforgiveness. Claude, I heard your vengeful prayers for Tamara. If death came for you today in hell, you would open your eyes at My command. Those who don't forgive their trespassers will be condemned to the lake of fire, as stated Wisdom."

After listing to the pep talk, Claude came to himself emotionally and intellectually rededicating his life back to Jesus. He went and baptized by Pastor Unique Preacher the evening before.

As Claude drove them to his house, he recounted and discussed the earlier conversation he had with Mother. He relayed to them that she brought up the idea of delivering my blessing at my house earlier today, and she also left the key to the limousine on the table. Pastor Unique Preacher commented, "I assumed the chateau had a limousine parked there."
Junior Jeffery confirmed that "She is using the one at Claude's house to take you back to the mansion and confuse your followers. The pastor's whereabouts will remain unknown to them."
The decision made by Mother Faye Esther shocked almost everyone. Rose Marie, Moses' wife requested assistance

in comprehending, stating, "I'm not trying to be humorous. Do you know who Mother Faye Esther is? Is she an ordinary human being?"

Miriam recently replied, and surprisingly, she was thinking about the exact same thing and even prayed about it. "He informed me that Grandma Faye is one of His specially chosen Super Humans with supernatural Power. Guess what? That Power intends to be passed down through generations."

"It's the truth, look at Moses and you, Miriam, and the rest of the immediate family," Claude replied.

Miriam revisited the conversation about her Grandma's blessing, suggesting to Claude that it might be Tamara. Just as he was about to say something negative about Tamara, he recalled the warning he got from God. He altered his attitude but cautioned, "Be careful what you say, Niece. Don't wish that upon me. Furthermore, she has nobody to bail her out of prison, and I won't either." Claude's answer hit a nerve with all three women in the truck. In unison, they all echoed, "Uncle, wait a minute." Everyone started talking at once, but Pachouco stepped in and suggested one person speak at a time. Claude thanked him for pointing it out since he couldn't hear what they said next. Rose Marie and Miriam chose to enable Pastor Leslie to pursue Claude for his comment. "Picture this scenario: you open your door and see Tamara waiting for you inside. How would you react?" Claude responded humorously, saying that "Waking up from that nightmare would only be possible in a bad dream. If I see Tamara at my door while fully awake, I'll eat both of my shoes. I have salt and pepper here, but even better, I will forgive her forever."

While the three guys were enjoying the conversation, Pastor Unique Preacher asked Claude about the size of his shoes. He answered with the number thirteen. The Pastor responded, "Uncle, Bon Appetit." Claude glanced at Junior Jeffery who replied, "Don't look at me, Uncle. You're on your own because I witnessed how God dealt with my wife." Miriam's thinking poses a significant danger, reminiscent of her Grandma Faye. Her thoughts had the power to become reality." Pachouco and Pastor both agreed, saying Amen, to indicate that their wives are similar. Claude told them that their wives will be totally lost tonight because he knows his ex-wife is locked up. "Yes, I said ex-wife and I meant that."

At the house, they arrived. As soon as they exited the truck, they headed directly to the white and black limousine with white tires, the epitome of luxury among limousines. Pastor Unique Preacher expressed his joy and admiration for his Grandma's classic choice. Like someone they know, they are a perfectionist through and through. After he made the last comment, Miriam caught the attention of everyone, even those who had met her as recently as yesterday. Claude told them that Mother never did anything halfway, especially when it came to matters involving God.

Claude left them in the limo and instructed them to come inside whenever they felt like it. Because of the white carpet, he chose to use the side door instead of the front door, which required shoe removal.
However, Claude eagerly awaited the surprises Mother Faye Esther had left for him. Inside his humble castle, Claude was unprepared for what he was about to

encounter. Even Mother Faye Esther, the blesser, could be in for a serious surprise if she's with Claude. On the contrary, nobody expected her to be the author of it, knowing she might. While retrieving his keys, Claude noticed a small smudge of ashes leading from the backyard barbecue pit to the door. He believed that Mother Faye Esther arrived early in the morning and prepared them a meal. He concluded that those were the blessings. Having her barbecuing for them should be considered a blessing, as it's not going to occur in this lifetime because she will have the barbecue catered.

Poor Claude opened the door and saw something that he had never seeing before in his entire life, but he read about it in the Old Testament of the bible. Startled by frightening surprises, he sprinted out while screaming, at the top of his lungs wondering what it all meant. Confirm that I'm not losing my mind, my Lord, and my God. Is this real or am I hallucinating?

He stood hunched over, gazing downward, hands on knees, murmuring softly. They rushed out of the limousine to come to Claude's aid. His attempts at explanation fell on deaf ears as they couldn't grasp a single word he uttered. His overpowering emotions rendered him unable to speak. Sensing his difficulty in communication, Claude motioned towards the door. Moses and Miriam both followed their twins' instincts and ran into the house simultaneously. The sight filled them with excitement. Inside a circle on the kitchen floor, Tamara was spotted wearing sack clothes and ashes from head to toe. "I am seeking God's forgiveness for my sins against Claude, Mother Faye, Oscar, and Miriam," she told them. Miriam respectfully requested Tamara's permission to join her in her penitence. Miriam invited everyone, including Claude, to come inside. They gathered in a circle around Tamara and offered prayers together. Pastor Leslie noticed Claude was still standing, so she stood up, took his hand, and placed him in the circle beside his wife. He obediently took a seat beside her. She opened up about her situation for the first time due to a lack of someone to confide in. Claude brought up her frequent remarks about him being her closest companion. Tamara, being completely honest, gazed into her husband's eyes and said, "Claude, I really need to talk to you, but not just one-on-one. When we have a private conversation about my situation, all you'll hear are lies because I love you so deeply. Claude, I trust this group enough to share my deepest feelings. Will you commit, in the presence of Pastor Moses, Junior Jeffery, Pachouco, Rose Marie, Miriam, and Pastor Leslie, to actively listen without leaving the circle? Claude, this meeting holds great significance for me. I believed that my salvation lies within this circle. I am Sick Claude, and my mind is plagued by wickedness."

Pastor Unique Preacher requested that Tamara allow Junior Jeffery, Pachouco, Claude, and him to step outside for five minutes before continuing. Tamara approved of that idea. The men outside offered prayers for Claude. Pastor Unique Preacher revealed that Tamara was under the control of a powerful sex demon. To cast out the sextortion devil, Claude was instructed to stay calm and avoid getting upset. Uncle, "I know her confession will be difficult for you, but with faith in Jesus Christ, I will overcome that demon."

Claude replied, "Let's do this but afterward, do I have to go back with her? While my intellect will say yes, my emotions will strongly object." Pastor Unique Preacher emphasized that love would prevail, but now let's focus on addressing the issue of that sex demon. "Let's pray for her to gather momentum and share with us."

When they went back inside, they found every one of the ladies was crying because they felt sorry for Tamara. The guys regained their sit on the floor in the same position.

A major surprise was about to come Tamara's way. When she comprehended the unusual nature of her situation, she reached out to Pastor Unique Preacher via mail, seeking aid with her spell. Her lack of personal connection with him prevented her from receiving a response, but she maintained her faith in his ability to assist her. She didn't know that Moses was Pastor Unique Preacher like most of his followers. If Tamara realized his identity, she would faint due to the intensity of her love for Pastor Unique Preacher. One thing about him, he did a boundless joy hiding his identity over the years.

Everyone was in their designated spot, except Tamara, who chose to kneel before her husband. With a tone of sadness and regret, she humbly requested Claude's permission to continue, apologizing for any discomfort her supplication might impose. Starting her tearful confession, Tamara uttered these words:

"Your wife, Claude, is suffering from a severe illness beyond your imagination. I sought assistance from multiple sex therapists, but none of them could provide a solution. My ongoing battle has been diagnosed by multiple doctors and root workers as PTSD, stemming from a brutal sexual assault. I recently learned from a dream that I have been contaminated by an invisible demon of a sexual nature. I battled that deceitful evil spirit who consumed me with the desire to sleep with multiple men, except you. I felt so polluted and contaminated that I couldn't allow you to touch me. As a result, my libido disappears whenever you're near me. I labeled myself as someone who was taken advantage of any man who showed attraction towards me. I had moments of forgetfulness about my marital status until I finished what I needed to do. The location wasn't important to me if I thought the spot was safe and no one was watching - whether it was at the mall, grocery stores, vehicles, or the field, wherever the urge struck. Demonic men seemed drawn to that demonic spirit; I never faced rejection or got caught until Miriam stopped that streak by catching me with Oscar. Claude, I am not the right person to be your wife as I am a woman of impurity. I embody the essence of a prostitute, as I don't typically have genuine financial hardships. Against my wishes, I was programmed to cause harm and ended up hurting you emotionally. I have brought disgrace upon you and your honorable family. I feel unworthy of being among you all. I despise myself intensely. You were outside in the limo waiting for me the day before when we picked up the welcome sign; a young man followed me to the limousine, and you were sleeping. Do you know I have the nerve to sleep with him that day in there with you present. I've reached my limit and think that Pastor Unique Preacher, a TV evangelist, is the only one who can exorcise this demon from me. My past online activity involved following him closely because I had a major crush on him. He had a deeper understanding of the demonic spirit compared to most preachers I've encountered. Upon hearing his lecture on "The side effect of sextortion after being delivered by God," I decided to write him about my abnormal sexual issues. My zip code and impoverished appearance could be the reason for not receiving a response until now. Finding myself near him would cause me to faint, anyway."

She managed to turn everyone's sadness into a smile, even her husband and Pastor Unique Preacher signaled for them to remain silent. Moses desired to keep her unaware of his identity until he expelled the demonic spirit she acquired from Joseph.

Pachouco asked Tamara if she could freely discuss her rape and how it occurred.

Tamara happily replied with a positive mindset, "I often lay in our backyard twice a week to tan after exercising. Our house is fully fenced, so I didn't think there would be any peeping Toms. Occasionally, I even liked basking in the sun without clothes. Our yard offers great privacy to the point Claude, and I decide to engage in some open-air lovemaking. Only immediate family, maids, and Joseph, who keeps the yard twice a month, a job Claude created to help him out financially, are welcome here. As usual, after my work out on a Friday morning, I took a shower outside and relaxed on the mat with Claude, our favorite spot under the cozy shade. Claude and Mother left for a four-hour drive out of town. I thought there was nobody else at home, especially since it's the maid's day off on Fridays. In that moment, I found myself in a state between sleep and wakefulness, thinking Mother had changed her mind and Claude came back home. Whenever my husband spotted me on the mat, he knew exactly what I enjoyed and would join in. Our own special love language remains a secret to everyone else. On that day, as usual, I pretended to be asleep while he started performing his magic on my body, but it didn't turn out as I had anticipated. When I touched Claude's head, I was surprised to feel hair instead of his usual baldness. When I opened my eyes, I uncovered his face only to find a knife stuck by my side. It's Joseph!

He threatened to stab me from the side, slashed my throat, and end my life if I moved. I was assaulted by him four more times in my own bedroom. One of the times, he turned me over on my stomach, I pleaded with him to not let his wickedness escalate to that extent. I witnessed an evil spirit emerge from him and become linked to me. Joseph, please stop, I cried." The spirit responded, "My name is PTSD now, and you belong to me forever."

"He used handcuffs to secure me to the bedpost and forced me to watch explicit videos of myself, both alone and with Claude. Pictures that Claude and I don't want on social media or circulate by any other means. By looking at the photos/videos I'm surprised by how nasty Claude, and I were. Some of the pictures he captured when I was by myself in my yard, I would not even want my husband to see them. Joseph informed me that he had placed a few cameras in our backyard, which is why he was able to seduce me by studying Claude's actions. He planned to rape me, knowing that day would eventually arrive. I pleaded for him to release me as Claude will be returning shortly." He reassured me by replying that "I shouldn't worry because he wouldn't be home soon." "Did you murder my husband," as I asked? "If you follow my instructions, your husband, pictures, and personal safety will be protected. I ran into your husband this morning and he mentioned that he and Mother Faye are going out of town and will return late tonight. That's all I wanted to hear from your husband, and I came straight here and used his cologne to fool you."

"I was exhausted from fighting and had no energy left. My hands were bound, but I had a handgun near my nightstand, which he didn't notice." "I'm going to set you free," he said with resignation. "The decision to live or die is up to you. Your life depends on keeping this secret between us; don't tell anyone."

When he freed me, I took hold of the gun and fired at him, but it turned out to be empty. Claude cleaned the gun the night before but forgot to reload it. That night, luck was on Joseph's side. After he departed, I experienced deep humiliation, diminished femininity, impurity, and an overwhelming desire for death. I reached for the phone to call the police and recalled his menacing warnings. My life was made miserable by him. Some of the pictures he took with me and him looked I was willingly engaging with him because of the hidden knife he had in his hand. I became enslaved to him, and he introduced me to sextortion and drugs. He manipulated using my husband's name and my pictures. Adding to everything, he had a photo of me in the nude on his bed with two other guys. To this day, I remain clueless about how that occurred. My self-confidence has plummeted to the point where I can't refuse Joseph. Each time I followed his orders and fulfilled his desires, he would delete two pictures. When I bought his clothes, three pictures got destroyed. If I went on a date with someone he picked, he erased three photos. Keep in mind that he had had over hundreds of photos therefore I got trapped in his trap. His blackmail caused me to live his lifestyle. He refused to take no for an answer. How can I escape from his bullying, I'm worn and tired?"

Junior Jeffery, one of the country's greatest lawyers, assured Tamara that he would be her legal representative if she decided to press charges against Joseph. According to Claude, Tamara had no option but to testify against Joseh to avoid prosecution by Mother. Junior Jeffery suggested that we let Pastor Unique Preacher handle that demonic story before discussing it further. Tamara asked the lawyer if Pastor Unique Preacher would really be able to help her and questioned how that could be possible, wondering if he was a relative of the lawyer. Tamara, emotionally no good after hearing Junior Jeffery's comment. She had a strong belief that her salvation was coming soon. She inquired of Claude if he would join her in meeting the Pastor if Junior scheduled it prior to their divorce. "Who told Aunt Tamara about Uncle Claude wanting a divorce?" Miriam asked. No one had to tell her anything, Tamara simply understood her husband. She requested Moses to join them in meeting Pastor Unique Preacher, as she required all the support she could gather. Her statement created a buzz among everyone in the circle. The room erupted with laughter, leaving everyone in tears, except for Tamara. The more she inquired about their laughter, the more it seemed to spiral out of control. Finally, Moses put Tamara's curiosity at ease by revealing that he was Pastor Unique Preacher, leading to her fainting for a few seconds. While Rose Marie and Miriam cared for Tamara, Pastor Unique Preacher instructed Claude and Junior to open all the doors and windows in the house. By obeying his commandment, they finished the task. He requested Pachouco to perform one of his gospel songs called "Satan, you can't touch this." The lyrics are well-suited for exorcism rituals. Pastor Unique Preacher successfully expelled five demonic spirits from Tamara through the power of Jesus Christ.

The sight of the spirits leaving Tamara's body prompted Pachouco and Pastor Leslie to sing the song incessantly. Tamara's immediate return to her senses stunned Claude, leading the singers to briefly stop singing. Pastor Unique

Preacher resumed the song and, suddenly, a choir group came together. Pachouco and Pastor Unique, who already had similar voices, sang the song together while the others supported them. Tamara couldn't assist since she was unfamiliar with the song's lyrics, but she adored it as it resonated with her own experiences.

Claude took hold of a pen and wrote down the lyrics for Tamara:

"I found myself trapped in a deep pit. In that moment, I was crying and pleading for mercy from the Lord. Satam confined me in a pit full of sins. I wept and confessed to Jesus, repenting for all my sins. He came to my rescue, forgiving all my wrongdoings and renewing my mind, body, and soul. Jesus told him, "Satan, you can't touch this. you tried Tamara and you failed, Satan you can't touch this.""

God allowed Pastor Unique Preacher to change Claude's mind about modern day exorcism, even though he didn't believe in it before. The singing interrupted to focus on the next stage of Claude and Tamara's problems, namely their separation. Although they understood Claude's reaction to his wife's actions, they still hoped he would forgive her by looking past her faults. Pastor Unique Preacher discovered that every aspect of human life, whether positive or negative, is connected to a spiritual entity. Most people with the spirit of God chose not to exercise the power to expel evil spirits. They willingly ignored the presence of Satan spirits behind the situation due to their harsh criticism and stereotypes of the victims. The gift will only appear when the recipient realizes that thieves possess stealing spirits. The spirits of the murderers have power over those who committed the murders. The same goes for the prostitutes possessed by spirits of promiscuity. Once the believers identified the culprits responsible for the inappropriate actions, they should not judge but instead expelled those spirits and liberated the victims through Christ.

The same group met Claude and Tamara. Miriam got right to the point and asked, "What's the plan moving forward?"

"You know my position," Claude replied to Miriam.

Miriam acknowledged that Claude had previously rededicated his life to God, but now she was asking him as a renewed believer. In a humorous whisper that everyone could hear, Pastor Unique Preacher told Claude, "Your niece and my sister is teasing you."

Claude sighed, expressing his inner conflict, stating that while his intellect desires to spend the rest of his life with Tamara, his emotions and moral values do not align.

"What do you mean by that, brother in love," asked Pastor Leslie. Claude responded, "I don't see myself with…"

Junior Jeffery interrupted him before he could complete his sentence, requesting a period to be inserted for now. He suggested, "Let's hear Tamara's thoughts on the same question."

Tamara looked up and smiled, thanking the Lord for sending these faithful believers to rescue her unexpectedly. "Honestly, if I were Claude, I wouldn't forgive him. After witnessing all the spirits that emerged from him, I would remain loyal to my man until death separates us. However, I am not Claude. I will respect his decision regardless, as I regret my unintentional wrongdoing. My husband holds the power over my fate as a wife. Thank you, Junior Jeffery, for agreeing to be my representative. I'm strongly advocate for pressing charges against my rapist, who was also my slave master. I thought

I could have saved countless girls and women from sextortion rings if I had been willing to sacrifice myself. I should have called the police right then that day." Surprisingly, Mother Faye Esther advised me, "Tamara, to prosecute anyone who sexually assaulted me, regardless of the cost. Remaining silent after being raped is equivalent to condoning it. It's a betrayal of what it means to be a woman. The person who raped you has and will continue to harm others because of their evil nature. Not too long ago, she shared with me one of the dumbest things someone who is a victim of a legally punishable crime can do: let the statute of limitations expire. The likelihood of experiencing the same abuse again is nine out of ten for individuals like this."

The sound of a car pulling up in the yard caught their attention. When Rose Marie peeked through the window, she couldn't help but laugh and commented that Grandma Faye knew how cool she appeared driving a two-seater sports car. Claude insinuated that she is utterly unique. Rose Marie captured everyone's attention with a serious expression on her face. Pachouco questioned her about what my mother is doing up there. Rose Marie, still serious, responded and she swiftly grabbed her Bible from the car. She then began reading a passage of scripture. She's now splashing holy water in the yard. Rose Marie kept saying that she's coming now. Claude, Tamara, and Miriam had finished cleaning the floor when she knocked on the door.

Curious, Miriam opened the door and questioned her Grandma about her unexpected presence. She described her yard and the streets as crazy. The tent is about to reach maximum capacity and an additional twelve officers were sent for security. Casting a quick look at Tamara, she commented that she seemed completely at ease. Tamara admitted that despite feeling great, she still felt guilty about how she treated Claude. "I understand," Mother Faye chimed in. Mother Faye Esther directed her attention to everyone in the group, leaving out Claude and Tamara. With her index finger pointed at them, she confidently stated, "I have a bone to pick with you guys" and Moses is unquestionably guilty. The act of not designating a place for a demon to go when casting is known as swapping demons. Sometimes, they would switch from one person to another within the same family, houses, or even complete strangers. I sent them to a location that God-fearing individuals will never visit or reside. God granted us the ability to cast them out and send them straight to hell.

Moses chuckled at his Grandma's accusation, wanting to understand her perspective. She interjected, who cast out those fresh demons that were near the gate? One of them audaciously asks, "Pretty lady, can I accompany you home this evening?"

Moses and the crew burst into laughter, exclaiming, "No way, Grandma! I told you, you're too cool! Now you're even attracting the devil!" Mother Faye Esther chimed in, saying "I opened my Bible that instead of me taking him home, I sent them to where they belonged with a one-way ticket on an express train."

"Where is the express train heading to, Mother?" Rose Marie repeated. Mother Faye Esther with joy replied, "Hell."

Tamara anticipated informing Mother Faye Esther about her decision to press charges against Joseph, which was what Mother Faye Esther had wanted. In response to Tamara's announcement. Mother Faye Esther said to her, Instead of seeking legal action for manipulation, what about suing him for assault.

Tamara, surprised by Mother Faye Esther's remark, asked her how long she had known about it.

The occurrence shouldn't have happened, but her husband's stubbornness was at fault, answered Mother Faye Esther.

In contrast, Claude was displeased with the trajectory of Mother's conversation as he foresaw that he would be the one to shoulder the blame. Pastor Leslie sought clarification on the measures that could have prevented the rape. Mother was not prompted to reveal what she knew, but Miriam took it upon herself to support the motion to hear about this prevention. Claude stood up with a bowed head while Mother prepared to burst his bubble. There was a vacant seat in front of her, and she asked him to sit there. Despite his obedience, embarrassment took over his inner self.

Despite not being present when they circled on the floor, Mother Faye Esther rearranged the sitting position back to its former position as before. She asked Tamara to switch seats with Pachouco so that she could sit next to her husband.

Moses swiftly understood his Grandma's methods, so he readied himself for a counseling session where Claude would face scrutiny. Mother Faye Esther kicked off the session by calling out Claude for thinking she was going senile based on her predictions. "Tamara," Mother said, Can I recount the day you experienced rape?"

"Mother Faye Esther, how can this be? You're not present but let me stop before you begin pointing to your gray hair as a symbol of heavenly insight. You may continue," reply Tamara.

Mother Faye Esther did exactly what Tamara and the others expected. While pointing at her hair saying, "Yes Baby girl, these grey hairs are a manifestation of Divine Wisdom." In a stunning manner, Moses and Miriam were amazed at Grandma Faye's ability to boast about the Lord. Moses constantly blames himself for not visiting his Grandma sooner. Just as Moses felt, he believed he had missed countless chances to sit at her feet and gain knowledge.

Mother started the story by asking Tamara if she was raped around noon on the day Claude drove her out of town for a four-hour drive. Mother's knowledge of the exact day and time of Tamara's nightmare surprised her. In her search for answers, Tamara curiosity continued to grow. "Yes ma'am," she answered hurriedly and with great intensity.

Mother Faye Esther kept her gaze fixed on Claude, her beloved adoptive son, who now brimmed with regret. The conversation his mother had with him came rushing back to him, as if it happened yesterday.

Mother said, "Claude and I were two hours away from home when I asked him to make a U-turn around ten o'clock because Tamara was about to get into trouble."

He assured Mother that nothing would happen to Tamara, but he also mentioned that Mother's intuition had been affected by negativity. He stressed the significance of this meeting for her and remained determined to move forward. He planned to call Tamara and prove her wrong.

Mother said they had to return home to save Tamara from the devil. He couldn't stop laughing as she told him the funniest jokes he'd ever heard. His words were that Tamara is perfectly capable of looking after herself.

Mother Faye Esther interrupted, warning Claude that he would regret this decision and that she would be there to witness its consequences.

Mother Faye Esther spirit remained unsettled when it came to Tamara that day. She inquired Claude to call the Police Department and connect her with them since she had left her phone at home. He chimed in "Mother, what's for?"

"I want a couple of Officers to be sent to your house because Tamara is in danger."

Claude shifted the conversation in a way that signaled the end of their interaction on the subject. When they returned from the trip, Claude confirmed that Tamara was okay upon seeing her at home. He made a sarcastic call to Mother, harassing her for needlessly being concerned about Tamara's well-being. Put Tamara on the phone, she asked, and he did. "Daughter, everything is fine."

"Mother, it turned out to be better than I thought, regardless."

"Tamara my Daughter, always remember that the law is on your side. It's important to consider that condoning someone's actions is the right thing to do, regardless of the cost, bye for now."

After the call, Tamara believed Mother Faye Esther knew, but reporting Joseph for assaulting her wasn't worth the potential consequences of him destroying her and Claude's lives.

The group was shocked by the unexpected news from their Great Grandmother. Right now, Tamara felt betrayed by her husband, the person who was supposed to protect her. Looking at his wife, he said that everything could have been different if he had just listened to his mother that day. Moses encouraged Claude to use his power and make the right decision, reminding him that the past is behind them. With all the information shared by Grandma Faye and Aunt Tamara's supernatural experience, what lies ahead for the marriage, Uncle? "Only God Knows," Nephew, replied, Claude.

Mother Faye Esther prayed, beseeching God to relieve Tamara of her distress. Immediately following this request, she prayed as if she had received classified information that Tamara was pregnant. The prayer failed to fuel the fire, but only the women heard it for some unknown reason. It became clear to Miriam that Tamara had gotten pregnant by the young man when she witnessed them together.

Soon enough, Tamara will learn firsthand the steep cost of living a sinful life. It seemed like everything was against her until she could have sung the song "when it rains, it pours" if such a song existed. Tamara has become someone she doesn't deserve to be. Not chosen by God, but by Angela to be Claude's wife. She possesses beauty, brains, and is a great photographer indeed. She married a wonderful man who adores her and believes she was specially created by God just for him. Could one imagine how he felt watching her with Oscar and hearing that Joseph was her lover.

Joseph's assault caused her body to reject her husband sexually. To disguise it, Tamara demanded that her husband present her with either valuable gifts or a sum of money in exchange for sex. The rule of "no money, no honey" was only for Claude, not Joseph and Oscar. Claude and Tamara's last involvement was six months ago. It's only been recently since the incident between her and Oscar. Pastor Unique Preacher and Mother Faye successfully expelled the demons of prostitution from Tamara that evening, but Claude refused her advances later that night. Rather than being intimate, his thoughts were increasingly consumed with Tamara and the possibility of divorcing her. Rejecting her that night turned out to be the right decision for him.

In Mother Faye Esther's prayer the Holy Spirit confirmed that Tamara is pregnant with Oscar's child. That's making him a father, on his first try as a virgin. Tamara is old enough to be his mother. The pregnancy will put an end to their marriage.

When Tamara's pregnancy was revealed, Pachouco and Pastor Leslie empathized with her woes. Tamara's painful love story reminded them of their love affair, which seemed to have some similarities. Their situation was much more pornographic than Tamara's. Prior to becoming a Pastor, Leslie's journey was chronicled in Tears of Deception. With a gun in hand, she kept her two lover's captives, and subjected them to three days of torment, including raping Pachouco. In comparison to the old Leslie, Tamara is like a saint.

CHAPTER 16

THE RESIDUE

Moses, the esteemed Pastor Unique Preacher, and his twin sister Miriam may have their faith tested in the days to come. Would they pass the test with excellence? Is the whole family, including Junior Jeffery, his wife Miriam, and their children, prepared to confront the truth?

The tent revival was successful, but he decided to shorten it from five days to four days for his followers. Moses' reaction caused both of his Grandmas to react. According to him, God has a different plan and requested that the fifth day of service be reserved exclusively for their family members. Without an invitation, anyone from the community can attend, but please refrain from inviting anyone. Upon hearing this, Grandma Faye asked Miriam, Patrice, Andre, and Fernand, who are the children of Pachouco and Leslie, to each pray for forgiveness on behalf of the family.

Mother Faye Esther contacted the tent company, who then arrived and took down the tent. The inmates from the nearby jail arrived to tidy up the yard. Moses convened with the family to determine the distribution of the nightly offering to the city. The funds were allocated to the city manager by their vote. Patrice couldn't believe it when Junior Jeffery revealed the amount the services generated. She kept saying $250,000, why give them all that money? Why not give me some to buy my dream car? Rose Marie told Patrice that ever since we arrived, all we've heard about was their dream car. Miriam said, yeah, what it is about this car" Junior replied, "You are right baby, I want to know too." "I'm tired of hearing about this dream car," Moses said to Patrice in a serious tone. Yvonne, his Grandma began to cry because she mistakenly believed they were teasing Patrice, who was defending herself. "I'm sorry, guys, I apologize, but I won't bring it up as long as everyone is here." Moses responded, saying "Sorry nothing and stop that crying, Patrice. Why not step outside and see if your dream car is there? Go outside quickly, trusting in faith, before the Good Lord changes his decision. Patrice ran, all the children and adults followed her, and she saw a brain new car, parked with a script on the windshield, I'm yours Patrice." They said in unison "Love you Patrice, take care of it." This morning, she witnessed a car crossing the street and captured a photo to showcase its beauty. Patrice didn't think it was her car, but she kept checking, hoping to see the driver. Patrica was the person who brought her the most happiness. She was so proud of Patrice for handling their jokes with great understanding. If Patrice hadn't been saved, her behavior towards them would have been awful. Patrica became a believer in Patrice's salvation because of that event.

Miriam noticed that her twins had stayed behind to admire Angela's picture once the crowd returned inside. She wanted to know where they got the picture from. As Patricia was heading inside, she overheard the question and told Miriam that they seemed to be fixated on my mother's pictures, perhaps because it reminded them of their Grandma Ester. It's possible that she might appear in their dream. This family is capable of anything and nothing will get past her when it comes to this family. There are individuals who possess great strength in the Lord," ended Patrica. Miriam pointed out to Patrica that she was referring to herself as well.

Miriam realized from her conversation with Patrica that she hadn't explained to the family that Moses Junior and Miriam Ester were adopted. She wasted no time in summoning the rest of the family, excluding the children, for a meeting, while sending them all to the playground with her brother Moses and his wife. There were no kids present in the chateau.

The door knocked, a feeling discussing Tamara entered the meeting room. Her sins were relentlessly chasing after her. Her priority shifted to contemplating suicide rather than repairing her relationship with Claude; she acknowledged it was a slim chance. Upon seeing her approach, Junior Jeffery and Miriam recalled Grandma Faye's advice on avoiding sharing personal matters with strangers. During that time, they understood that their grandma's response was specifically aimed at Tamara. Tamara was already teetering on the edge of her deception and couldn't bear being pushed any closer. Mother Faye Esther, contrary to widespread belief, understood the dilemma of Junior Jeffery and Miriam without being a mind reader.

Tamara had everyone's attention, and some of the glances seemed to convey, "Why are you here, after betraying their brother?"

Rose, Yvonne, and Barbara truly considered Claude like a blood brother and that's how long he had been with them as Mother Faye Esther's chauffeur. Claude, along with Pachouco and the girls, is an equal beneficiary in Mother Faye Esther's Will.

Mother Faye Esther gave Miriam a nod, indicating that she could join the meeting. Miriam received the memo and requested a seat.

Junior Jeffery enthusiastically shared they were becoming the parents of twins. According to him, he and Miriam were fully prepared to become adoptive parents. On the day of the meeting, he had a client who needed to have a conversation with him. She worked as a female Pastor in an all-female prison. In an unexpected manner, she managed to conceive. Once she had the baby, she couldn't continue to keep him in jail. She wanted him and Miriam to take custody of her child. Miriam was already aware that his client was having twins before he arrived home. To make the story short, he brought his wife to meet her. She was crazy about Miriam because she resembled her sister. Miriam had a certain emotional reaction to being in my client's company before. On the day they were finalizing the adoption, his wife expressed that she felt like she was adopting family members. The pastor saw her children during the initial three days after giving birth and then instructed them not to visit anymore. She wanted to remain anonymous to her babies if they ever saw her, though she doubted He and Miriam would acknowledge that. The Pastor assured them that God instructed her to allow them to adopt the babies because they will love them unconditionally. Later, Junior Jeffery and Mirian welcomed their baby girl Evonne and thanked God for their children.

Barbara, who is equally beautiful as her mother, gestured with her hand to catch her niece Miriam's attention, and she responded. According to Barbara, "Junior Moses and Miriam Ester strongly resembled the Casimir family, especially Patrice and Patrica. Is their mother still serving her sentence?"

"Oh yes, she's out. Although she had the opportunity to come out earlier, she did something unprecedented. She took legal action against the government, and she emerged victorious. However, before signing her release papers, she met with the board and demonstrated her manipulation of the system. She stated that if her love for God was genuine, she would admit the truth as He had instructed her to do. She confessed and got sentenced to a maximum of ten years. The Pastor truly converted, and her conversion helped reshape the women's prison all over." Rose called it a dumb move, but Yvonne completely disagreed and even called it a great salvation story.

Mother Faye Esther picked up the phone and greeted the Pastor, asking about the congregants. "At the start, you had to face some rough patches. Oh, so you're aware of that too. So you've been following him for ten years, that's quite impressive. That's right, the address was accurate. How do I know Pastor Unique Preacher? It's a story that will take a while to tell, child. You would have loved to meet him. Perhaps one day you will. I experience how God has dealt with you, just like I have heard and seen. When the timing is appropriate, he may include you in his company." "When did I see you in operation?" "I've seen you in action numerous times at your church. God's gift of wealth and fame includes the skill of concealing one's identity to avoid interference." "Alright, you asked for a clue about me visiting your church." "That guy you talked to? He's married. Ignore him completely. He's absolutely no good, I mean seriously, no good." 'Yes Ma'an, it was me and no mere clue. I'm no longer interested in buying any more wardrobes."

" If you decide to let them know at any time, that's perfectly fine. If you don't speak up, I won't either, but it's unfair to distance ourselves when life is short. No need to ask me about anyone, you already know where they are." "The noise!" "we have company." "Don't be concerned about your church lease, it's been paid for the next five years. The spirit instructed me to assist you." The power of love acts as a magnet, uniting families without being affected by the inevitable loss of loved ones. I'll hang up the phone, go ahead and search yourself, Pastor. Remember, we love you."

Everyone is wondering who Mother Faye Esther was speaking with. They only heard her response. Whoever that was, may not want to deal with the rest of the family and she gave her space to follow her heart.

Miriam was inexplicably bothered by the phone call, without knowing why.

Junior Jeffery exited the meeting room to catch up on the news. He nearly sat on the picture that his twins are completely fixated on. He grabbed it and inquired about its proper placement. Patrice directed him to put it on the shelf in the room she specifically indicated. Upon entering the room, he followed instructions and placed the picture before stealing a quick look at it. Junior Jeffery was astonished. He was acquainted with the person depicted in the room's pictures. Unsure of what to do with the information, he carefully examined each picture to confirm his eyes weren't deceiving him. Tears blurred his 20/20 vision, prompting him to compose himself before leaving the room. Yet, his feet were not in sync with the rest of his limbs. Without waiting for all the details to emerge, he began to speculate about the outcome of his marriage. Instantly is almost on the brink of hating this vacation that he thought was the ultimate. Being a lawyer, he had the capability to guide others on what steps to take in a specific scenario. His personal affairs have been devoid of this ability. Surrounded by the Fabulous Mother Faye Esther Casimir, he was confident that he had found the ideal location for free counseling. He would rather have someone else to prevent any conflicts of interest. Despite this, his distrustful and overprotective family made him unable to trust anyone, including his pastor, in this situation.

In the meantime, Mother Faye Esther entered the room and offered Junior Jeffery her presence in her prayer room if he required someone to talk to. She grasped Junior Jeffery's dilemma because she knew more about the situation than he and all the party involved thought. She said to him, "Until the Good Lord unveils the reason behind his stumble upon the truth, he should keep certain things to himself."

As they exited the room together, Miriam observed that something seemed off with her husband. She believed he sensed her neglecting him. Her emotions ran high as she reunited with the family she had lost and finally found. She reached the conclusion that he had been thoughtless. Leaving the table, she joined him and inquired if he felt lonely due to her spending quality time with others since she arrived. He asked why he should not stand in favor of something he had prayed for daily, and God finally came through. Like her, he had funds and considered himself fortunate to be part of this wonderful family. It's understandable that there are dramas associated with it, like they are prevalent in most wealthy and famous families. Miriam kissed and thanked her husband for praying for this day secretly.

Miriam stood up to return to entertaining her Grandma Yvonne and Aunts Barbara and Rose. When her husband called her, he encouraged her to consider any knowledge gained from the trip as God's perfect plan and to bravely accept them, whether they are positive or negative.

Without wasting a moment, she responded to him by embracing her Grandma Faye; "Please Tell her husband after her time together with Grandma Faye, how powerful she became. She is ready to encounter any situation, even if it means meeting her parents again through divine intervention." Mother Faye Esther amusingly relayed the message to Junior Jeffery who stood right there.

She answered like that to introduce her new strong nature to her husband. The three of them laughed, and it's possible that Miriam will be haunted by those words someday.

None of the guests, including Moses and Miriam, were ever interested in seeing the family photo album. They made use of it as a flat, stable platform for exchanging contact details. They might have saved the idea of opening the album for later, considering they had a few days remaining. It seems logical that they would have started by looking at pictures of their parents Yves and Ester, their own baby photos, and the family. That decision would address Miriam's twins' attraction. By experiencing it firsthand not long ago in the picture's room, her husband learned the lesson and hopes it remains undisclosed at present.

The phone call Mother Faye Esther received earlier is still on Yvonne's mind. She grew weary of attempting to determine the identity of that individual. She inquired her mother about the person on the phone earlier. Mother Faye Esther expressed her suspicion of being eavesdropped on during her conversation. The person is waiting for God to provide opportunities to apologize to anyone they have hurt. Although the list is long, "Nothing is impossible for God." Rose and Barbara reminded their Mother that she hadn't revealed the person's name yet. Mother Faye Esther implied, "The person's name is minding your business." Yvon heard Mother's response and said, someone walked straight to that one, all of them laughed and Mother didn't crack a smile.

The time has come for the family's exclusive one night revival. To maintain the sanctity of the family's spiritual gathering, Pastor Unique Preacher requested Claude to lock the chateau gate and keep unwanted guests out. The chateau has a secret passage known only to the immediate family, and it's lock-free.
Pastor Unique Preachers launched the service. Miriam and he delivered a TagTeam sermon, resulting in the outpouring of the Holy Spirit upon everyone. By donning his preaching gear, Pastor Unique Preacher cleverly disguised himself as Moses. He and Miriam headed to the pool to check if any family member was interested in being baptized.

Meanwhile, the person who spoke to Mother Faye Esther on the phone was sleeping at home. In a dream, the Angel of God instructed the Pastor to quickly rise and go to my Faithful Servant Mother Faye Esther for baptism by Pastor

Unique Preacher and his Sister. Since the front gate is locked, enter through the gate in the backyard past the pool. Start off with Pachouco's song, I'm walking the king highway, on the way to the water. The pastor stood up and hopped into her car to pursue the adventure.

As the pool transformed into a sanctuary, Pachouco emerged and gave a concert to the worshippers. The spirit-filled Pastor Unique Preacher asked his Uncle to sing softly, as the Holy Spirit has an important message to convey. Two more individuals will be baptized tonight, but they are not present here. He requested that everyone leave the pool, excluding Miriam and Patrice. He instructed his Grandma Faye to stand by the pool gate and welcome them in, while signaling Pachouco to keep singing.

Claude and everyone are confused because they overheard him asking Claude to lock the Gate. While everyone forgot, Tamara remained inside, fast asleep. She had no knowledge of the service. The voice she heard called sinners to repent and be baptized, saying the Man of God is summoning them. Upon hearing the singing outside, she quickly rushed out. The Man of God urged the backslider to embrace Jesus. Making her way to the pool, Tamara's presence causes the ground to shake from the people's praise. Tamara and Mother Faye Esther both cried tears of joy as she guided Tamara to the pool. She had recently accepted Christ. He asked Pastor Leslie to join them in the pool and assist in immersing her in the water. Following the profound experience, Tamara spoke in an unknown language, glorifying God.

Upon exiting the pool, Tamara received congratulations from both children and adults. While embracing her, Claude wept tears of happiness for her salvation, but it didn't stop him from thinking of divorcing her.

To their surprise, a voice could be heard singing, "I'm walking, I'm Walking, walking the Hing Highway. I dare not stumble. If I stumbled, it's not God's fault."
Upon realizing the source of the sound, they turned around to see Pastor Angela from the female prison. Yvonne, Angela's Mother, Junior Jeffery, Claude, and Tamara all passed out. Thanks to Patrica and Antoinette's expertise, they were able to bring everyone back to consciousness. Everyone else rushed to her, showering her with their hugs of blessing. Pastor Leslie and Patrice departed from the water to offer her their embraces. Pastor Unique Preacher found solitude in the pool. While Miriam was beside him, she was lost in her own world, giving thanks to God. She was completely unaware that her husband and others had blacked out. Pastor Angela gently moved everyone aside and proceeded towards the water. She told Pastor Unique Preacher that she was a Pastor, but God had revealed to her that if she confessed her sins and was baptized by him, her territories would be expanded. "Pastor, do you have a sister by any chance? He responded, "There she is, in the spirit." Pastor Unique Preacher, along with his Grandma Faye, and Miriam baptized Pastor Angela in the Name of Jesus, according to her faith.

Pastor Angela, standing in the water between Moses and Miriam, expressed gratitude to God for the time spent in prison for her mistakes. "I've made the decision to distance myself from you all until I can sort out my life and ministry. I have been out for three years, and I established my own church. In some way, Grandma Faye found me but chose not to reveal herself. I discovered that earlier today during my conversation with her. She kept it a secret that Pastor Unique Preacher would be here this evening. Anyway, whenever I look at all of you, I see an opening to seek forgiveness if I must crawl on my knees to receive it, Lord knows I deserve the humiliation. I've intentionally transgressed against the entire family. Can you find it in your hearts to forgive me, please? Family, I ask for your forgiveness as I have transformed into a new person since accepting Christ. There's one thing that I can't forget and will never forgive myself for: causing the death of Moses and Miriam. If the roles were reversed, my sister Ester and my brother-in-law Yves would never treat Patrice and Patrica that way. Grandma Faye and my dear Mother Yvonne, please accept my apology for acting out of greed and hurting both of you. I've changed for the better, but I wish I knew where Moses and Miriam were buried. I will continue to visit Yves and Ester's graves twice a month, just like I'm doing now. Upon my release, I admitted to them that I had killed my sister's twins and expressed my desire to be held accountable for the crime. I described to them all the suffering I caused Moses and Miriam before their deaths. They conveyed to me that I am stuck with this for the entirety of my life. Please pray for me, recently I contemplated ending my life due to the harm I caused others. The moment Pastor Unique Preacher took the stage on TV, he delivered a powerful sermon, "Urging against suicide and reminding us that our lives are not ours to take. It belongs to God." "I withdrew the gun from my mouth. While incarcerated, I had twins, and I allowed a kind couple to adopt them. They expressed their desire for an open adoption, but I declined. Now I accept the fact meeting them again will be a miracle from God. Without a doubt, this couple will not treat my twins in the same manner I treated Moses and Miriam until their passing. I frequently wondered if they would forgive me if they were still alive."

Moses and Miriam exchanged signals, prompting everyone else to burst into laughter. "What's causing the laughter?" Pastor Angela questioned.

Pastor Unique Preacher stated to Pastor Angela that "Had I known earlier about you are being a murderer, I would have avoided baptizing you into the water. What a terrible act to commit, killing your own sister's children."

Upon hearing Pastor Unique Preacher's remarks, Pastor Angela looked up towards the heavens and uttered, "Lord, My fear of being ostracized wherever I go for the damage I supposedly inflicted on the kids, it's real. My beloved evangelist, Pastor Unique Preacher whom I would have blindly followed, is now torturing me for the crime. I'm exhausted from living, Lord, please."

With tears in his eyes, Moses removed his disguise and sincerely apologized to Pastor Angela, explaining that his previous statement was just a joke. Contagiously, Miriam, tears also streamed from her eyes like raindrops. They spoke simultaneously, saying, "Auntie, we forgive you!" "I'm Miriam and this is Moses, but his supporters known him as Pastor Unique Preacher."

They all celebrated by jumping into the pool and giving each other hugs. Little did they know, Pastor Angela collapsing in the arms of Moses and Miriam. Pastor Angela appeared to be falling under the spirit, but Junior Jeffery and Miriam knew they were the reason of passing out. Junior Jeffery carried her out of the pool, and Patrica and Rose Marie helped her regain consciousness.

It's a fact that whenever Moses preaches, bizarre incidents occur, except for tonight when he and his family are in the spotlight. What happened to Pastor Angela? Witnessing Pastor Angela's grand entrance at the baptism caused Junior Jeffery to faint earlier. Her presence there caught him by surprise and left him in a state of confusion. At first, he accidentally found her pictures and it dawned on him that she was the Aunt Miriam detested for the abuse they suffered. In addition, she was his client and the birth mother of their adopted twins Moses Junior and Miriam Ester.

Following her baptism, Pastor Angela delved into the stories of Moses and Miriam. Junior Jeffery perceived that his wife was having a feeling of melancholy. He slid into the water to provide solace and console her in case Pastor Angela's narratives became overwhelming for Miriam. However, he recalled her boasting about the empowering effect her Grandma Faye had on her ability to tackle any challenge. Unbeknownst to Pastor Angela, there was a third person present in the water. Moses and Miriam revealed their identities to Pastor Angela. Excitedly, she turned around to celebrate the good news that her nephew and niece were alive and well. They are exceptional preachers. Pastor Angela witnessed her lawyer and his wife, who adopted her children. The complexity was too much for her mind and heart to handle, resulting in her fainting. The Miriam that Pastor Angela mistreated, along with her brother, is now raising Pastor Angela's children as her own.

Inside the chateau, Mother Faye Esther and her children led Pastor Angela for a meeting. Pastor Angela was asked by Pachouco why she didn't consider him and Pastor Leslie for adopting the children. Yvonne suggested that it would be preferable for them to be raised by their uncle. Before Yvonne finished speaking, Moses Junior and Miriam Ester opened the door. They hurried to Pastor Angela and inquired about her well-being. They asked if they could say a prayer for her. She gave them the leeway. Moses Junior sang, Miriam Ester prayed, impressing Pastor Angela who inquired about their parentage. Junior Jeffery and Miriam twins, replied to Barbara, her aunt. The other oldest aunt, Rose, said that she told their mother how those two children reminded her of Angela. Mom replied, the truth is right around the corner it will get here today before the night ends.

 Pastor Angela glanced at her Grandma and remarked, "I have a feeling you were already aware." She revealed that they were adopted by relatives when answering Pachouco. I only discovered it tonight in the pool, but I had no idea before. Understanding their confusion, she made plans to convene a meeting. Once everything was complete, Moses and Rose Marie called for Junior Jeffery and Miriam to join them. Upon arrival, they immediately delved into a discussion about Pastor Angela's impactful confession.

Even so, Moses and his wife were perplexed about her fainting spell. In Moses' recollection, Pastor Angela observed Junior Jeffery and Miriam were sharing an affectionate hug. She displayed an emotional reaction as if she had seen two celestial beings, leading to her fainting. Antoinette asked Junior Jeffery and Miriam if they had met Aunt Angela prior to this. Miriam warned Moses and Antoinette that they should both sit down before she answered the question, as the answer might be mind-blowing. They replied to try them out since they are familiar with delivering good, bad, and shocking news. Miriam explicitly warned Moses and Antoinette, and Moses suggested that Miriam should stop meddling with their curiosity. Miriam and her husband exchanged glances, both smiling, before he grabbed two chairs asking Moses and his wife to sit down and comply with Junior Jeffery's request. He stated that Angela is the mother of both Moses Junior and Miriam Ester, our children. Moses leapt up and exclaimed, "Please tell me you're joking, "How long have you been aware of this?"

Rose Marie's behavior became outrageous as she confronted Junior Jeffery, asking if he had an affair with her sister-in-law's aunt, and expressing her disappointment. Miriam defended her husband against two individuals who claimed to know how to handle difficult news. She urged Moses and Rose Marie to stop making hasty assumptions and start paying attention. Similar to them, her husband found out tonight. Her husband disagreed, saying "not really." This morning, he stated that he came close to sitting on a picture without really looking at it. He asked Patrice where to place it. Upon her gesture, he turned his gaze towards the picture room and realized the picture in his hands was Angela's, creating a sense of connection for their children. He went on to describe his morning feelings and expressed thanks to Grandma Faye for sharing some wise advice. He now had faith in their Grandma's clairvoyant abilities.

Now Miriam wanted to know why she had just heard this. Her husband reminded her about her statement regarding her preparedness while being around her Grandma. She reached the conclusion that she is equipped to handle anything. He was about to tell her that, but she shut him down with her statement. After a few moments of thought, Miriam burst into laughter. Moses, known for his listening skills, recollected his sister mentioning her husband's knowledge in the past. Let's hear your response to the same question, Miriam. Based on her dreams and visions, she informed them that she had an intuition about the adoption. She believed that both she and her husband would adopt a child from a family member. When she encountered Angela in the prison, she couldn't remember Angela from her childhood. Yet, as she reached the parking lot, a feeling of confrontation washed over her. Upon laying eyes on her, she questioned the origin of her acquaintance with Angela. The feeling of being connected with the children, even there, was unbelievable. She thought the babies that Angela carried were Junior Jeffery's. After sharing this with Rose Marie, the Lord showed her that her husband was a faithful man. Seeing her face in the pool, Miriam concluded that she, too, was in a state of shock. Moses was completely shaken and unprepared for the news. He repeatedly uttered the phrase, "Lord has mercy." "The way we treat others badly or good doesn't always return to us in the same manner. Whenever it returns, ensure that love is the prevailing force."

She seized the opportunity to apologize to Moses and her husband for keeping her discovery a secret. Junior Jeffery and Miriam visited Pastor Angela and her inmate friends with the babies for one last time. On that day Miriam uncovered her and Moses' abuser. She shared the findings with Rose Marie that day. Pastor Angela assumed that Miriam exclusively spoke English. A Spanish-speaking inmate in the jail asked Pastor Angela, "Quien es esa bella dama?" translating, "Who is that beautiful lady?" "Ella es muy bonita." Translating, "She is beautiful." Pastor Angela responded in Spanish, "Ella es mi sobrina pero ella no lo sabe." Meaning, "She is my niece, but she doesn't know."

Miriam kept on explaining that night, feeling the urge to punch her in the mouth and knock out a few teeth. Miriam chastised the evil thought in her heart and sought forgiveness from God. After discovering Angela's true identity as the abusive Aunt Angela, she was prepared to bring her children and first cousins back home. Miriam was convinced her family and Aunt Angela would never cross paths again. The inmates all believed that Pastor Angela's decision to have the Jefferys adopt the twins came from a divine source beyond the sky. They felt the love of Miriam for the babies.

Yvon and Michelle were sent by Mother Faye Esther to gather everyone for a family meeting. Prior to entering, Moses and her husband thanked Miriam for keeping the secret from them. Otherwise they would be missing out on the most challenging test of love from God for our family. We've successfully passed the test so far, but the final exam awaits us within the mansion, concluded Moses.

When Pastor Angela and Miriam first met regarding the adoption, did she remember who Miriam was? Although the answer is no, there was a strong magnetic pull when they first met.

Pastor Angela had a vision the night before, where she said a final adieu to her children and saw her sister Ester. Pastor Angela was informed by her that "Miriam, your niece, is the new mother of your babies. It was your old self who nearly destroyed her and her brother. Those residing in the realm of the Saints of God have obtained forgiveness since the day they were converted, that goes for you too. Pastor Angela, please don't reveal yourself to her as I instructed, as she hasn't forgiven you yet. She and her spouse will shower your babies with parental love, and you'll be proud of them. Miriam and Moses will eventually find it in their hearts to forgive you. Anyone who read "Sold Out With a Kiss" will know what I mean."

Startled, Angela leaped from the dream and found herself disoriented on the bed. A prisoner rushed towards her to check if she was alright. She notified her that in her dream, she saw three deceased family members: her sister Ester and her two children Moses and Miriam. Pastor Angela playfully responded to the Spanish speaking prisoner about Miriam being her niece, alluding to the dream. However, Miriam was fully aware that it was real. Pastor Angela will deliver a sermon titled "A Message From The Dead" after piecing together the puzzle of her life story. The subtopic is making a U-turn on the busiest highway.

Every single person, including Tamara, was inside the chateau. Before Mother Faye Esther began the meeting, she asked Yvon and his wife to take the children upstairs. Moses Junior and Miriam Ester, both ten years old, seemed to know that the conference will focus on them. Miriam Ester asked Grandma Faye if she and her brother could sing a song for Pastor Angela since she was sick. Her demand resonated deeply with everyone, resulting in laughter. The family will be in for an unforgettable surprise if Great Grandma gives them the go-ahead. She gave them leeway, oh goodness. No one knows that is coming except their Parent, Moses, and Had their parents not been firm, their children would already be in show business. Many song producers who wanted to record Moses Junior and his wife.

Miriam Ester singing together were turned away. Miriam Ester began to sing a song by Pachouco called "I Have Jesus in my Heart, Mind, and Soul. I Have Jesus all over me." And Moses Junior joined in with the chorus, "In my mind, I got Jesus, in my soul I got Jesus all over me. It's all over, it's all over, no more sickness, no more, no more family separation because it's all over." Miriam Ester leaped onto Tamara's lap and Moses Junior did the same to Pastor Angela while they finished the song together, singing "It's all over, yes it's all over," and they hugged them. The natural gifts of those two children made them outstanding performers. Their souls blended in perfect harmony. Their performances were never rehearsed or planned, only guided by God. Through their anointed, many have found their breakthrough. It's amusing that they often chose to sing their Great Uncle Pachouco's songs during their recital. They all met for the first time and had no idea they were related. Those kids made a lasting impression on everyone's hearts. "The significance of this day will forever be etched in the history of our blessed family," said Mother Faye Esther.

Inside the chateau that night, they treated their family and everything else to a mini concert. Tiger and Trickcy, the two cats, came running and jumped on the table to watch and listen to Moses Junior and Miriam Ester's melody. Even Zorro, Patrice's dog who was napping upstairs, came down and jumped onto her lap to enjoy the festivity.

Just when everyone thought it was all over, Pachouco, a skilled and renowned recording artist, testified that he had never heard such a pleasant singing voice in his decades-long career. He informed Junior Jeffery and Miriam that whenever they're ready for their children to record, they should let him know because he has the best recording studio in the state. Miriam took the opportunity to state that "The decision is no longer in her or Junior Jeffery's hands alone. We should include Aunt Angela in the decision-making process for Moses Junior and Miriam Ester." In response, "Pastor Angela requested her niece's compliance with their agreement and emphasized the importance of not violating the contract." "Love had found its way back into the family at the pool," Miriam said. "The agreement we made was violated and the contract torn up by love," continued Miriam. "This task will be done by Junior Jeffery, myself, and you, Auntie. Your Niece and Nephew in law will handle everything except for your input when needed. Moving forward, we will honor the love instilled in this family by our Mother, Grandma, and Great Grandmother Faye Esther Casimir, through Christ our Lord."

Miriam said: "Family, I have been preparing for this day from the very start. Right here, right now, I can provide concrete evidence. Moses Junior and Miriam Ester, can you please let Mommy know how many mothers and fathers you have?"

They confirmed that they have two mothers and one father.

"Can you name them?"

"The world's greatest dad, Junior, Angela, and Miriam are our mother," they replied.

Moses Junior added that "We are unaware of our first mother because Mommy informed us that she is currently on a mission in a foreign country far away. Mommy made a promise that we would meet Angela our first mother before we reach eleven years old, and we're currently ten." Miriam responded to her son, "Who is she right here, pointed at Angela?" "Aunt Angela," he replied. Miriam answered, "That's Angela, your other Mom." Moses Junior's stubbornness frustrated Miriam Ester, who had already informed him that Angela was their first Mommy because of her name. In a display of emotion, they joyfully embrace Angela. Junior Jeffery and Miriam are praised by every family member for their Godly understanding.

"When did you realize that my mother was your aunt?" Patricia asked her cousin.

"Let me explain, I met Aunt Angela nine years ago but didn't recognize her at the time However, while I was retrieving you know who, a Spanish woman praised my appearance to Aunt Angela." She asked, "Who am I?"

"My aunt replied to her in Spanish, my niece, but she doesn't know that. My aunt was under the impression that I couldn't speak Spanish. Satan attempted to persuade me to abandon the infants and return home. I made it clear that under no circumstances will they be raised by strangers, as they are the only relatives Moses and I have left. I swiftly rebuked that devil. I didn't tell anyone and eventually shared it with Rose Marie my confident."

Mother Faye Esther observed them all and detailed what she had heard. Blaming herself, she thought that love had departed from her immediate family since the death of Veronique, Yves, and Esther, and the disappearance of Moses and Miriam. Their reappearance reignited love in this place. Angela's arrival was the perfect final addition. Speaking truthfully, she stated that she would be extremely satisfied if God called her to her mansion in glory. She finally got to see her longing fulfilled - both of her daughters healed, Moses, Miriam, and their family are home, and Patrice, Patricia, and Angela reunited.

She created space for Moses to talk to Pastor Angela, who was left in awe by how Junior Jeffery and Miriam raised her twins. Moses formally introduced his family to his aunt, acknowledging her unwavering support throughout the years without knowing their connection. It's time for her to stop feeling guilty about Miriam and him. During adversity, those who had knowledge of God could witness His miraculous presence. Spending excessive time on past hurts can impede God's purpose for our lives. Moses proceeded to describe to his aunt and the rest of the group how his heart had been consumed by hatred, transforming him into Miriam's worst nightmare. He directed his index finger towards Miriam and admitted that he had always been curious about the type of heart his beloved sister possessed. He described how he deliberately showered her with bitterness instead of love. A strong disdain for her developed within him, and he derived pleasure from it as well. Miriam's kiss, which felt like a betrayal, was a barrier he couldn't overcome. She kissed him as a reassurance of her intent to come back, but then vanished without a trace. He grew up believing that Grandma Faye, Aunt Angela, and Miriam colluded to eliminate him because of his speech impediment. Miriam's mission to save him prevented her from retaliating with hate, even if she wanted to. He was one step away from hell when she pulled him out from the grave's mouth. Moses shared with his aunt that he had the same sentiment towards her and the whole family. As Pastor Unique Preacher, she followed him, unaware of the darkness he hid when no one was watching. His sister, Miriam, helped him rediscover love. Once he regained his awareness and conquered his blindness, he expressed gratitude to God for his upbringing, including the painful experiences. If Miriam hadn't wanted to see him speak, he wouldn't be speaking today. When his parents' death wish was fulfilled, he finally spoke, and they died. If Grandma Faye hadn't followed Aunt Angela's fake will, he wouldn't be living with her. If he hadn't stayed with Aunt Angela, he wouldn't have experienced mistreatment and betrayal. If he and Miriam hadn't escaped, he wouldn't have discovered what had been left behind or crossed paths with Mother Irma. If Grandma Faye hadn't agreed to his emancipation and granted Mother Irma permission to raise him, he wouldn't have gone to seminary, met his wife Rose Marie, or become a father. If he hadn't joined the church, he wouldn't have the title of Pastor Unique

Preacher. If he wasn't mean to his sister, he wouldn't n recognize the need to be saved. Without his sister's liver donation, he would not have survived. Why did he go through all that trouble just to demonstrate that Handy Hands of God played all the role in everything that happened to him, including being in the presence of a loving family who shaped him into who he is today? Now Moses said that he is without hate but overflowing with love. Today, Miriam, Junior Jeffery, and Aunt Angela showed us the incredible resilience and capacity for forgiveness and love within our family. His wife Rosemarie, Junior Jeffery, and his daughter Antoinette played a crucial role in convincing him to listen to Miriam's voice and seek their root, resulting in the healing of Grandma Yvonne and Aunt Rose today. Without his persistent Grandma Faye, the revival wouldn't happen, and the town wouldn't receive a quarter of a million dollars. If Aunt Tamara hadn't gone through what she did, she wouldn't have become a new person in Christ and Joseph would still be free, despite his offenses of assault and sextortion. Had Pastor Angela not obeyed God's instruction to come to the pool, he wouldn't have had the chance to meet and baptize his aunt. God asked his wife to bestow $900,000.00 upon Aunt Angela for the purpose of building a church. Everything happened for a reason in God's people lives, preparing the way for greater blessings. Let's sing about

Joseph, Jacob's son, and how he went from the Pit to the Palace. It's one life to live and count all things for joy."

After Moses revealed his wife's generous gift to his aunt, an overwhelming amount of praise built up within the people, waiting to be expressed. Right after Moses completed his last statement, a new worship service came into existence. Pastor Angela's worship was so powerful that it spread uncontrollably, infecting every believer inside the chateau, including the children, with her praises to God. Adding to the unexpected twist, Moses' little girl ended with another Pachouco song, "Oh Jesus Loves Me and He loves all of us." Worshiping was bound to happen. A girl, appearing quiet yet having a great spiritual aura, shocked everyone with her unique and talented voice.

Pachouco used his role as a well-respected Great Uncle to facilitate his nephews Moses, Junior Jeffery, and nieces Rosemarie and Miriam taking their children to the studio. Then he proclaimed, "Everyone in favor, say I," and they all chimed in with I.

Pastor Angela was appointed by Mother Faye Esther to lead the closing prayer before everyone goes to sleep. Since Pastor Angela had her own room, she asked her to stay overnight in the chateau. Prior to praying, she mentioned that there was something she needed to do to confirm if she had been forgiven by everyone.

Yesterday morning, Claude approached Mother Faye Esther, requesting permission to post bail for Oscar and have him resume his duty. Claude's compassion left a strong impression on her, but she mentioned that he had previously been in prison and was subsequently fired. "For my sake, hire him back," Claude told Mother Faye Esther, "I don't want him to be exploited on the streets."

Mother Faye Esther glanced at Claude, shaking her head, and said, "Go find him. Welcome to the family of God. I sensed your compassion."

Upon Claude's arrival at the shelter, Oscar spotted him and quickly scurried to hide beneath a bed, just enough to conceal his head. Since the incident caused by a demonic spirit, that was the first time he laid eyes on Claude. Claude suggested returning home by saying, "Come on, let's go."

Oscar remained skeptical of the offer and persistently begged Claude for forgiveness. Feeling Oscar's genuine remorse, Claude comforted him, saying, "Son, I have forgiven you, and God has too."

Covered in dirt and a strong odor, Claude embraced Oscar and showered him with affection. Oscar's dirtiness was overshadowed by love, even after he ruined Claude's white outfit.

Oscar showed up at the chateau wearing new clothes bought by Claude. Oscar's initial assignment was to fill the kiddy inside pool for Pastor Angela. He made a hand signal to Pastor Angela, notifying her that the pool was good to go.

Pastor Angela invited everyone to join her at the kiddy pool. Six months ago, Mother Faye Esther had a vision of this move of Pastor Angela. She saw Pastor Angela was leading people to the pool. In the dream, Mother Faye Esther was about to intervene, but a voice from above said, "Let it be. I am guiding and preparing her for a greater purpose for the family's benefit."

Moses, the exceptional Pastor Unique Preacher, humbly sought his Grandma Faye's approval to follow his Aunt's spiritual guidance, given his training. His Grandma empathized with his discomfort, as he is a devout preacher who values hierarchical protocol. The affairs of God should be conducted in a respectful and orderly manner, honoring the shepherd of the house. To satisfy his hesitation, Mother Faye Esther revised Pastor Angela's request by inviting everyone to follow her if they wished. No one in the house had any clue about Pastor Angela's procession, except for Miriam and her Grandma who were informed by Divine Power. This family didn't take their relationship with God lightly, and it was a truly beautiful sight to behold. In their creation, they were programmed to spontaneously worship and praise the True Living God. When Pastor Angela arrived at the pool, she stepped into the freezing water and she spoke sorrowful words from her sorrowful heart, asking her family to listen. The family present could tell that her confession came straight from the heart, filled with remorse and truth. She articulated in her plea:

"I wrongly assigned myself the role of a black sheep, wrongly accusing my family of this identity. I caused you pain. I must take responsibility for causing you distress. I made the choice to become a disgrace and a nuisance to society. I intentionally tried to make my daughters Patrica and Patrice turn against all of you, so they would feel like outcasts too. I can vividly recall the day I was afflicted with this incurable jealousy disease, as if it happened yesterday. I didn't find relief from this invasive and aggressive sickness until I discovered Jesus in prison seventeen years ago. The disease first entered my heart when my sister Ester invited Yves, her only love in life, who eventually became her husband until they passed away, to a picnic before I had the chance. All is written in "Sold Out With A Kiss." On that day, Ester extended an invitation to Derrick, Yves' brother, whose death I caused and whose Will I manipulated, making myself the only beneficiary. I was imprisoned partly because of this deception. While Derrick loved me, my affection was solely for his wealth, not him. Stanley and Joy came along. I have a strong dislike for that evening because of Yves' open declaration of love for my sister Ester. My anger towards them was so intense, I wanted Ester and I to swap partners. Something Ester with her classy and conservative self will ever allow. Even though I was beautiful and had many admirers, Yves was the only young man in my circle who didn't fall for me like a puppy. Yves, a talented soccer player, proposed to Ester, who was seated beside me, and that's when jealousy consumed me. Amid his college's championship victory, he dropped to one knee on the soccer field and proposed to Ester. Yves' voice echoed across the field from loudspeakers positioned at the four corners, asking Ester, "Ester, will you marry me immediately?" The crowd began to serenade, pleading, "Ester, say yes." On the flip side, Ester was captivating the crowd with her singing, oblivious to the fact that Yves was requesting her hand in marriage. My sister reluctantly agreed, under pressure from fans who wouldn't accept no as an answer, and her acceptance broke my heart. Yves and Ester's well-known status brought joy to both the family and fans. As everyone around me expressed their happiness by screaming and jumping, I stayed seated, displaying my lack of consideration. Your parents tied the knot on that day, Moses, and Miriam. The unfortunate part is that they both loved me deeply. Although I loved them as well, my body still craved Yves. My low self-esteem caused me to be unconcerned about him marrying my sister or me dating his brother. I'll stop boring you with my past, Angela has been gone for a long time, and I'm grateful to God for the transformation my family has witnessed in me through Christ Jesus."

Moses and Miriam desired Pastor Angela to continue sharing her hurtful testimonies so they could learn about their parents. It was an occasion for them to give thanks to God once again for their aunt's transformation from bad to good, from wicked to righteous. Miriam encouraged Pastor Angela to finish sharing the life lesson that helped her grow and move on from her previous actions.

In the midst of the pool, Pastor Angela tearfully apologized once again to Moses, Miriam, and Mother Faye Esther. Jealousy, she retorted, is a soul destroyer that can spread rapidly over the heart. "I deeply envied your parents and was ready to do anything to ruin their marriage. Yves' feelings towards me were misunderstood, leading me to make an unsuccessful attempt to kiss him. He took offense that day and scolded me mercilessly. Instead of feeling ashamed about trying to kiss my brother-in-law, I went home and started criticizing him to my husband, who was obsessed with Yves and Ester's flawless relationship, so he shut me down. One day at the airport, I went to pick up my boyfriend's sister, only to discover she was his secret girlfriend. Yves was at the airport, engaging in conversation with a woman, grasping her shoulders. I took out my phone and captured the moment when he kissed her goodbye. I initially believed it was a passionate kiss, but I later realized it wasn't after getting myself in trouble. Feeling hangry, I reached out to Ester to inform her that I caught her husband cheating and have proof. Ester, who was expecting, informed me that her husband was not that sort of individual. I confirmed that he was indeed a dog, with a capital D. I will be right over to shut your mouth, Ester. I can't tolerate an adulterer; your husband is a cheater. Upon my arrival at Yves and Ester's house, I recounted the story and Ester expressed interest in watching the video. I told you it's on your phone, I sent it to you and my husband earlier because I knew you wouldn't believe how dirty Yves the perfect was. Upon watching the video, Ester started exhibiting signs of wanting to abort her babies. What she witnessed was too much for her emotionally, and it wasn't her husband kissing another woman. I escorted her to bed and contacted her doctor to come check on her. I began to apologize profusely to my sister. I should have thought twice before sending you the video, considering your strong love for Yves. Ester asked me if I had already sent the video to your husband. Yes, I responded, and I truly didn't mean to hurt you, Ester."

"Your mother, Moses, and Miriam had a deeply ingrained conservative nature. She held moral values that aligned with the word of God."

With a look, Ester asked "Angela did our mother drop you over your head when you were a baby? Angela, in the video you sent your husband and me, you can be seen engaging in a make-out session with a young man who could possibly be your son. It seems like he's younger than your son. Angela, my sister, I love you, but you bring shame to our family. I pray that someday you will choose to give your life to Christ."

Pastor Angela continued to say, "I learned a valuable lesson that day: never dig a pit for someone who fears and loves God. I tried to undermine Yves and cause problems in his marriage. My life took a devastating turn as I ended up losing my marriage, my son through death, and my husband divorcing me due to adultery. Since that time my life has been a living hell for the past thirty years, until my sister's prayers were answered by God. God acknowledged my plea, took note of Ester and Grandma Faye's prayers, and bestowed upon me the privilege of existing in Him. I want to let my family know that I am a completely changed person through Christ. I have given my penance to God and He grants me forgiveness. Family, I seek your pardon, just as God showed mercy by not dwelling on my fault."

Patrica moved closer to the edge of the pool, bent over, and embraced her mother Pastor Angela, who had eloquently revealed her troubling imperfections. Patrica released her embrace and questioned the family, "Didn't we forgive my mother before? Moses, Miriam, and the rest all replied, "Yes, we did."

Pastor Angela replied, saying, "That God has put it in my heart to wash your feet as a sign of receiving forgiveness from her family."

Moses removed his shoes while accompanied by his sister Miriam, and Pastor Angela washed and kissed their feet after drying them.

Reaching out to her Grandma Faye and Mother Yvonne, she washed and kissed their feet, just as she did for everyone else after that. Pastor Angela's actions while washing Oscar's feet demonstrated that God was working through her. Claude and Tamara were called by her in the water. Claude and Tanaea were next to Oscar when the spirit delivered a shocking bombshell. Pastor Angela's spirit informed Claude that Tamara is pregnant with twins for Oscar, and he will be the surrogate father of the twins. The spirit mentioned that Claude might not be inclined towards it, but it's God's divine plan. The same spirit advised Junior and Miriam to refrain Pastor Angela from participating in the upbringing of Moses Junior and Miriam Ester. She confessed and repented for every sin, fully converting to God. Pastor Angela prophesies to Moses and Miriam, as directed by the spirit speaking through her. According to the spirit, Pastor Angela will be launching an orphanage specifically for children who have experienced abuse. With the help of Moses and Miriam, Pastor Angela will launch it successfully. The way she treated them would lead her to see each child as her own, as a perpetual consequence of her sin.

The Casimir and the Day had their most memorable immediate family reunion ever. They left with novel perspectives on the unknown and the exciting possibilities of tomorrow. "One never knows if the person they mistreat today could end up being a lifesaver for them or their siblings. Having a good condition now doesn't guarantee a successful tomorrow. Approach each day with caution and be mindful of your actions, as they may shape tomorrow's outcome. Remember, the lingering effects of a difficult past are like a relentless skill seeker that constantly pursues you in the present, never fading away."

The above words of wisdom from Mother Faye Esther the Godly will be needed by Rose, Claude, and Tamara someday.

Mother Faye Esther revealed the prayers she had been praying for ages, which made this day possible for the family to come to know God and experience abundant prosperity in all things, just as their soul prospered. It's the prayer for the Ephesians found in Ephesians 3:14-21, quote:

14 For this reason I kneel before the Father, 15 from whom every family in heaven and on earth derives its name. 16 I pray that out of his glorious riches he may strengthen you with power through his Spirit in your inner being, 17 so that Christ may dwell in your hearts through faith. And I pray that you, being rooted and established in love, 18 may have power, together with all the Lord's holy people, to grasp how wide and long and high and deep is the love of Christ, 19 and to know this love that surpasses knowledge—that you may be filled to the measure of all the fullness of God. 20 Now to him who is able to do immeasurably more than all we ask or imagine, according to his power that is at work within us, 21 to him be glory in the church and in Christ Jesus throughout all generations, for ever and ever! Amen.

Mother Faye Esther used five envelopes to symbolize the fivefold Gospel and put various NIV Bible verses quote inside each one. Placing them on the table, she inquired which of them desired an envelope and was willing to follow the scripture's instructions. Those envelopes had no name written on them. The first five people to raise their hands were Pastor Angela, Pastor Moses, Tamara, Rose, and Claude (not Rose Marie, Moses' wife).

Her words were, if someone opts to stay and hear the verses, they must also put the lessons into practice. Everyone willingly agreed to stay of their own accord. What is the objective of that? Mother Faye Esther aims to demonstrate the immense power of her God. She believes that each participant will choose the verse or verses that relate to their personal story and expand on them if they wish.

Pastor Angela picked the envelop with John 3:16,17. She emphasized the importance of John 3:16 to the family at the pool, reminding them that without reading and focusing on John 3:17, they won't fully understand its significance, quote:

16 For God so loved the world that he gave his one and only Son, that whoever believes in him shall not perish but have eternal life.

17 For God did not send his Son into the world to condemn the world, but to save the world through him.

Romans 3: 7 was Pastor Moses' verse, quote:
Someone might argue, "If my falsehood enhances God's truthfulness and so increases his glory, why am I still condemned as a sinner?"

After Pastor Moses read Romans 3:7, Miriam and Rose Marie exchanged a high 5 to show that he felt the same way about them. He believes that no matter his position in God, those two special women in his life always blame him.

Romans 5 : 5 was Rose's verse, quote: 5 And hope does not put us to shame, because God's love has been poured out into our hearts through the Holy Spirit, who has been given to us.
Eventually, everyone will comprehend the reason behind God letting Rose, Daughter of Mother Faye Esther, come across Romans 5:5. Eventually, someone will share the lengthy tale. Her loss of sanity was immense, but Pastor Moses recently facilitated her miraculous healing through God's intervention. Those who knew her story and lived with her clapped their hands when she finished reading her scripture.

Tamara, overwhelmed with emotion, cried uncontrollably after reading the scripture from John Chapter 8: 1-8 in her envelope. Tears spread like wildfire, infecting others. No one else knew what it was, except Tamara, but everyone, including Mother Faye, Esther, and Oscar, shed tears while lending her their support. As she read the verses, she realized it didn't justify ongoing sins. It reassured her that Jesus heard her plea for repentance and forgave her based on her sincere remorse. Her actions will be forever remembered by many, a testament to God's Merciful nature after cleansing a sinner. Then, she read, quote:
John 8:1-8, 1 but Jesus went to the Mount of Olives.
2 At dawn he appeared again in the temple courts, where all the people gathered around him, and he sat down to teach them.

3 The teachers of the law and the Pharisees brought in a woman caught in adultery. They made her stand before the group

4 and said to Jesus, "Teacher, this woman was caught in the act of adultery.

5 In the Law Moses commanded us to stone such women. Now what do you say?"

6 They were using this question as a trap, in order to have a basis for accusing him.

But Jesus bent down and started to write on the ground with his finger.

7 When they kept on questioning him, he straightened up and said to them, "Let any one of you who is without sin be the first to throw a stone at her."

8 Again he stooped down and wrote on the ground.

Soon, they will witness the divine intervention of God Handy Hand in Mother Faye Esther's scripture-filled envelopes, as Claude reads the final verse. When Claude first read it silently, he exclaimed, "Is this a setup from you, Lord?" The family waited patiently for Claude as he conversed with his God. The family's curiosity multiplied rapidly beyond imagination. They couldn't wait eagerly to hear his chosen verse, which turned out to be Galatians 6:1, quote:

Galatians 6:1   Brothers and sisters, if someone is caught in a sin, you who live by the Spirit should restore that person gently. But watch yourselves, or you also may be tempted.

This information was a tough pill for Claude to swallow and he did not know how to react. It will not be long before we find out about Claude's decision.

MAY THE READERS OF THIS NOVEL BE BLESSED
BY GOD!

Patrick Pierre

Made in the USA
Columbia, SC
03 May 2024

35214182R00154